AGAINST THE STARS

Christopher Hartland

Tiny Ghost Press

The characters and events portrayed in this book are fictitious. Any similarity to real persons, living or dead, is coincidental and not intended by the author.

ISBN:
E-book 978-1-915585-02-8
Paperback 978-1-915585-03-5
Hardcover 978-1-915585-04-2

Cover artwork by: Samantha Lee

To find out more about our books visit www.tinyghostpress.com and sign up for our newsletter.

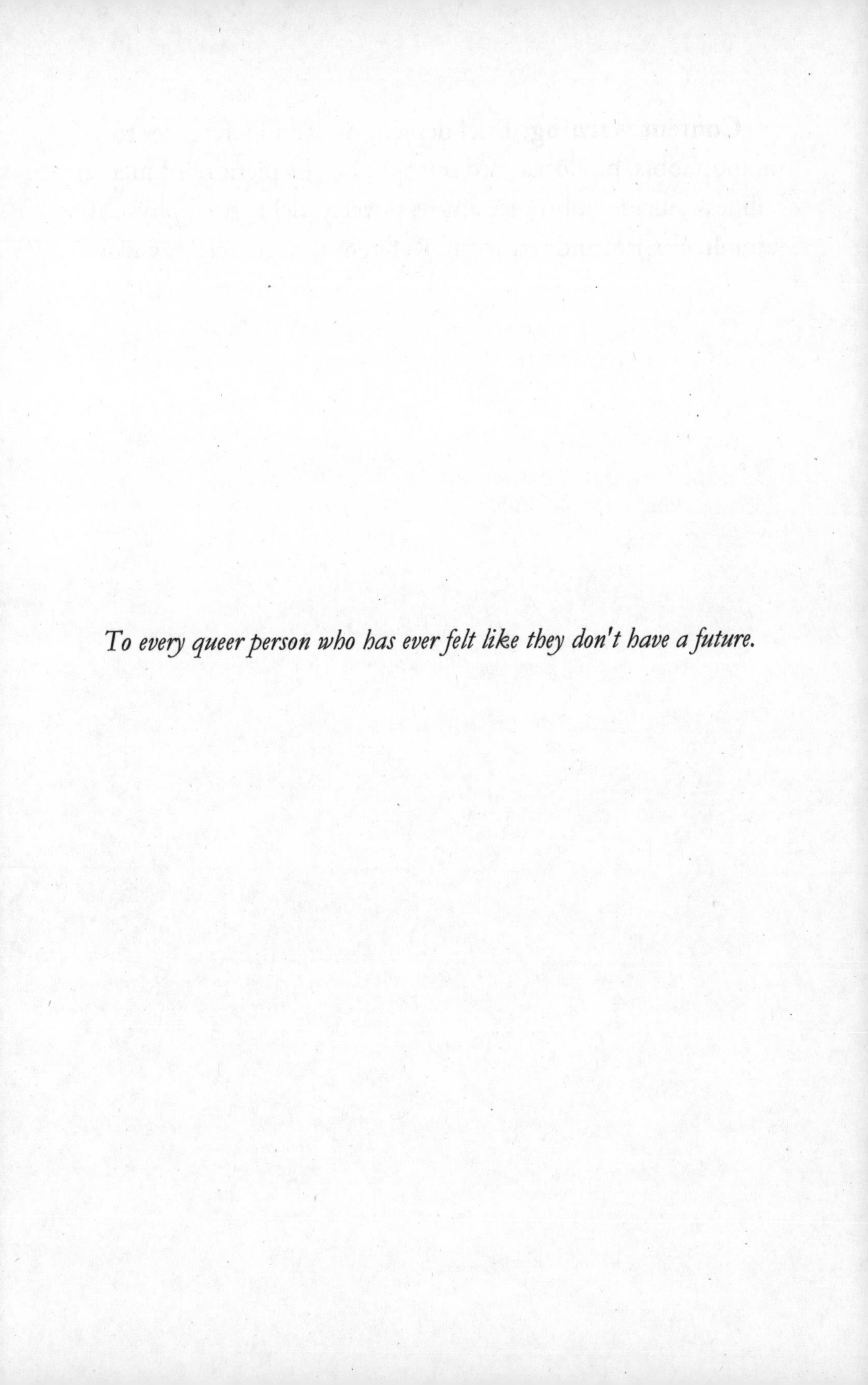

To every queer person who has ever felt like they don't have a future.

Content warning: Brief depictions of and references to homophobia, biphobia, and transphobia. Depictions of mental illness, suicide, substance abuse, poverty, debt, grief, physical assault, classism and terrorism. References to coerced sex-work.

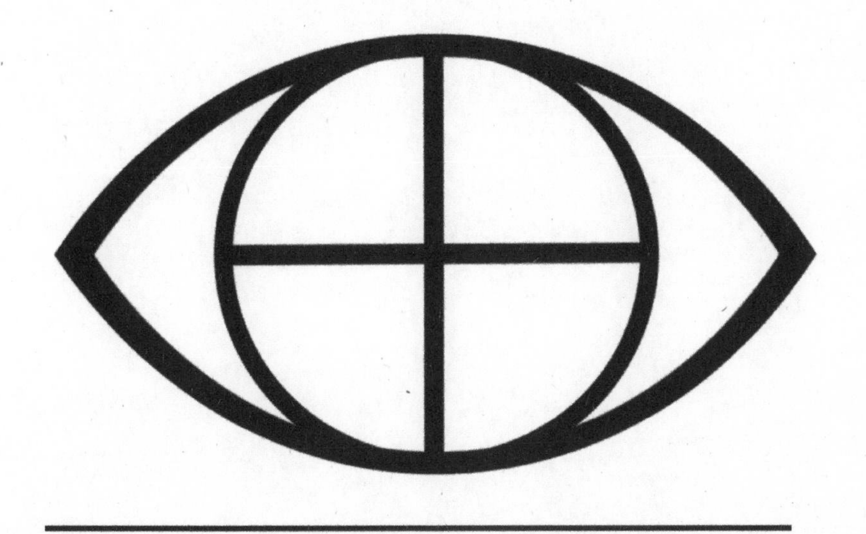

PART ONE

SEEING

GlimpseNet Post #1529B7

Subject: Eliza Delaney

Date Glimpsed: 21st June

Verification Status: Verified

All I could see was this symbol: a wide-open eye with a plus sign for a pupil. It was printed on a flyer on the windshield of my car. I turned on the wipers, shoving the flyer away and revealing a group of protesters blocking the road. I honked my horn, but they stayed, waving their placards about. A crowd had formed on the pavement to the side, but my attention was on a single figure: a man with short, blond hair. He was strange. Everyone else was angry, but not him. He didn't look like he felt much at all. But he was staring at me, right into my eyes, clutching his stack of flyers. Then, just as my Glimpse was coming to an end, his mouth twisted into what I can only describe as a maniacal grin.

Elliot

I don't know why they bother broadcasting election results anymore. Everyone's known who the winner's going to be for at least a year; even the news started confirming it when enough Glimpses had been verified. And yet, every channel has been reporting on it all night as the votes come in. Mum says it's a part of tradition, a relic of the days before the Glimpses, back when the news was only ever about the present. Apparently, people used to stay up into the early hours of the morning, nervously watching the votes being counted with no idea what the result would be.

"And there we have it," the news reporter says from the TV in the living room, "the Alethia party have secured another seat and have won the election. We'll go live now to London, where Maria McBride will give her acceptance speech."

I roll my eyes and look down at my revision notes. The acceptance speech is as obsolete as the rest of it–Maria McBride has said her piece a thousand times already, ever since the first reports came in about people Glimpsing her victory. The words she's about to say have already been shared on GlimpseNet by countless people. They're set in stone. My exam results, on the other hand? I can't rely on fate for those. So, instead of listening to the news, I reread my notes and pray that I've done enough to at least pass.

"Elliot," Mum says, snapping me back out of focus. "You need to eat." She nods at the plate of cold, untouched toast beside my notes.

"I'm not hungry."

She raises an eyebrow.

"Fine." I grab the toast and take a bite, despite the nerves that have already filled my stomach. I guess it's probably not the best idea to go into an exam without breakfast. Still, with each bite I feel like I'm going to throw up.

"You'll be fine," Mum says after a moment. "At the end of the day, you can only do your best. I've seen how much work you've put in." Here she goes with one of her classic headteacher speeches, making me eternally grateful that I don't go to her school. She prattles on and I only half listen, letting my eyes drift back to my notes and taking another bite of cold toast.

"The Anti-Fates are out in force again," Dad says as he enters the dining room. He's wearing his nicest suit and has caked his hair in way too much gel, but I don't comment.

Mum scoffs. "Of course they are. There's nothing they won't protest these days."

I can hear the distant chants of the Anti-Fates on the news: "Restore free will!" They were saying the same at the last election. I remember Mum and Dad rolling their eyes at the sight of the measly protests on TV. The Anti-Fates was a much smaller group back then, but that was before the rumours about the Last Day.

"Honestly," Mum continues, "some people really have nothing better to do." She dismisses the topic with a shake of her head and looks Dad up and down. "You look nice, darling."

"Thanks. Can't be looking scruffy when I've got interviews to run." I hide a laugh–he says it like he doesn't wear a suit every day. "And on that note, I'd best be off."

"Have a great day!" Mum kisses him goodbye. I take that as my cue to wolf down the last bit of toast and leave the room before she has the chance to carry on her motivational speech.

There's a nervous crowd waiting outside the exam hall when I arrive at school. The air is filled with quiet voices, some whispering last minute revision to themselves, some trying to distract each other with conversation. I spot Callum and Nikita on the edge of the crowd, next to the water fountain. Callum has his back to a wall while Nikita stands mere millimetres away from him, their eyes locked on to each other's and a smile on both of their faces. They stand out a lot, not just because they're a happy couple pressed against each other while the rest of the crowd looks terrified, but also thanks to their matching red hair. And I mean red as in the literal colour red, not ginger like mine.

"Oh my God," I say as I approach them. "You actually went and did it."

They both face me with ridiculous grins. If it weren't for the fact Nikita's skin is a light brown while Callum's is white, they could almost pass for twins.

"Yep," Callum says, "and if it gets us some laughs at prom it'll be worth it."

"If you're even allowed to go," I say.

"Wait," Nikita says, "you don't think they'll ban us, do you?"

"They wouldn't dare," Callum says. "And besides, we already know we win prom king and queen."

Callum told me his absurd plan months ago. Thanks to his Glimpse, he knows he's going to win prom king and pass all his exams with flying colours, so he thinks if he breaks a bunch of school rules there'll be no consequences. The plan, therefore, was to do just that...but it's been months and he has maintained his head boy image perfectly. Until now.

"And you're *sure* you didn't mishear?" Nikita asks.

"I'm sure." He turns back to me and gestures at his hair. "So, what do you think?"

"I think it looks awful."

"Cheers, El. I can always count on you for compliments."

"You're welcome."

He smirks. "So, are you feeling ready for the test?"

"No," I answer honestly. "But I revised as much as I could."

"Same."

"Except you already know you're going to pass."

"True, but I still revised."

I roll my eyes, and I can tell Callum knows what I'm about to say because he does the same. "Don't you think that makes the Glimpse completely pointless?"

"Here we go again."

"What?" Nikita chimes in.

Callum turns to her. "Elliot's been reading up on Glimpse conspiracy theories."

"Oh?"

"What? No, I haven't! I'm just saying, the fact you still revised even though you know you're going to pass makes the whole thing unnecessary. It's a self-fulfilling prophecy. You saw yourself pass and responded by revising to make *sure* you pass."

It's a debate we've had a lot recently, especially since my birthday. Immediately after wishing me happy birthday, Callum asked when I'd be having my Glimpse. I told him that I'm not sure. I used to think I'd do what most people do and have my Glimpse as soon as I could, but the closer I got to sixteen the more I started doubting it. Callum's not entirely wrong about what I've been reading–it's impossible to avoid conspiracy theories when you research the Glimpses, especially with the Last Day approaching. But most of what I've read has been healthy debate about whether the Glimpses are beneficial to us.

"Whatever," Callum says now, dismissing any form of doubt about the Glimpses as he always does. "We've both revised. We'll both be fine."

Easy for him to say.

There's a sudden silence in the crowd as the exam hall doors swing open and the examiner, a short old man, hobbles out. After two weeks of exams, we all know the process, but he still runs through the list of rules before letting us enter in silence.

"Good luck," Callum whispers behind me as we walk in.

"It was fine. I think." I repeat the words for the fifth time. Callum smirks at the face I pull. He's sat across from me in the park, Nikita resting her head on his lap while she lies down.

"I told you it would go well," Mum says through my phone. "You're following in your brother's footsteps. I'm so proud."

Much like any of her motivational speeches, I've heard this one many times before. Ever since Simon got into Oxford, the slightest achievement on my part is me 'following in his footsteps.' Actually no, not since he got in, it's ever since his Glimpse showed him that he would.

He was halfway through year eleven when he turned sixteen, and he didn't even wait a day before marching his way into GlimpseTech. When he got home that day he was practically bouncing with excitement, and the front door had barely closed when he recounted his Glimpse to us in a loud, breathless stream of words.

"I SAW MYSELF AT OXFORD UNIVERSITY STUDYING MATHS AND I WAS IN A LECTURE AND I WAS MAKING ALL THESE NOTES AND I FELT LIKE I UNDERSTOOD IT ALL AND–"

After that it was plain sailing for him through sixth form, and soon enough he was packing his bags and on his way to Oxford, leaving me behind with the hefty expectation of doing just as well. I guess that's one of the reasons I've been so wary about having my own Glimpse–I'm scared it'll show me failing...or that it'll confirm I'm bound to be a disappointment.

"Anyway," Mum says through the phone, "I'd better be off. I don't have much time for a break today. I'll see you this evening."

"Yeah. See you."

She hangs up and I let out an unnecessarily dramatic sigh as I lean back on the sun-dried grass, taking in the summer warmth. The park is full of year elevens from all the local schools, ties and blazers off, school shirts untucked, buzzing with the freedom that the end of exams has brought.

Callum, Nikita, and I have planted ourselves on a slope beside the fountain. A rainbow has formed in its spray, and the occasional breeze sends cool droplets over us. It would be a perfectly nice sight, were it not for the graffiti on the fountain's base: END FATE, RESTORE FREE WILL.

"They're planning a protest here next week," Nikita says, nodding at the graffiti.

"How do you know?" I ask.

"My sister's going to it."

"Yeah, you'd probably get along with her, El," Callum. Says "She's big into the conspiracy theories too."

"For God's sake, I'm not into conspiracy theories. I'm just not sure about the Glimpses, that's all. I'm not about to protest against them."

Callum looks sceptical. I get it. His Glimpse was another step in his ascension to popularity, asking Nikita out was the first. He climbed the popularity ladder and continued to do well at school. While I watched from below.

"Look, I know how much you loved your Glimpse. That's fine, that's great, I'm happy for you. And I'm not saying I'll never have one, I'm just not sure. Now can we just *not* talk about Glimpses for a bit? Please." It comes out a lot snappier than I intended, but it seems to work because Callum nods.

"So," Nikita says, sitting up now as if the sudden tension made resting on Callum unbearable, "Elliot, have you got your prom suit ready?"

If I could bury my head in the ground, I would. "Damn, that's tomorrow, isn't it?"

"Um...yeah. Did you forget?"

"Well, I've got my suit and everything, I just forgot it's so soon." I guess exam stress has had more of an effect than I realised. Prom is tomorrow evening, but I haven't thought about it in weeks.

"You have sorted out how you're getting there, right?" asks Callum.

"I mean... I figured my dad would drive me or–"

"Your dad?!" He looks like I just slapped him in the face. "El, you can't turn up to prom in your dad's car."

"Why not?"

"Because everyone else will be turning up in limos and fancy cars, and don't act like your parents can't afford something like that for you."

He's not wrong–my parents paid for my brother's prom transport without question, but the difference is Simon went to prom with his friends and my only real friends are going together as a couple. I'd always assumed I'd be sharing a car to prom with Callum, until a couple of months ago when he revealed his plans for him and Nikita to have a romantic car ride together.

"And anyway," Callum continues, "aren't you going with Matt and that lot?"

Ah yes, the Matt plan. After Callum told me his prom plans, he suggested I ask Matt if I could join his group. Matt and I were close friends back in primary school, but we kind of drifted apart at secondary. We were in different forms so didn't see each other much, then I met Callum and Matt met some other people. Soon enough, we were more like friendly acquaintances than anything else.

After Callum and Nikita got together, things changed again. It felt a bit weird to be hanging out with a couple all the time, so every so often I'd leave them to do their own thing and ended up tagging myself on to Matt's group. They're all nice enough and are happy to talk to me, but it's obvious I'm just a spare part to them. They made this pretty clear when I asked about joining them for a ride to prom and they said they'd already booked a car with no room for me.

"Oh yeah," I say, "that kind of fell through."

"Oh. Sorry about that." He looks at Nikita and then me, sympathy all over his face that does nothing to make me feel better. "I mean... I guess there's room in our car if you wanted to–"

"No, no. Don't be stupid. I'm fine. You two should enjoy yourselves."

"You sure?"

"Yeah."

It's no secret that mine and Callum's friendship has become strained since he got with Nikita. It's no fault on her part–I get on with her quite well and, to be honest, think of her as more of a friend than Matt–but it's just always a little bit weird when the three of us are together. Unfortunately, that's what it's like most of the times I get to see Callum nowadays. Any time he used to have just for me is now reserved for Nikita.

"At least you'll be on our table," Nikita says, smiling a little too kindly.

Yeah, that's going to be weird too. For the prom meal, everyone has to be on tables of eight, so I'm going to be on a table with Callum, Nikita, and all of Nikita's friends, most of whom I've barely ever spoken to.

"True," I say. A feeling rises in my stomach, one that could so easily consume me if I dwell on it. A longing for what could have been. A prom without failed friendships or new girlfriends getting in the way. I cough the feeling away and pull out my phone, checking the time. 12:07. I've only been here half an hour and had every intention of staying longer, but all this prom talk isn't what I signed up for. It's all just a big reminder of what's changed. "I need to go."

"What? Why?" Callum asks.

I stand up and brush the grass off my clothes. "I've got stuff to do."

"I thought we could hang all afternoon?"

"No, it's fine. You two have fun. I'll see you tomorrow for prom."

I move to go but Callum jumps up and blocks my way. "El?"

"Yeah?"

"I'm sorry about the Glimpse thing. I was just joking. If that's why you're leaving, I-"

"That's not why I'm leaving. It's fine, really. See you tomorrow."

He lets me go.

Mum and Dad spend the entirety of dinner doting on me and comparing me to Simon. They make it all the more dramatic by video calling him and having me recount yet again that the exam was 'fine.' I try to tell them not to get so hyped up–we won't know my exam results for weeks yet–but they insist, and to top it all off they bring out a 'congratulations' cake for dessert.

When I finally get up to my room, I collapse onto my bed, completely drained of all energy. Beside me, the letter from GlimpseTech flutters in the breeze from my open window, taunting me. I've read it a few times since receiving it and have recounted the words in my head more times than that, but I still don't know what I'm going to do. Should I brave the Glimpse and seize my chance to find out my future? Or should I leave it up to fate?

My parents once told me that they used to doubt the Glimpses; everyone does at some point, I guess, and they spent a long time refusing to have one. For years after their marriage, they'd been desperate to have children, but no matter how hard they tried Mum just couldn't get pregnant. They were checked by doctors and told it was very unlikely they'd be able to have kids of their own. They were devastated, of course, but then Mum had her Glimpse and saw herself giving birth to Simon. Dad followed and saw himself playing in the park with both Simon and me. Mere weeks later, Mum found out she was pregnant.

I know what the protesters would say. They'd tell me the Glimpses eradicate our free will, that the world was better off before we could see into the future. But what if they're wrong? What if it's a good thing? What if, like for Callum, my brother, my parents, and countless others, my Glimpse could be something good?

Seb

"Fuck!" I drop the cigarette from my burnt fingers and watch as it falls off the crag. The orange embers fade away as it drops beneath the treeline below.

Aym is almost doubled over in laughter beside me. She's clutching the rock, probably trying not to follow the cigarette. "Thought you were meant to be a natural?"

"Fuck off. I am. I was just distracted."

"Sure."

I light another cig and take a drag but immediately let out a stream of coughs. I haven't smoked in months, and even then, I've only tried a couple of times before. It shows.

I offer it to Aym.

She shakes her head. "I'm good. Quit a couple weeks back, didn't I tell you?"

"Yeah. You did. Sorry, there's just been a lot of shit going on since then."

Aym doesn't ask what I mean. She's good like that– knows I'd have told her if I wanted her to know.

"I like your new hair, by the way," I say, admiring the jet-black braids.

"Thanks. About time I got something long." She's been changing her look a lot recently–I guess she's been figuring herself out. It's not just the clothes and hair either. Sure, she's swapped the t-shirts and jeans for a dress, and she's wearing bolder and brighter makeup, which is impossible to miss against her dark skin, but it's also in the way she holds herself. Like she's more comfortable in her body.

"How'd yesterday's exam go, by the way?" she asks.

"Shit."

"Fair."

"Just like the rest."

"Yeah?"

"Yeah. Failed everything."

"You don't know that."

I look at her with a raised eyebrow. "You know I didn't revise. Or do any work. Like, at all."

"Fair point. It's not the end of the world, though. I failed all my exams and look at me now."

She's not wrong. She's managed to get herself into an art college starting September, but it took two years and a couple of resits to get there. I'll probably have to do the same, not that I've got the time to waste on dream jobs right now. I lean back, ignoring how uncomfortable the rock is against my head. Aym does the same, and I feel her kick my foot lightly. I laugh, kick her back, and wonder if anyone's watching from below. If they see the scrawny pair of white legs and the thicker brown legs dangling off the edge of the crag, kicking each other while giggles echo from above, they'll probably think we're just a pair of carefree kids. Not a pair of queer teens hiding from all the shit at home we should be too young to deal with.

Our laughter dies down eventually, and we both lie still, staring up at the clouds, the smoke of my forgotten cigarette obscuring our view.

"So," Aym says, "did you get your letter?"

"Yep."

"And?"

"I'm not having a Glimpse."

Again, she doesn't question it, and this time she knows all the details. I've never kept my feelings about Glimpses a secret, just as she hasn't kept hers. I hadn't known Aym for long before she had her Glimpse; I think that might be why she's so close with me, but I was there to see how big a change it made in her life.

"Oh," Aym says, "I almost forgot." She dives into her handbag and pulls out a box wrapped in brown paper with a green ribbon tied in a bow around it.

"You got me a present?"

"'Course I did!"

"You didn't have to."

"Well, I did, so shut up and open it." She thrusts the present into my hands.

I untie the ribbon, tear off the paper and open up the box. Inside it, strapped around a small black cushion, is an insanely expensive looking wristwatch. "What the fuck?"

"That's...not the reaction I expected."

I stare at the watch, open mouthed, as the sunlight glints off its golden rim. The strap is dark brown leather, and the spinning gold cogs can be seen beneath the face. "No, I love it, but...how the fuck did you afford this?"

Aym laughs. "Oh, I didn't buy it."

My stare shifts to her. This is a weird way for her to tell me she's a thief.

The laughing stops when she sees my expression. "I didn't steal it either, idiot. It was a gift from my dad. To me."

"I don't understand."

She rolls her eyes. "When you look at that watch, would you say it's made for a man or a woman?"

I nod, realising what she's saying. "He's still on that, is he?"

"I don't think he'll ever accept that he's got a daughter instead of a son."

Aym's family have been awful to her since she came out as trans. You'd have thought her Glimpse would have convinced them, but they all claim she's making it up or that she's mentally ill.

I cast her a sad smile and carefully remove the watch from its box. "Thank you." I wrap it round my wrist. It looks pretty weird next to the rest of my clothes– a too-big, too-creased T-shirt plus jeans that have a few too many rips to pass off as intentional. The watch isn't subtle at all, either. The face is huge, nearly covering my entire wrist with the time.

Shit. The time. "I've got to go." I swing my legs onto solid ground and force myself up. "I'll see you tonight."

"Not changed your mind about going to prom then?"

"Fuck that."

Aym laughs. "Then yeah, I'll see you tonight."

"Thanks again for the present."

She gives me a thumbs up as I half-run away.

It takes about ten minutes to walk to my house from the crags, but I need to be back in five. I should have just waited till after Dad visited to meet Aym, but Mum was fast asleep this morning and I didn't want to wake her–sleep is such a rare thing for her these days it wouldn't be fair to not let her have it when it comes. But since she was asleep, I didn't have a chance to warn her about Dad, and if she sees him before me then that's a recipe for a breakdown.

I speed up and am out of breath in seconds– maybe smoking wasn't the best idea– but I push on, past the detached houses in the village on the edge of town with their identical gardens, along the pavement by the independent bakery and bookshop, until I cross the main road that divides the village from the outskirts of the town centre. Here, opposite the ugliest hospital known to man, is my street.

The sunlight is only just hitting the row of terraced houses; mornings here are dark thanks to the hospital blocking the sun. Instead of a bright beaming sunshine greeting me every morning, I get to stare at the sad-looking cement block that claims to heal people. We might not be far from the tourist-trapping village with its cute little shops and landmarks, but our street is a slum in comparison. Just two doors down from mine is a house with cardboard and newspaper over its broken windows, and there's a stream of litter on the edge of the pavement that never seems to move.

Just as I cross the road, I spot Dad's car pulling up near the graffitied bus shelter. I'm surprised I still recognise it; I've seen his car maybe three times in the last two years, and never for more than a few minutes. I wasn't expecting to hear from him at all today, not after last Christmas when all I got was a boxing day text wishing me well, but I woke up this morning to a text saying he'd be coming round with a birthday gift.

"Hey," he says, waving at me as he gets out of his car. I glance at my house. Mum's curtains are still drawn. If I can keep Dad outside maybe she won't have to see him at all.

"Hey."

"Happy birthday." He looks good. Too good. His hair has been cut and styled, his face is clean shaven, and he's wearing a creaseless button-up shirt. I've noticed changes like this every time I've seen him since he left us. The scruffy man who raised me–if you can call it that–is long gone. He's even holding himself differently. Confident. Happy.

He hands me a red envelope.

"Thanks. How are you? How's..."

"Samantha? She's good. We're good." There's a smile on his face that he's failing to hide. "I have some news on that front actually."

"Oh?"

"Yeah." He glances at the front door of the house. The brass number twenty-five is glinting ever so slightly in the sunlight. "Can I come in?"

"I'm not sure that's the best idea." I move myself so that I'm directly between him and the door. It's not a threat, but I think he gets the message. "So, what's your news?"

"Samantha's pregnant."

Oh, so that's what this is. He's not just here to wish me a happy birthday. He's here to say goodbye. He just doesn't have the balls to actually say the words. The red envelope in my hand suddenly feels a lot heavier.

"Oh," I say. "Cool." I know I should be telling him how happy I am for him, and I suppose a tiny part of me is. I've spent long enough without him fully in my life that I don't miss him, but this feels like an ending I didn't see coming.

Dad looks to the ground. That's the shame kicking in, I bet.

"Well," I say, "if that's everything?"

"Um, well, I..."

I nod. "Thought so. Thanks for the card." I turn and head for the front door but give him one last look before I turn the key. "Bye, Dad."

I spend a minute with my head pressed against the door once I'm inside, listening as Dad drives away for the last time.

"Sebastian?" comes Mum's voice from the living room. "Is that you?"

I find her sat on the sofa in the dark, curtains drawn. So, she wasn't in her bedroom after all. I wonder if she heard me and Dad.

"Yes, it's me. Can I open the curtains?"

Enough light is creeping in from the edges of the curtains that I can see her shake her head.

"How about the lights?"

"Okay."

I flip the switch and see Mum properly. She's slumped on the sofa in her pyjamas and dressing gown, her long, dark hair a matted mess. Another day without a shower. How many is that? Five? She's gone longer in the past, I suppose.

"Have you taken your pills yet?" I ask.

She looks unsure. "I was going to, but..." she gestures weakly toward the coffee table. It's a cluttered mess– newspapers, unwashed plates and mugs– the table is almost invisible under the pile, and there, on top of it all, is Mum's pillbox. Empty.

I try not to sigh. "You're out?"

Mum nods.

"Mum, I said you need to tell me when you're nearly out."

"I know. I just forgot."

"Well, you need to start remembering! I shouldn't be the one going to the chemist for you!" I feel my face flush with heat and my breaths come fast.

Mum looks at the floor and I feel like slapping myself in the face. This isn't her fault. I know that.

"Sorry. I didn't mean to shout." I sit down next to her. The sofa is stiff with age and covered in frayed cushions. I clutch Dad's envelope in my lap.

"What's..." Mum looks at the envelope and then quickly to my eyes. "It's your birthday."

It's a punch to the gut as I realise she's forgotten. Especially after what just happened with Dad. All I can manage is a nod. I feel like I'm about to cry, but then Mum gets up and darts out of the room, suddenly full of energy. I hear her move about in the kitchen cupboards, before she walks back into the living room, dragging a wrapped present almost as tall as her.

"Happy birthday," she says. It's the first time I've seen her smile since... I don't even know when.

"What...? What's...?"

She lays the present down on the floor. It's almost triangular in shape, thick, and wrapped in blue paper. The shape sends my mind in one direction immediately...but it can't be that. There's no way.

"Mum, what's...?"

"Open it!"

I join her across the room and start tearing off the paper, revealing the plain box underneath. I shake my head, because this really can't be what I think it is, but as I lift off the lid, I'm proven wrong.

It's a guitar. Not just any guitar, but *the* guitar I've been admiring for years. Every time I walk past the shop in town. Every time I watch a YouTube tutorial where someone's playing it. It's the one I pretend I have whenever I'm playing the old, scratched and battered guitar I've had since I was ten. It's an electro-acoustic, with a gleaming, dark, rosewood body. I stare in disbelief at the instrument, not even wanting to touch it in case I stain it with fingerprints.

I look up at Mum, who is still beaming in a way I haven't seen in years, and I'm about to say thank you but what comes out instead, and for the second time today, is, "How the hell did you afford this?"

"I've been saving up."

"Mum, I know how expensive this is. You can't waste your benefits on–"

"It's not a waste." She puts her hands on my shoulders. "It's your birthday present. You deserve it."

"But you must have saved up for ages. I can't take this, Mum, I know you don't have enough money."

She shakes her head. "I promise, it's fine."

I stare at the guitar again, already hearing myself play it in my head.

"Look," Mum says, "I'm gonna go have a shower, then go to the chemist, and then we can do whatever you want. Okay?"

It feels like emotional whiplash. Just a moment ago, I was ready to cry at the idea Mum had forgotten my birthday, and now here she is trying to make plans. It's rare these days that Mum will have this energy, so when it happens, I know I have to embrace it fully.

"Okay," I say, matching her smile.

THREE

Elliot

Bright spots of colour fill the room in every direction, both from the decorations and the girls' dresses. Even some of the boys have gone for bright colours in their suits. I spot Harvey Smith–resident football star and all-round twat–wearing an aqua blue blazer, something I wouldn't be able to wear without being called gay. I have to pause at the entrance to take it all in, this heaving mass of everyone in my year gathered together for one last celebration. Most of them don't even know my name.

Over at the drinks table, Callum has his arm around Nikita. They're both chatting to some girl I don't know and are impossible to miss with their dyed red hair and outfits to match. Callum spots me and waves me over; by the time I reach him the girl has moved on.

"Looking good, El," he says, giving my plain-as-possible suit a once over.

"Thanks, you too. And you, Nikita."

I already hate this. The music is quiet, and most people are chatting with each other, leaving the dance floor empty. I know where things are heading, though. Soon enough, everyone will be having a good time while I hang in the background, alone.

I can tell from Callum's smirk that he's already read me like a book. "You're bound to hate tonight if you don't let yourself go a bit," he says. "The night is young, my friend."

I roll my eyes.

An hour and a half later, everyone's eaten their meals and the dance floor opens up. Some rush straight to it, jumping into a dance with the first beat of the music. Others hang back, feeling out the vibe of the song before joining the eager dancers. And some, like me, stay sat at their table, watching.

Nikita and her gang of girls are part of the first group, and with a tug of his arm Callum follows. The couple skip straight to a close, intimate dance, while the rest of the girls start some sort of group dance that makes me think they've been practicing together.

It doesn't take long for the other tables to empty. Soon enough there's only a smattering of people left in their seats, and suddenly I feel exposed. I catch people glancing at me from the dance floor. They don't laugh, at least not obviously, but I can see the judgment in their eyes. I can hear the words they're thinking. *Loser. Loner. Freak.*

It shouldn't get to me, not when this is the last time I'll see of most of these people, but it does. This feels like the culmination of everything I've been feeling for the last few months. Sat here, while everyone dances with their friends and while Callum dances with his girlfriend, I've become a beacon of loneliness.

Even Matt and his friends are having a good time, on the opposite side of the room, laughing with each other while they pull the most ridiculous dance moves I've ever seen. They don't even seem to care that Harvey Smith's gang are pointing and howling at them. I guess they're doing what Callum keeps telling me I should do–letting go.

"Hey." Callum plants himself in the chair beside me with a thud.

"Hey."

I spot Nikita still on the dance floor with her friends. The song has changed. I didn't even notice.

"So, exactly how long are you gonna keep up this whole depressed loner vibe?"

I stare at him as if he's just slapped me in the face. It's one thing to think the people staring at me are thinking that–but my own friend? What the–

"I'm joking," he says. "Well, kind of. But mate, you really can't just sit around being sad all night. It's prom!" He throws his arms wide, as if he's attempting to reveal prom to me in a whole new light. Like the shining night of perfection it's always made out to be in the movies. "Just come and dance? Just once? Please?"

I meet his eyes. Eyes that are hard to say no to. "Maybe. But I don't know. I just–I don't want people staring at me. I mean, I know they already are, but I–"

"Dude." He puts a hand on my leg, which I hadn't even realised was shaking before, and suddenly my every focus is on that point of contact. "Calm down."

I try to slow my breathing but find it falters. My heart races and the music seems to fade away until all I can hear is my own pulse. And I can't stop staring at Callum's hand. His perfect, smooth–

"Elliot?"

I look straight back at his face. "Yeah?"

"Are you listening?" He removes his hand and I feel instant relief. The music returns.

"Yeah. Sorry." I shake my head to clear it. I was just overwhelmed, that's all.

"Look, I know you kind of hate all this, and I get it, I swear, but I've heard Harvey's throwing an afterparty at his house and pretty much everyone's going. Do you want to join?"

I immediately ready myself to say no.

"And I know you're probably thinking that's not your scene either," he goes on, "but I think it'd be different. There's no dancefloor. Just music and chatting, you know?"

"And alcohol?"

"Well yeah, probably, but just because it's there doesn't mean you need to drink it."

The last (and only) time I was at a party with alcohol was Callum's sixteenth. I remember how surprised I was when I turned up at his house to find rows of bottles just sitting in the kitchen. But when Nikita and her friends showed up, they acted like nothing was out of the ordinary. Like it was an expectation. I hadn't realised until then that underage drinking at parties is kind of the norm. At least among the popular kids.

When everyone started drinking, I was tempted to join. But I just found myself panicking whenever I got near a bottle. All I could hear was my mum's voice in my head, ranting at me about the dangers. So, I went for lemonade instead.

"What do you think?" Callum says now. "Nikita's getting an early night, so I figured it could be fun for you and me to g–"

"Nikita's not going?" I say a little too quickly.

"No. She's going on holiday tomorrow, so after prom she's going straight home."

"I see." When I imagined prom back in younger years, one thing was always clear in my head. Though I could picture a thousand different themes, and any random people joining our table, I always saw me and Callum laughing and smiling together. Best friends celebrating the end of school. No girlfriends. No distractions. That's obviously not the prom I've ended up getting, but maybe this party could be an alternative.

"So....?"

"So, yes. I'll come."

Callum beams, and for a moment my heart races again. "Amazing."

"I need an excuse to tell my parents though. They're not going to want me to be at this party. Can you imagine their reaction?"

"Fair point. Just tell them you're staying at mine for the night."

I nod. That'll work. My parents have always liked Callum. Staying over at his isn't that unusual. At least, it wasn't before Nikita was in the picture.

"Callum!" Nikita calls from the dance floor. She's waving him over as a new song starts. I vaguely recognise it but can't place the name.

"Back to it," he says, getting up off the chair. "Are you joining?"

I look at him, and then to the dancefloor. "Go on then."

Harvey lives quite close to the hotel, it's just a short walk up a hill. The promgoers divide into two groups as soon as they're outside–one is composed of almost all the popular kids, who set off walking to Harvey's house with him leading them like the pied piper; and the other is everyone else getting into their parents' cars to head home. It feels wrong to be following the first group, and I can't help but glance back at Matt and his friends getting into cars, wondering if I made a mistake not joining them.

I've seen Harvey's house a million times, but I've never crossed the gates; it's hard to miss–set back from the village but raised up on a hill for all to see. Up close, it's even more impressive. Gardens almost as big as the school field surround it, perfectly mown and with a large fountain in the centre. The house itself looks like it should be a hotel, pillars flank the front door and ivy decorates half the walls. It's way too big for just one family, especially since I'm pretty sure Harvey's two siblings are at university.

By the time Callum and I reach it, most people are already inside and music has just started blasting. Callum gives me an eager smirk before we step through the front door. My every sense is immediately under attack. Music mixes with the voices of everyone inside, forming a swamp of noise to wade through. In front of us is a grand staircase, already littered with people, some of whom, I notice, aren't dressed in formal clothes and look a little older than us.

"Must be his brother's friends," Callum says, only just audible.

"Huh?"

"Those guys." He points at the older people. "I think one of Harvey's brothers is back from uni. Must have invited some people over."

I loosen my tie, suddenly feeling suffocated. I didn't think there'd be anyone except people from our year here, and now everything feels more intense.

"Come on," Callum says, heading to the living room.

I follow closely, as though being near him will keep me safe.

The crowd is much more concentrated in here, and the music is even louder. I spot the speakers in the corner– they're huge, professional standard, which I guess shouldn't surprise me. Sofas, crammed full of boys with their ties undone and girls with their dresses sprawled all over the place, span the length of the room. A TV screen fills an entire wall on which people are playing some car racing game–not that I can spot who has the controllers when there are this many people.

Harvey is stood by the speakers, can of cider in hand while he chats to a group of girls who I've said hello to no more than once in my life. A cheer emanates from a crowd of boys stood in the middle of the room as one of the virtual cars wins its race.

"Fancy a drink?" Callum asks.

I spin around to find him stood at a table covered in drinks which I hadn't even realised was there. I'm reminded of the selection at his birthday party, except there's a whole lot more to choose from here. And not a soft drink in sight.

"It's okay if not," he says, grabbing a can of beer (I think).

"I, uh." I scan the drinks again. I recognise some names, but I have absolutely no idea what any of them taste like. I loosen my tie a little more; I swear this place is getting hotter.

"Hey! Callum! How's it going?" A boy I only vaguely recognise walks up to Callum with a hand raised, ready to collide with Callum's in some weird cool-guy handshake thing (which I've never seen Callum do until now).

"Hey Carl. Long-time no see."

Carl? The name doesn't ring a bell. He's black, with short-cropped hair, intense cheekbones, and dressed in a T-shirt and denim jacket. Not in our year, I guess.

"I know," Carl says. "Too long. What you been up to?"

"Ah, you know, exams and shit. Got a girlfriend."

"No way! Nice job, is it going well with her?"

"Yeah, really good, she's great. How about you? You still with...what's his name? Seth?"

"Seb. And no, that's over."

"Shame."

Seb...I recognise that name. There's a Seb in our year, though I've never spoken to him. Bit of an outsider I guess, even more so than me. Scrawny guy, with messy dark hair and blue eyes. I used to hear people chat about him sometimes, spreading rumours that he was gay. I've only ever really seen him on his own, or occasionally with–ah, I do recognise Carl. He's from the year above us. Around the end of year ten I used to see him hanging with Seb. Looks like the rumours were true.

I cough. And I'm not actually sure if it was an accident, but it gets Callum and Carl's attention.

"This is my friend," Callum says. "Elliot."

"Hey," Carl says.

"Hey."

There's a moment where we all just stand in silence, until Callum and Carl get back to their conversation. I feel my cheeks turn red. My attention turns back to the alcohol. I remember the day after Callum's party, when I asked him what it had been like to get drunk for the first time. He answered in detail, but the main thing I remember was how he said it made him feel free. Free of worries or anxieties. I could really do with a feeling like that right now.

I reach out, grab a can of I-don't-know-what, and take a gulp.

I don't know how long it's been since my first drink. All I know is that I love this song and listening to Callum singing along has me howling with laughter. We're both moving to the music. It's weird and I'm not used to it at all, but it's fun all the same. Callum guides me, laughing when I mess up and helping me get back on track. At one point, when the chorus of one of the few songs I know swells, he throws his arm over my shoulder and sings up at the air with me. For some reason, I feel like grabbing his hand to keep his arm around me a little longer.

Soon, when a new song starts and a spot finally opens up on the sofa, I follow Callum down onto it, naturally leaning against him. Heat radiates off his body and I take it in, staring at his face as he leans back, eyes closed, relaxing.

He opens one eye and notices me looking. "Hey," he says.

"Hey." I take in every detail of his face. His sharp jawline, his smooth skin, the dyed-red hair still held in place by the product he must have put in it, his eyes, now open, blue, beautiful. I lean in closer. And closer. And–

"Woah there." He shuffles back a little.

I go rigid, realising what I almost did.

"I think you've had a bit too much to drink, El."

My heart is racing. A cold sweat breaks out across my chest.

"I'll go grab you some water." He gets up and walks away, leaving me to myself. My shaking, terrified self.

What the hell did I just do? What was I thinking? No wonder Callum's walking away from me; he's never going to want to speak to me again! And why should he? He's my best friend. My *only* friend. And I tried to kiss him.

I look around, checking to see if anyone is looking. If anyone saw. But they're all engaged in their own conversations or bobbing their heads or singing along to the music. No one's looking at me. But what if they were before? What if they know what I almost did? What if–?

I get up. I can't stay here. I have to get out. I push through the crowd to the entrance hall, but the front door is blocked by a group of new arrivals, their hands filled with bags of snacks and boxes of beer cans. They cheer as they walk in, ready to turn up the energy of the party even more. As if it needs that. I turn instead to the stairs. There has to be somewhere in this huge house without people, where I can sit and think. And hide. I grab hold of the banister and walk–no, run–up the stairs, darting down a corridor and throwing myself against the door of a random room.

It's a bedroom. Empty and quiet. I can't even hear the music from here. But that means I can hear every single one of my thoughts loud and clear. I stumble to the bed, throw myself down on it, and cry.

Seb

"If this is shit, I'm gonna kill you." I tell Aym when I meet her at the end of my street.

I left Mum sleeping on the sofa after watching a film trilogy. I was planning on going up to my room, maybe playing a bit of guitar before bed, but then I got a text from Aym: **Party tonight at that twat Harvey Smith's house. You down?**

I can't say I jumped at the chance–'Harvey's a right bell-end who called me all sorts of shit when he found out I was gay–but getting drunk with Aym in a massive house on my birthday does sound fun, so I agreed.

"If it's shit, we'll leave," Aym says, throwing her arm round my shoulders. She's wearing the tightest dress I've ever seen her in, plus high heels and a blonde wig. I feel underdressed in my T-shirt and jeans, but why should I dress up for a bunch of dickheads from school? Even if they are all still in their prom gear.

A taxi pulls up on the curb and we get in. Harvey's house isn't that far, but I didn't even bother asking if we were gonna walk–not while Aym's wearing those shoes.

"Good birthday so far?"

"It actually has been, yeah." I fiddle with the watch Aym gave me; it feels heavy on my wrist. "I got a new guitar."

"No way!"

"Yeah...not sure how Mum afforded it. I've wanted it for years though."

Aym shrugs. "She must've saved up."

I nod. I'm not sure I'll ever believe that.

"And, uh...did your dad show up?"

I give her a look that says it all. "Yep. For the last time. His girlfriend's pregnant."

Aym nods and, like always, doesn't question it.

The taxi turns a corner, heading up a hill where the houses die away and the trees take over. We're heading straight into rich country. As the ground flattens out, the taxi pulls to a stop, I can hear the music blasting from Harvey's house before even opening the car door. The ground is practically pulsing with the beat.

Aym pays the driver, and we hop out. I feel like laughing at the sight of Harvey's house. I mean, it's just stupidly big. I don't even know what I'd do with that much space.

"Jesus," I say.

"Yep." Aym sidles up beside me and throws an arm over my shoulder. "Welcome to 'how the other half live.'"

We start heading up the driveway, which–of course–is paved with slabs of polished white stone.

"I knew he was rich," I say, "but this is something else. Why doesn't he go to a private school? His folks obviously have the money."

"People used to ask his brother that back when he was at school. Apparently, their dad thinks sending them to state school is like 'character building' or something."

"Right, so we're supposed to train him to be able to handle himself around poor people?"

"Basically, yeah."

"Sounds like a challenge."

I push open the overly heavy door, revealing the swarm of people on the other side. You can tell the party's been going on for a while because everyone looks just a little bit shit. Of the ones who went to prom, there are missing ties, untucked and unbuttoned shirts, stained dresses, and even one couple who've stripped down to their underwear. A crowd is egging them on while they make out at the bottom of the staircase.

Aym hauls me away from the live porn and into the living room, where people are clumsily dancing to music across from a selection of drinks covering the dining room table.

"Guess we'd better play catchup," Aym says, grabbing the closest drink to her. I know full well she doesn't care what it is.

I shrug, "Guess so," and do the same.

It's been a while since I last got drunk, so whatever's in this drink hits me pretty quickly. I don't get invited to many parties, especially not since the night I broke up with Carl. That one was messy. I remember my throat hurt from the never-ending cycle of screaming and crying. He got way more tears out of me than he deserved, even though it was me that broke up with him and not the other way round. I called Aym and had barely started speaking before she told me to come round to hers. So, I did. I spent the night with her, talking about what an absolute nob her so-called cousin was while downing drink after drink. Maybe not the best way to cope but hey, it made having my heart shredded to bits a lot more fun.

That's why, when I see Carl chatting with some guy I don't know, I have to laugh. It's like I've summoned him into existence with my memory.

"Wha's so funny?" Aym slurs. Like me, her tolerance is pretty low, and we're both drunk after basically just one drink. Or three. I don't even know.

I grab her arms and sway with her to the music, laughing. It's not even a sway'y song. Is that a word? Sway'y? Like sway-E? Doesn't matter.

"Nothing," I say. I spin her around in some corny dance move, facing her away from Carl. He might be my ex, but I think Aym would be more upset to see him. I'm not the one he hurled transphobic abuse at, after all.

The funniest thing is, I wouldn't even know Aym if it wasn't for Carl. When we first started dating at the start of year ten, before he was ready to come out and be near me at school, I spent a lot of time at his house. His parents didn't love the idea of him being gay, but it sort of became a case of as long as we didn't kiss in front of them, it was fine. My mum was fully okay with it, but I didn't really want Carl to see my house. Not while Mum was, well, the way she is now. In any case, I was at Carl's a lot, and his family is (or was) pretty close, so his cousins were round all the time. Enter Aym–not that she went by that name back then.

Aym and I hit it off pretty fast. She used to chill with me and Carl whenever the parents were nearby, and she was super invested in our relationship. But then Aym had her Glimpse and, as most things have these past few years, everything went to shit. I broke up with Carl as soon as I found out the stuff he was saying to Aym.

Seeing him now, much as I hate him, the good memories are still there. I keep swaying with Aym, stealing glances at Carl over her shoulder. I can't help but picture us pressed together in his bed. I still remember the taste of his lips. The smoothness of his skin. The–

Carl's friend walks off, and Carl looks up. Right at me. A million feelings flash across his expression all at once. Like a TV screen has appeared right in front of him, replaying our entire relationship, blasting it into his eyes. But then he looks away, grabs a new drink, and leaves the room. Asshole.

Since he's in the year above me and at a sixth form halfway across town, I haven't seen him at all since the breakup. I never got the chance to make him feel as shit as he made Aym feel. It was all over in a flash. Me and him, arguing at a party. Me crying. Him leaving. I barely got to see his reaction. I just cried tears that should have been his.

The song changes and I grab another drink.

"You look angry," Aym says, almost spilling her own.

"I'm fine." The drink burns my throat as it goes down.

I scan the room, recognising most faces as people from school, except for one boy stood in the corner on his own. He's wearing a polo shirt and tight, checked trousers, so I guess he's older than me. Probably Carl's age. Maybe even eighteen. He has short, blond hair and cheekbones so sharp you could use them as a razor.

"I'm going to the toilet," Aym says, sauntering away. She's already out of earshot before I can reply.

The blond boy's eyes scan the room. I wonder why he's alone. Did he not come with someone? Maybe his friend is one of the two dry-humping on the stairs. His eyes finally land on me, and my lips morph into a smile. He raises an eyebrow and bites his lip. Suddenly the memories of Carl are swapped out with fantasies of this guy.

I'm sober enough to be able to stop myself, but I decide to let the alcohol take control. Why the fuck not? I walk over to him, immediately getting way closer than I would with a stranger normally. I can practically feel his body heat.

"Hey," he says. His voice is deep. It reminds me of Carl's. And I guess that's all it takes.

I lean forwards and his hand moves to the small of my back. Suddenly my lips are on his, then his tongue is on mine and his hands are all over me and I can already feel something going on below the belt.

"Jesus, take it somewhere else you fucking faggots."

The voice comes from behind me. I don't recognise it, but it's quickly joined by others.

"Benders!"

"Fags!"

"Poofs!"

Before I have chance to respond someone grabs me from behind and throws me to the floor. This face, I recognise. Steve Macintosh, one of Harvey's mates from school, a mutated ball of muscle with a face that's permanently pissed off. This isn't the first time he's laid hands on me. I'll never forget the bruise he left when he punched me behind the sports equipment shed. I didn't give him any sign of weakness then, and I'm certainly not about to now.

I stand up and face him. The boy I was kissing has already vanished from the wall behind him. Must've run away.

"What's your problem, Steve?" I say, definitely not slurring my words. "Did you want to join in?"

He raises his fist. "What did you just say, you gay piece of sh–"

"Stop! Stop!" Out of nowhere, Carl throws himself in front of me. He's taller and wider than me–looks like he's been working out since we broke up–so he completely blocks my view. "I know you're not about to start a fight, are you Steve?"

I don't hear him respond, but I can feel the tension fade from the air. The crowd that formed around us slumps with disappointment and some people even turn away.

"Thought not," Carl says, turning to face me, as Steve heads for the drinks table. Carl smiles at me like he's expecting me to call him my hero.

"What the fuck was that?" I say instead.

His smile vanishes. "What do you mean? He was about to punch you, I came to–"

"To what? To save me? I don't need saving, Carl. Especially not by you."

"I wasn't just gonna stand back and let him say all that shit to you!"

I almost laugh. "Right. So homophobia is a no-go zone, but you're all for transphobia towards your own cousin?"

"That's different. That's–"

"No, it's not any different, Carl! You're just as bad as Steve and all the rest of them. Worse, even, because you do it to your own family!"

"Carl?" It's Aym. I don't know how long she's been listening, but she's stood beside me now, giving Carl a look so vile I can almost feel it, like the heat from a flame.

Carl stares at her. As far as I know, they haven't seen each other since I broke up with him, which means Carl's never seen Aym truly expressing herself. He's never seen her in full makeup, or a dress, or heels, and certainly not in a wig. He looks disgusted.

"Come on, Seb," Aym says, looping her arm through mine. "Let's go."

She turns me around to leave, and I notice people are still staring at us–the crowd from the almost-fight hasn't fully dispersed. These people are hungry for any sort of drama, no matter who it hurts.

We're almost at the open living room doorway when Carl speaks up, voice laced with anger and bitterness. "See you around, Andy."

Both of us stop in our tracks, as if the ground grew hands and grasped onto our feet. He just deadnamed Aym. Just like he used to do every time he saw her after she came out. Just like so many members of her family keep doing to this day.

I feel her arm tense, and I can't even imagine how hurt she must feel right now. I'll never know how she truly feels, but I can do something about it.

Maybe it's still the alcohol taking over, but I spin loose of Aym's grip and run full pelt at Carl.

I punch him once. Twice. Five times. He struggles beneath me. Then he's on top. I take a blow to the face. I dodge another. I get free and force him down again. Noise surrounds us. Cheering. Screaming. Laughing. I can't keep track. His fist connects with my face again. I feel a wetness under my nose. Red drops fall from my face to Carl's shirt.

A force on my back pulls me to my feet, away from Carl, leaving him squirming on the floor. In a blur, I find myself being led out of the room and up the stairs. The world around me is spinning. I can't see properly. Or hear. Or–

Aym shoves me against a door. We're in a corridor upstairs. The bright lights that dot the ceiling hurt my eyes and there's a ringing in my ears.

"Care to explain what the hell just happened?" Aym says, giving me the same foul expression she gave Carl minutes ago.

"I... I..."

"I'll tell you what just happened. You just beat up Carl in front of *everyone*!"

What was blurry in the moment is now becoming clear in my memory. I see myself running at Carl. I see myself forcing him to the ground and punching him. And him punching me back. And all the people going wild around us.

"I wasn't... I just... He deadnamed you, Aym! What was I supposed to do? Just let it slide?"

She sighs. "It's not last year anymore, Seb. I can fight my own battles. I know you care about me, and I love you for it, but beating up my cousin isn't going to help anyone." She's right. Of course, she is. And it doesn't escape my notice that I said almost the exact same thing to Carl after he got between me and Steve.

I take a deep breath, but almost choke on the blood that's still pouring from my nose.

Aym rolls her eyes. "Let's get you cleaned up." She pulls some tissues out of her handbag and forces them against my face. "Pinch your nose and *don't* tilt your head back. I'll go grab some more from the bathroom. You wait in there." She nods at the door behind me and runs off.

I do as she says and pinch my nose while wiping away the excess blood. What must I look like right now? I stumble through the door, guess I'm still a little drunk, which means my nose probably hurts a lot more than I realise.

It's a bedroom. Perfectly tidy and way too white to be in here with a bleeding nose. And I'm not alone.

A boy stares at me from the bed. He's wearing a simple black prom suit with a loose blue tie and is sitting cross-legged on the bed. His eyes are red and puffy, like he's been crying, and his curly ginger hair is all messed up. I recognise him, but only faintly. I've never spoken to him before. His name's something like Ethan or Edward or Elton.

"Um..." I start. "Sorry, I, er, I didn't realise anyone was in here." I stop looking directly at his eyes. He's in here alone, so anyone seeing him cry is probably the last thing he wants. "I'll just..." I grab the door handle.

"No," he says, voice shaky. "It's fine. I'm leaving anyway." He pushes himself off the bed and barges past me, right out the door before I can respond.

Immediately after, Aym walks in. "What's up with him?" she says, glancing back at the boy who I assume is running away. She's carrying an entire roll of toilet paper.

"God knows."

Elliot

Sure, universe, go ahead and taunt me. Send in the one kid from my year I know for sure is gay right when I'm crying about almost kissing my best friend. Perfect timing. Really solid. And to make things even better, it's starting to rain. I know I should call a taxi, or even just call my parents and admit I lied about going to Callum's. They'd be furious, but at least I'd get home quicker, into a warm bed and out of this drizzle. But no. I'm not ready to talk to them yet. Or anyone, for that matter.

I amble down the hill, the music from Harvey's house growing ever more distant as I go. I wish the same could be said for my memory. I keep reliving the moment I almost kissed Callum. What was I thinking? It was a stupid, drunken mistake that has ruined everything. There's a long string of texts from him on my phone, checking that I'm okay, asking where I am. He hasn't mentioned what happened, but part of me thinks that's even worse. If he won't acknowledge it or brush it off with a joke, he must be thinking about it. Just like me, he's probably replaying it in his head. He'll be pulling all sorts of conclusions and putting pieces together. If there are any pieces to put together–I mean, I don't even know what happened. I don't find him attractive. I don't find *men* attractive. I like girls. I'm straight.

My phone buzzes as another text comes in. From Callum.

Are you okay?! Where are you???

I feel sick. Like any second I might turn and throw up at the side of the road. And I don't think it's just because of the alcohol.

I'm fine, I text back. **I'm going home. Enjoy the party.**

I've always loved Callum. As a friend. He's always been there for me, and we've been so close throughout high school. Well, at least before Nikita. Not that I'm jealous. How could I be jealous? She's his girlfriend. Sure, I'd love to spend more time with him, but as friends. Nothing more than that.

But then why did I feel so alone when I watched them dancing together at prom? Because I want a girlfriend too? Because I want to be in a relationship instead of being a third wheel? That must be it. But there was also the moment he put his hand on my leg, where my heart raced, and I couldn't think straight. And the way I looked at him at the party. His face... I thought it was so cute. So...kissable. But why? It was just the alcohol! It had to be! Except I wasn't drunk yet at prom.

I remember my first proper crush, back in year nine. I'd found girls attractive before, but I'd never really thought of asking someone out until I met Jessica. It was the start of a new term, so the teacher did what they always seem to do in a new term and changed the seating plan. Miss Jackson was usually nice and let us sit next to whoever we wanted, but thanks to some idiots by the names Harvey and Steve, she decided the class's behaviour was too bad to let us sit with our friends.

In the new plan, I was sat next to Jessica Adams. I'd never really spoken to her before, but I'd certainly noticed her. It was hard not to–she had this dark blonde hair that curled ever so slightly, big brown eyes, and the cutest smile I'd ever seen. I fully expected to not have anything in common with her, but it turned out we were equally clueless when it came to chemistry and that made us find every practical lesson extremely funny.

One evening, when I was gaming at Callum's house, he mentioned how he'd noticed Jessica and I getting along. I immediately went bright red, so it was already impossible to hide the fact I had a crush on her. Callum found it way too exciting and started begging me at every opportunity to ask Jessica out. I was against it at first, scared of the potential embarrassment, but he wore me down and after a few weeks I plucked up the courage and asked her.

She said no. So, you know, that didn't feel great, and it solidly put me off asking anyone out for the rest of my school life, but if there's one thing it proves, it's that I like girls. I find them attractive–even my internet history backs that up. And when I imagine my future, I see myself marrying a woman.

And yet...the closest I've ever gotten to kissing someone was with Callum at the party tonight.

By the time I get home, my blazer is heavy and my shirt is clinging to my skin, completely soaked by the drizzle. I open the door, trying to make as little noise as possible, but that proves entirely pointless when I find a dishevelled Mum and Dad stood on the other side, car keys in hand, both pulling on coats.

"Elliot!" Mum howls, throwing herself at me and pulling me against her into a hug.

"Mum? What's–?"

She lets me go as quickly as she grabbed me, now looking furious. "What the hell do you think you're doing going to a party this late without telling us? Get inside, right now!"

I step in, wet shoes squeaking against the wooden floor, and close the door behind me. Rain drips from my hair, getting caught in my eyelashes. I know I'm supposed to say something, but I don't know what.

Dad speaks first. "Callum called us."

"What?"

"He said you'd run off from this party and he didn't know where you were and wanted you to get home safe."

My chest tightens.

"You lied to us!" Mum chimes in. "You said you were staying at Callum's. I can't believe this!"

"I'm sorry, I–"

"Damn right you're sorry! I've never been more disappointed in you!"

A lump forms in my throat and the tears come before I can stop them. Mum and Dad glance at each other; they've never been great at handling me when I'm upset.

"We'll discuss it in the morning," Dad says.

Mum looks like she's about to disagree, but Dad raises his eyebrows and that seems to do the trick.

I nod and walk past them, pulling off my soggy (and quite possibly ruined) shoes before heading upstairs. I leave my clothes in a damp pile on my bedroom floor and climb into bed, sobbing uncontrollably.

Tonight has been too much. All of it. Too. Much. I've never been less sure of myself and no matter how hard I try, I can't shake the image of Callum's face from my mind. The way he looked at me after I nearly kissed him. The surprise. The confusion. I hear Dad's words again: 'he didn't know where you were and wanted you to get home safe.' No matter what Callum thinks of me after what happened, he still cares. He's still my friend. Right?

I roll over. A sliver of moonlight cuts through the gap in my curtains and falls on the letter from GlimpseTech, still sitting on my bedside table.

I've always had this image of what my future would be. Me, a wife, maybe even children. But now it's all a blur. I know how I feel about girls. I thought I knew how I felt about boys. But now, my certainty's been shaken. That future I thought I knew has all but disappeared. It's in flux. Hidden away. Falling apart because I can't get a closer look. But there's a way to fix that, right here in a letter next to my bed.

Everybody knows the so-called Last Day is coming up–the twenty-eighth of July– the day beyond which no one has ever seen in their Glimpse. There are all sorts of theories about what this might mean; the one about the world ending is how the Anti-Fates gained so many new supporters. GlimpseTech denies it, of course, but I don't know what I believe. Maybe the chance of me winding up happily married to a woman has never been on the cards. But maybe my Glimpse could show me something. Something *certain*. Something to hold on to. Right now, that's all I need.

Seb

I wake, lying in the bed in Harvey's house, head throbbing. Aym is next to me, passed out on top of the covers. The dim, early morning light peeks through the curtains and reveals a red stain across what was once a clean, white pillow beneath my head. I think it's safe to say Harvey's gonna get all the grief he deserves when his parents discover the mess.

I sit up and check my nose. It's painful to the touch, but my hand comes away dry. A digital clock glares at me from the bedside table: 6:07 AM. I can't have been asleep for long, and I could definitely use some more, but I reckon now's the perfect time to sneak out without anyone in the house noticing.

I shove Aym and speak in a hurried whisper. "Psst. Hey, Aym, wake up."

Aym groans and twists her body round to face me, opening her eyes the smallest amount possible. "What?"

"We need to go."

"Huh?"

"Now. Come on!" I roll off the bed and drag Aym with me, much to her annoyance.

"Slow down," Aym says, sounding like her vocal cords have been through a shredder, "My head is killing me."

"I know. Mine too." I grab her by the arm and try to drag her off the bed. "Get your shoes on and let's get out of here."

Downstairs is a mess—people are passed out on every flat surface, some only half dressed, some less than half, bottles and cans lie everywhere, and it absolutely stinks. Quiet chatter is coming from the living room; all the awake people must be in there, probably having the deep chats you can only have after a night with no sleep. I wonder who's in there. Would Carl have stayed the whole night?

"For God's sake," Aym mutters as she stumbles down the stairs. I glance back to see her rolling her eyes and pulling off her heels. She walks the rest of the way down much more steadily. "Right. Taxi's outside. Let's go."

"One second," I whisper. It's a stupid idea, since the last thing I want right now is another confrontation, but I walk towards the living room anyway.

"What're you *doing*?"

"Ssh."

I get as close as I can to the living room door without being seen by anyone inside and listen. They're talking quietly, in the intimate way people do at times like these, so I can't hear everything, but I get the gist. Something about school ending. Something about college. One person talks about their Glimpse–yawn. But I'm not here to listen to the conversation, I'm here to listen for one voice in particular.

"Honestly, I'm pretty hyped for college," Harvey says, his pompous tone impossible to mistake for anyone else.

"Same," Steve grunts.

"What subjects are you doing?" comes an unfamiliar girl's voice.

They go on, a few other voices adding to the mix, some I recognise, some I don't, but no Carl. I lean a little closer, just enough that I'm able to peek into the room, keeping my fingers crossed that no one sees me.

The group is sitting in a deformed circle, some on the sofas and some on the floor, and there he is. Carl. Barely in the circle but awake and listening to the conversation. My body relaxes as I study him. There's a bloodstain under his nose, but other than that he doesn't look too bad. I didn't hurt him as much as I thought I did (at least not visibly). Much as I hate him and think he deserved payback for what he said to Aym, beating him up was a very drunk idea. I don't want to be the reason someone ends up in hospital.

"*SEB,*" comes Aym's almost-too-loud-to-be-a-whisper from behind me.

I back away from the living room and join her. "Sorry. Let's go."

When I get back home, I keep quiet, figuring Mum will still be asleep. Usually, I'd try to get her up early–especially after a good day like yesterday, since she might be at the start of a streak of good days–but right now all I want to do is sleep. I head straight to my bedroom and pass out as soon as my head hits the pillow.

My headache is even worse when I wake up, and the pang of hunger in my stomach does nothing to help. I check my phone: 3:35 PM. Jesus, no wonder

I'm starving. I haul myself out of bed and head downstairs, pressing one hand against my throbbing temple and using the other to text Aym.

NEVER. LET. ME. DRINK. ALCOHOL. EVER. AGAIN.

It's quiet downstairs. No sign of Mum at all. The living room remains a mess and the kitchen is still unused; it's been at least a week since either of us properly cooked anything. I guess she's still in bed; so much for thinking she's on a good streak. I'm hungry enough for a full-on feast but as soon as I open the fridge and see my options, I feel sick. I settle for toast instead.

A text comes through from Aym: **Sure, so long as you don't let me drink either.**

Deal, I reply.

I lower myself gently onto the sofa with my plate of toast, every movement causing my headache to flare up even more. There's nothing good on TV, just a boring news segment about the new prime minister. She's making a speech about her plans to launch an investigation into GlimpseTech. Honestly, who gives a shit? It's not like it'll make a difference. GlimpseTech would fall apart if everyone just stopped having Glimpses, no need for some big investigation to 'expose the truth.' I don't know what 'truth' people are expecting to find out anyway. We already know how the Glimpses work. We know about the rules. And we can read people's Glimpses online. What more is there to find out?

If I were prime minister, I'd make Glimpses illegal altogether; life would be better that way. There'd be no more people building their lives around what they see in their Glimpse, no more people desperately trying to avoid their inevitable future, no more people giving up on life because they Glimpsed nothing but blackness. No more dads abandoning their families because they Glimpsed a life with a new wife and kid.

Hours of dull TV pass by–I only watch it to distract me from my hangover–and there's still no sign of Mum. It's not completely unusual, she's spent days in bed before, entire weeks even, but I figure I should check on her. If nothing else, then to make sure she's taken her pills.

I head upstairs, bringing a glass of water with me, and knock on her door.

No answer.

"Mum?" I call softly. "Are you okay?"

No answer.

"Mum?" A little louder now. "I'm just gonna come in, okay?"

No answer.

I push open the door. It's almost pitch-black inside; her curtains are drawn tightly against the sun. "Mum?"

No answer.

I turn on the light, flinching at the sudden brightness, and walk closer to her. Then I see the pile of empty pill bottles.

Without hesitation, I reach for my phone to dial 999 and use my free hand to check Mum's pulse. My body is driven by instinct, and all the while, I feel like I'm floating above it all, watching my body at work while I remain a silent observer, held aloft by fear.

"I'm at twenty-five Rodrick Lane," I hear my voice call out to the phone. "I need an ambulance. Quickly."

Mum attempted suicide once before, a month after Dad first left. I was eleven. I found her in the living room, slumped on the sofa, mouth wide, a bottle of wine and an empty box of pills on the floor beneath her. I didn't really understand what had happened at the time, but I was trying to wake her up and she wouldn't respond. I called Dad first, but he didn't even answer. I tried again and again. Then I finally called for an ambulance.

That night felt endless: sitting in the hospital, waiting, desperate for someone to explain to me what had happened. Where was my mum? Why was it taking so long? Was she going to die? When the nurses tried to explain it to me, they didn't really tell me anything.

"Your mummy has just had an accident, but she'll be okay."

I hated when they referred to her as 'mummy.' I was eleven, not five; I was ready to be spoken to like an adult.

"When can I see her?" I asked.

"Not quite yet, sweetie." The nurse patted my shoulder, smiling at me with far too wide a grin. "The doctors just need to do some tests on her and then she'll be right as rain."

I remember finding that phrase stupid–'right as rain'–as far as I was concerned, rain was annoying and there was nothing right about it. I didn't want my mum to be compared to rain, I wanted her to be a shining sun.

It wasn't until the next morning that the hospital managed to get through to Dad. He came and took me to his house before I got a chance to see Mum, and he never hid the fact he thought she had done a stupid, selfish thing. I didn't like the way he spoke about her, but I didn't know what to say. I just wanted to wake up and discover it was all a nightmare, and that Mum was fine.

But she wasn't fine. She was alive, yes, and she was discharged after a week, but she wasn't fine and never would be again. For a long time, I worried almost every day that she'd make another attempt, always checking on her before she went to bed, even counting her pills to make sure she was taking the right amount. But she seemed okay–at least, as okay as she could be in the circumstances–and eventually, I convinced myself that she wouldn't try to kill herself. Not ever again. Not as long as she had me.

Until now.

Elliot

The local GlimpseTech building is the most modern building in town. It stands out between two concrete husks as a shining, jagged structure, like broken shards of glass stuck together in an artistic statement. Even if it didn't look so striking, it would still stand out as an oddity: we're the only town in the country to have our own GlimpseTech building. There's one in every city (even two or three in the biggest), but for some reason about five years ago the company decided to build one here. It baffled a lot of people at the time, even triggering a few protests. They said it wasn't fair that in every other town people had to travel for ages to reach their nearest GlimpseTech building while those of us in Millfield can just waltz into our town centre. GlimpseTech claimed it was because Millfield is a fairly large town with a good geographic position, whatever that means. People are still confused about the decision, but I suppose it doesn't really matter.

It's hard not to take a deep breath as I step up to the door, as if the building itself fills me with trepidation. So, with a breath, I walk through the automatic door and into GlimpseTech. It's painfully clean inside, giving the same shining effect that the shattered glass structure does outside. The floor, walls, and ceiling are all a gleaming white, save for the black tiles on the wall above the front desk which form the logo: an infinity sign with an arrow cutting across it.

Staff, dressed all in black, wander through the foyer, fiddling with their tablet screens and occasionally glancing up to check where they're going. The front desk is curved, with multiple people behind it, grinning intensely as they greet visitors. I walk up to the nearest person–a blonde woman with her hair tied back and the brightest red lipstick I've ever seen.

"Welcome to GlimpseTech," she says through her relentless smile. "What can I help you with today?"

"Yes, hello, er, I have an appointment?" I don't know why it comes out as a question.

"Wonderful. Can I take your name?"

"Yes, it's, ah, Elliot Dove."

She scrolls and makes a few clicks with her mouse, waits a second, then turns back to me. "Perfect. If you want to head over to the lifts, your appointment is on the fifth floor in room 117." She points round the curve of the desk to a wall of three elevator doors.

"Great. Thank you."

"I hope your Glimpse shows you a bright future."

I nod, feeling my stomach twist at her words, and head to the lifts.

Upstairs, the white tiled surfaces continue. I walk down the fifth-floor corridor, passing each glass door with their etched-in room numbers until I find room 117. I knock and it slides open. Inside is a room full of strange angles and slopes, with the furthest wall from me being sheet glass, exposing the world outside. It seems the broken, jagged design of the building doesn't just apply to the outside, but the rooms within as well.

A man with short, dark hair and a smile much like the people downstairs sits at the edge of a ring-shaped control desk. Thousands of controls span the entire ring, but what draws my eye more is what the ring surrounds. A large, golden hemisphere sits on the floor in the very centre of the room. A seam divides it in two, as though the hemisphere might open up like an eyelid. Around the rim, where the hemisphere connects to the floor, wires poke out and connect it to the control desk.

The man looks from me to a screen on the desk in front of him and back again.

"Elliot Dove?"

I nod.

"Please, take a seat." A chair moves by itself around the desk until it stops a few feet from the man. Both this chair and the one he's sat on are fixed to a track around the edge of the desk.

I take another breath and head to the seat, the door sliding closed behind me. I know I could leave at any point, but the click of the door as it seals makes me feel trapped.

"It's nice to meet you, Elliot," the man says as I sit down. "My name is Dr James, and I'll be guiding you through your Glimpse today."

I nod again.

He smiles like he finds it amusing. "It's entirely normal to feel nervous, but I assure you there is absolutely nothing to worry about. The process itself is entirely painless, and for many it can be incredibly enlightening. I am, however, obligated to mention that you undertake this process at your own risk, and we take no blame for anything you might see, or indeed not see, during your Glimpse. There are, as I'm sure you know, very rare instances where a person will see nothing at all during their Glimpse. Many people interpret this to mean they will be dead, but not enough tests have been carried out to prove this is true."

"But no one whose Glimpse showed them nothing has ever lived past the date they saw, right?" It slips out without warning, but I can't help myself. One of the main criticisms of GlimpseTech, that's always brought up in debates, is how they refuse to admit for certain whether a person Glimpsing nothing means they're going to die.

Dr James' smile falters, but only for a moment. "That is correct, but as I said, it is a very rare phenomenon." He flips one of the switches on the control desk and a small panel close to me lights up. "Now, before we begin, I just need to check your fingerprint. If you could please place your thumb against that panel."

I do as he says. The panel feels warm against my skin, and it glows a little brighter before going dim. A picture of me flashes up on Dr James' screen along with lines of text that are too small for me to read.

"Perfect," he says. He flips another switch, and a vial rises from a hole in the panel. Within it is a swab which Dr James removes. "And now, for the system to sync with your biology, I need to take a quick sample of your DNA. If you could just open your mouth, I'll swab the inside of your cheeks."

I hadn't expected anything so intrusive, but I open my mouth and let him take a swab. When he's done, he returns the swab to the vial and pulls the same switch as before. The vial lowers, Dr James presses a button, and a bunch of lights turn on across the desk. A sound emanates from the golden hemisphere–a gentle whirring. I feel my breath quicken as the reality of what's about to happen sets in. Is it too late to back out?

"Excellent. I must now remind you that your Glimpse could take you to any date and any time in your future. It is impossible to predict when it might be."

Except that it won't show me anything beyond the Last Day, or so the theories say. I don't bother to mention it. The Last Day is yet another thing GlimpseTech refuses to explain.

"The Glimpse will last for forty-four seconds exactly, but you can end it early if you wish."

"How?"

He raises an eyebrow, then reaches down below the desk. His hands return holding what a miniature version of the hemisphere. It has the same seam and everything.

"This," Dr James says, "will be on your head throughout the Glimpse. If you want it to end you need only remove it from your head."

"But...I'll be in the Glimpse."

"Though your consciousness is being projected into the future, your body remains here, and you are still in control. If you want to remove the helmet, you'll be able to, even while you're observing your future."

He holds the helmet out to me. "Ready?"

No, not at all, but I place the helmet on my head anyway.

"Okay," Dr James says. "Preparing." He flicks more switches and presses more buttons, then his chair moves along the track, sending him around the desk so that he can turn dials, adjust sliders, and flick more lights on.

The whirring becomes more intense, and my helmet vibrates. The seam in the large hemisphere widens, the eye opening, and now I can see inside. Rings of metal twist and turn around each other in gyroscopic motion, and a bright light glows from within the very centre. The whirring keeps growing, as do the vibrations in my helmet, and though I can't see it I know the seam in the helmet is open now, too.

Dr James returns to my side and grips the most intense looking lever on the desk–one which matches the same golden colour of the hemisphere and helmet.

"Three..." he begins.

My heart is racing faster than ever before.

"Two..."

I feel sick. This was a mistake.

"One..."

I should just pull off the helmet. I should get up and run.

Dr James pulls the lever.

I'm happy. That's what I notice first. Happier than I've ever felt, in fact. Euphoric. My eyes are closed, so I see nothing, but I know I'm alive. And awake. I can feel another body against mine, their bare flesh pressing against me, their warmth and their quickly beating heart almost indistinguishable from my own. I feel their lips on mine, and their tongue in my mouth. And it's like nothing I've ever felt before. It's like every part of me is buzzing, every nerve ending primed to *feel*.

My hands move down the other person's back, gently stroking their smooth skin. I feel their breath falter and their lips leave mine, opting instead for my neck. With my spare hand, I run my fingers through their hair–short and soft, it slips through my fingers like silk.

It's strange. I'm here, but I'm not. I can feel and hear, and I'm sure if my eyes would open then I'd be able to see. But I'm not in control. I'm a passenger in my own body. A witness to the future.

My eyes open, revealing a plastic sheet above me. The light is dim, and flickering, but I recognise the crinkled orange vinyl as the ceiling of the tent my parents took me camping in years ago.

The mouth leaves my neck, and the person rises, their face now in my view. It's Seb. Seb, the quiet boy from school. Seb, who walked into the bedroom I was crying in at Harvey's party. Seb, who is now smiling down at me, bare chested, with a hunger in his eyes that makes me feel things I've never felt in another person's presence before. Not to this degree.

It's excitement, desire and nerves all rolled into one, sending my heart into overdrive. I can feel my body tremble slightly, but it isn't scary. I'm comfortable. I'm safe. At least, that's what my body is telling me. My mind, on the other hand? That's in two places at once. There's the me of the future, who wants nothing more than to feel Seb's lips on mine again. But there's also the me of the present, the silent observer, who doesn't understand how this can be happening. How I could possibly feel this way about this boy I've barely spoken to.

His face comes down to meet mine, devouring me in a passionate kiss that my body reciprocates with all its will. His hands caress every part of me they can, pausing just above my pants.

"Is this okay?" I hear him ask. His words send shivers through my body, their intent filling me with excitement.

"Yes." The word escapes me in barely more than a whisper.

His hands undo the button of my trousers. My breath catches, and it's like I'm paralysed by an electric shock. But as it ebbs away, I'm left with nothing but excitement and joy. I let his hands wander, and I explore him with mine.

The floor of the tent crinkles as we roll over each other, turning to feel every angle we can, and all the while still locked in a tight embrace. And those future feelings intensify, taking over completely, so I almost forget that this is just a vision, that I'm not really here. I let the euphoria flood my mind. I want it to never end. I want to live in this moment forever.

The vision fades and I'm staring out at the whirring gyroscope once more. The hemisphere begins to close, and the whirring lessens to silence. My heart is pounding so strongly I can hear it and I'm covered in a cold sweat.

That can't have been real. It can't have been. Seb? And me? No. No no no. It doesn't make sense. It can't–

"Would you like to know the timestamp for that Glimpse?" asks Dr James, still sat in his chair and looking at the screen in front of him.

"Huh?" I feel unsteady, like I might fall from my chair at any moment.

Dr James lifts the helmet from my head, and I feel my hair stick to the sweat on my forehead.

"Not everyone chooses to," he continues, "but most do."

The timestamp...the exact time and date that my Glimpse will come true. Perhaps if I don't know, then it'll never happen. Everyone always says it's a self-fulfilling prophecy–by knowing the time the Glimpse is meant to come true you end up forcing it to happen. Maybe if I just ignore it, I'll be fine. Maybe it'll never happen. But is that what I want? I can't shake what I felt in there. The happiness. It was like nothing I've ever experienced. Can I deny myself that?

And I know full well that the Glimpses are absolute. What I've seen will happen, whether I want it to or not.

"Okay," I say. "Tell me."

"Your Glimpse showed you a forty-four second moment beginning at exactly twelve minutes past ten PM, on Sunday the fourteenth of July."

I don't know why I say it, because I already know the answer, but instead of just accepting what he's told me I ask, "Have the Glimpses ever been wrong?"

He looks down, eyes filling with pity. He must get this question all the time, and the answer must disappoint a lot of people. "Elliot, I'm afraid–"

"I know what everyone says, I know you claim every Glimpse is a hundred percent accurate, but what if you're wrong? You can't monitor everyone. Not everyone posts their Glimpses online."

He nods. "You're right. We can't know for certain, but the evidence suggests–"

I jump off my chair and head straight to the door.

"Elliot, wait."

"Did you watch it?" I ask, feeling heat rise in my face. It's either cry or get angry and I'm choosing the latter.

"Sorry?"

"My Glimpse. Did you watch it? On your little screen?"

He shakes his head.

"But you do record them, don't you?"

"Yes, the Glimpses are stored on our system in order to allow our staff to verify any posts on GlimpseNet."

I knew this already; it was all outlined in the letter. You can only have one Glimpse because having multiple could result in brain damage (although some conspiracy theorists debate that idea), but once you've had your Glimpse you can view it again as many times as you want.

"I want you to delete it."

Dr James sighs. "You know I can't do that. You agreed to those terms when booking the appointment."

I clench my fist, trying to keep my tears at bay. "Please."

"I can't. Look, Elliot, I–"

I walk out. Because I can't avoid crying any longer.

Seb

I hate the smell of hospitals. There's something too clean about them. Too clinical. It makes you even more aware of what the cleanliness is trying to hide. It's been hours since I got here in the ambulance with Mum. Hours of not knowing how she is, only that she's alive. All sorts of people have passed through the waiting room: an old woman with bruising all down her face, a man clutching his arm so tightly he must have been scared it'd fall off, and a kid with the worst cough I've ever heard in my life.

All the while, I've stayed sat on my cold plastic chair. I should count myself lucky though, there are a couple of others who have been here longer. A woman in a hijab has been crying on and off since I arrived, and a balding man has been on his phone the whole time. God knows how strong his battery must be. I've been texting Aym, but my phone is almost dead at this point.

Any news? her new text reads.

Nothing, I reply.

When I first got here, the nurses asked me if there was someone for me to call. "Your dad, perhaps," they said. I lied to them, saying he's living in another town and that I'd call him to let him know what happened. I didn't call him, of course. He'd only make things worse, calling Mum selfish like he did the last time. Besides, why would he even want to help? He's got a new family to worry about now.

"Sebastian Glass?" comes the voice of a friendly looking nurse. She stands at the nearest door, a polite smile on her face, looking round the room to find me. She has light brown skin and black hair cut into a neat bob.

"Yes?" I say.

Her eyes jump to mine. "Could you come with me, please?" She says it calmly enough, but I can't help thinking the worst.

I follow her through the door.

"Your mother is doing well," she says before I even have the chance to ask.

I feel tension I didn't even realise was there vanish from my body.

"She's awake and talking, but the doctors want to keep her in the mental health ward for a few days just to monitor her, review her medication, all of that. We wouldn't normally keep her very long, but what with her history and the fact the medication doesn't seem to be helping..."

"I understand."

I hate to admit it, but I'm glad they're keeping her here. At least she'll be safe, and I won't have to check on her every second.

"I assume you want to see her?"

"Yes. Please."

Mum fiddles with her hands on the hospital bed and keeps her eyes down.

"Hey, Mum," I say, approaching slowly.

She looks up, but she's hesitant. "Seb," she says in a low, tired voice. "How are you?"

I remember this from last time–the doctors explained that it's normal for people to feel guilty and ashamed right after an attempt. She's not likely to talk much.

"I'm good," I say. "You?"

She nods, which I guess means 'I'm fine.' A lie, but not one I'm going to question.

"That's...good." I force a smile.

The nurse clears her throat. "I just explained to Seb that we'll be keeping you here for a few days."

Mum doesn't react.

"I'll visit you as often as I can. Okay?"

She nods, and she gives me the smallest glance, a tiny moment of eye contact. I walk over and hug her as best I can while she's sat up in the bed. She's weak, but she hugs me back.

The nurse chimes in with a question I've already been asked. "Do have someone to stay with, Sebastian? We will need to contact a social worker if not, just to make sure you're safe."

I curse under my breath. I'm not sure what the rules are when it comes to children being left alone when their parents are in hospital. I mean, I'm sixteen, surely that's old enough not to need a babysitter? It's not like I haven't been caring for myself for years. Still, there's probably some law that means I can't be by myself. Guess it's time to lie again.

"I do," I say, "I'm gonna stay at my dad's house. I already called him, so..."

It's a good thing Mum's so subdued. She'd definitely know I'm lying.

"That's good," the nurse says. "Well, you can stay with your Mum a little while, but she does need to rest."

"Thanks."

I take a seat beside Mum's bed. The blue surface of the chair has a torn slit at the edge, exposing the foam underneath. I pick at it, avoiding eye contact with Mum and the nurse. No one says a word.

Aym is waiting for me at our usual spot up on the crags. As I walk through the heather, which slowly gives way to bare rock, I spot Aym's silhouette against the morning sun, still low in the sky. She's sitting, legs dangling off the edge of the rockface, so I join her. She gives me a nod to say hello, a wordless agreement passing between us that we should just sit in silence for a moment. I breathe in the outside air, it's cool and clean, and carries the faint scent of Aym's floral perfume.

Mum and Dad brought me here when I was a kid. I can't remember the first time, but I remember plenty of others. We'd go on weekend walks together, often with my grandparents before they died, and I remember once coming here for a picnic. It's strange to think back on those times, as though they're from someone else's life. It was a time when Dad was always around, when Mum was truly happy. Before either of them had had their Glimpse.

I don't know if it's because of rose-tinted nostalgia, but the crags seemed nicer back then. The heather was more vibrant, there weren't cigarette butts scattered around, and there was no graffiti on the rock face. Or maybe that was all there, and I just didn't notice.

"She seemed okay when I left," I say, breaking the silence. "As okay as she can be, anyway."

Aym fidgets with one of her braids. "How long are they keeping her in?"

I shrug. "At least a few days."

"Are you gonna be okay on your own?" She leans against me. "Want me to stay with you?"

"I'll be fine."

"You sure? I don't mind if you –"

"I *said* I'll be fine."

Silence again. We both stare out at the village below. I wonder how many people down there are feeling the same as me. How many other lives are being turned upside down for no good reason?

"Sorry," I say. "I'm just...tired. Of everything."

Aym throws an arm over my shoulders. "I know. And it's okay to be angry."

I nod and wrap an arm around her too.

"Now how about a coffee to wake you up?"

"Coffee sounds good."

Coffee *would* be good–if we could actually get to the shop. A group of protesters blocks the street. Car horns flare up around us as the traffic piles up, and Aym and I try to push our way through the onlookers. The protest itself is small, only about a dozen people, but that's enough to stop traffic, and all the people watching are making it worse.

"Restore our freedom!" shouts one of the protesters–a stumpy middle-aged woman holding up a placard that shows the GlimpseTech logo with a large red X painted over it.

"Restore our fate!" shouts another, a younger man this time.

The rest join in, repeating each phrase and holding up banners and placards that read the same. It's quite the mix of people, different ages, races, genders. I guess GlimpseTech haters span all walks of life. I get where they're coming from–I hate the Glimpses too–but I don't see the protests doing much good.

Protests like these are what got the new prime minister in power. Her campaign was built on exposing GlimpseTech. But it's been a couple of days since she took office, and nothing's changed as far as I can tell. Seems the protesters think the same.

"For fuck's sake," says Aym, pointing at a group joining the protest, a gang of barely-older-than-teenagers, linking arms and spreading themselves across the road. "Do you want to go back to mine for coffee instead?"

"Might be for the best," I say, shaking my head at the sight.

Just as I'm about to turn and join Aym, I spot someone new join the crowd. He wouldn't stand out much normally–a man in his twenties, wearing jeans and a blazer, with short, dark blond hair that sits un-styled on his head–but it's his expression I can't help noticing. While everyone else around here is either angry or amused or frustrated, this man is strangely calm. He sidles through the crowd with a completely blank expression. When he reaches the protesters, he hands something to a few of them. A piece of paper–a flyer, perhaps–and though I can't make out much detail from this far away, I do notice a symbol printed on it.

A wide-open eye with a plus sign for a pupil.

Elliot

There's a woman in Swansea who claims her Glimpse showed she'd be dead within a year, but she outlived it. And there's an old man in Leeds who says his Glimpse showed him chatting with his wife even though she's been dead for years. And there's a married couple in Birmingham who saw themselves getting divorced, but they're still together now, way beyond the time stamp of their Glimpse. There are countless posts like these online, all of them claiming to be proof that the Glimpses aren't concrete. That what you see can be changed. But there are even more comments disputing each and every claim.

None of the claims are verified on GlimpseNet. And many people bring up studies which have shown time and time again that Glimpses are absolute. Like the so-called 'Freedom Jump' that happened about ten years ago.

A group of sceptics who had seen things they didn't like in their Glimpses got together and made a suicide pact. They climbed onto the roof of the GlimpseTech HQ in London and jumped off, deciding to sacrifice themselves in the belief that their deaths would prove the Glimpses could be changed. But it didn't work. A few of them were too scared to jump, and those that went through with it ended up injured instead of dead. Two of them became paralysed for life and their Glimpses still came true.

The 'Freedom Jump' is used all the time as a cautionary tale, proof that Glimpses come true, no matter what. So, basically, I'm screwed. No matter how much I don't want my Glimpse to be real, it's going to happen. It's inevitable. And that's fucking terrifying.

I blink away the stinging feeling in my eyes, and the screen in front of me blurs as I yawn. I've been up all night, searching for a shred of hope, even though I know how pointless it is. I close the many windows open on my laptop but stop at the final one. The one that isn't about Glimpse conspiracy theories. It's a page about bisexuality.

Bisexuality, I read for what must be the billionth time, **is the attraction to people of one's own gender and others.**

It's something I've heard of plenty of times before, but I never thought it might apply to me. After what happened with Callum and what I saw in the Glimpse, my first thought was that I must be gay and I've lied to myself my whole life. But maybe it isn't that simple. I find girls attractive. I'm sure of it. I think. I mean, I definitely am. I had a crush on Jessica from school, for God's sake. Or did I just make myself think I had a crush because that's what all the other boys were doing, and I just wanted to fit in?

No. Maybe. I don't know.

I slam my laptop closed and bury my face in my hands. My chest is fit to burst with a thousand different feelings. Sad that my future is nothing like I wanted. Ashamed of how I know people would view me if they found out. Afraid of what my family might think. It's all swirling around in a poisonous cocktail. And perhaps most surprising is guilt.

I've never thought of myself as homophobic. I never liked seeing the way Seb or any rumoured-to-be-gay kids got treated at school. I never used the word 'gay' as an insult like so many others. And yet now I'm terrified by the idea that I might be some level of gay myself. Does that make me a hypocrite?

Despite all the negative feelings, there is one spark of light that flashes in my mind every so often. The memory of how I felt during the Glimpse. That closeness. The way I felt so safe. How, in that moment, I wanted nothing more than to be with Seb. It faded as soon as the Glimpse ended, but it's still there at the back of my mind. Calling to me. Tempting me.

I've thought about watching it again, as though replaying my Glimpse might give me some new answers. But it feels wrong. I know it's me in the Glimpse, but it's also Seb, and what we were doing was so...private. It feels like an invasion to even think about it.

My phone buzzes as a text comes in from Callum. It's one of a few he's sent since the night of the party. Most have asked how I'm feeling, and I've brushed them off with an 'I'm fine.' I know what he wants to ask. He wants to understand what happened between us. Why I almost kissed him. But I'm not ready to face that question yet.

You free today? the new text reads.

I don't know how to respond. Part of me wants nothing more than to spend time alone with Callum, but that's also the part that tried to kiss him and I'm terrified of how he'll look at me now. Things can't be the same between us anymore, not when we have that memory hovering over us. But...maybe I'm wrong. Maybe Callum won't care. I mean, the boy decided to dye his hair bright red–he's not exactly the stereotypical straight man. I can't see him abandoning me just because I'm maybe-not-straight.

But what am I supposed to say to him? Do I just confess to everything that's happened? Tell him all about my Glimpse? Come out as whatever the hell I am?

Am I ready for that?

Yes, I reply to Callum's text.

I pace around the park while I wait for Callum to arrive, ridiculously tired but jittery with anxiety. I don't know why I agreed to meet him. I'm still far from decided about what I'm going to tell him. I guess I just want to see his face if nothing else. And maybe I'm hoping just seeing him will give me a sign of where to go next, or at least an answer about where we stand now. Have I lost him as a friend forever? I don't think I could cope with that.

"Hey." Callum's voice snaps me out of my pacing-trance. He walks towards me with his usual smile, as though nothing has changed since we last spoke.

"Hey," I say, though it comes out as more of a whimper.

"Elliot, what's wro–"

"I'm sorry!"

He stops in his tracks. "What?"

"I..." I shake my head and burst into tears. I try to speak, but all I can muster are more sobs. And they won't stop. I'm not sure they ever will.

I don't see him approach, but after a moment I feel Callum's arms around me and hear his soft, familiar voice through my cries. "El, what's wrong? It's okay, I promise." He puts his arms on my shoulders and starts guiding me somewhere while I'm still blinded by tears. When I finally manage to breathe properly and open my eyes, I find we're sat on a bench.

"What's wrong?" he repeats.

"Everything."

He doesn't speak, but I can see in his eyes that he wants to listen. He wants to hear me out. And he doesn't hate me...at least not yet.

"At the party," I start, "I... I tried to..." I glance at his lips, picturing myself moving towards them again, ready to kiss him, but the words don't come. I can't tell him. I can't.

"Do you want me to tell it how I saw it?" he asks, voice calm.

I nod. I knew it. Of course, he noticed.

"I think you wanted to kiss me, is that right?"

Hearing him say it brings back that feeling of shame, but I nod again.

"Listen, El, you're my best friend. You can tell me anything you want to. But if you're not ready, then–"

"No," I cut in. "No, I... I am... I think..."

Callum nods. "Take as long as you need."

I look around the park, taking in the noon sunlight and the smell of honeysuckle on the warm summer breeze. We're all alone here. Callum is my best friend, that much is still true. And telling something to your best friend isn't the same as telling it to the whole world. Callum would keep a secret if I asked him to. And right now, I think keeping everything to myself might kill me.

I take a deep breath. "I always thought I was straight, right up until prom night, and then...then something changed." I look at Callum. Those blue eyes that made my heart race that fateful night. "And I don't know if it was the alcohol or whatever, but I think there was maybe always part of me that wanted to...wanted to..."

"Kiss me?"

"Yeah."

There's a moment of silence. My words dangle in the air between us like bait, just waiting to be snapped up.

"Elliot, it's okay if you're gay."

"I'm not," I say a little too quickly.

"Really, it's fine."

"No, but, I'm not. I mean, yes, I...like guys. I think. But I'm also pretty sure I like girls."

Callum stares at me, but it's not a look of horror. He's listening. He's taking it in.

"Right," he says, "okay. So, you're bi then?"

"I don't know. I think...maybe?"

I hadn't noticed till now, but the cocktail of emotions in my chest has started to froth a little less. The pain is slightly muted. I breathe a little easier. Even the tears have started to dry up.

"Okay," Callum says. "Cool."

"You're...not angry?"

Callum almost laughs. "Angry? Jesus Christ, El. What sort of a friend would I be if I were angry at you coming out to me?" He throws his arms back around me. "I'm glad you told me. Honoured, in fact."

I start crying into his shoulder again, but these tears feel different. More out of relief than sadness. I sniff and wipe my eyes when Callum releases me.

"And I really don't mind about the whole almost-kiss thing," he adds. "You're still my friend, and I know you wouldn't have done it sober. But if you ever need me to give you some space, just let me know."

I smile. "Thank you."

"Have you told anyone else?"

"No. I'm only just figuring it out for myself, and even then, I don't know for sure."

"Fair. Well, I won't tell anyone. You've got all the time in the world."

The time stamp of my Glimpse flashes in my head. Maybe not *all* the time in the world. And talking of the Glimpse...

"There's something else, too," I say.

"Oh?"

"Yeah. I...er...I finally had my G–"

I stop mid-sentence because we're no longer alone. A pair of voices echo across the park from the path between the honeysuckle bushes. And at least one of the voices sounds vaguely familiar. I glance across the field and there, emerging from the bushes, is a skinny white boy and a tall black girl. Seb and his friend.

My body tenses up as my mind is thrown back into the Glimpse. Seb's face smiling down at me inside the tent. His bare chest against mine. Our lips pressing together. An overwhelming sense of happiness. Of closeness. The two of us, together.

"I have to go." I say, darting up off the bench and running out of the park, following the path away from Seb. I don't look back when Callum calls, not even once, and before he gets the chance to catch up with me, I'm already halfway home.

Coming out to Callum was enough vulnerability for a lifetime. I'm not ready to face the rest of the world. Not ready for my parents or my brother or anyone from school to know. Not ready to confront Seb. Not ready to let my Glimpse come to fruition. Not yet.

Not yet.

TEN
Seb

A couple of days pass without much change at the hospital. They're still keeping Mum in and say she's doing okay, but she doesn't look to be improving much whenever I visit. Not that I've been that often. I want to, of course, but...it's hard. Seeing her there, in that bed. And the more I go the more I get questioned about staying with Dad. At least with Mum there all my worrying stays in the back of my mind instead of the front. Plus, it's kind of fun to have the house to myself.

Aym comes over a few times and helps me tidy. She's the only person I trust to come into the house while it's in this state. Any other friends I've had over the years have never been let in. My choice, not Mum's. I felt ashamed of the mess. I still do, but I know Aym doesn't judge me.

After a few sessions of cleaning, the place looks much better. Still untidy by most people's standards what with all the piles of papers and other random crap Mum doesn't want to throw away, but it's way better than normal. There's not as much dust, and the curtains are open for the first time in a while, reminding me of what it looks like in natural light. It exposes a couple of damp spots on the wall, but other than that the room feels much brighter.

When Aym's not around, I play my new guitar. It's amazing how much different it sounds in comparison to my old one. Each strum sounds so much richer, sending beautiful waves of music right through me. After the first few play-throughs of my go-to songs, I decide to try something new. My old guitar has been missing a string for a while, so nothing ever sounds quite right and some songs are just downright impossible. But not now.

Some of my earliest memories are of music. Dad used to have this record player he'd play at any opportunity. I remember thinking it was a bit weird that he didn't just use his phone. He told me it was a family heirloom, and that music doesn't sound as good in any other form.

Dad introduced me to the musicians I love now. He'd play records from years back–stuff no one really listened to anymore. The 90s, the 80s, even further back than that. And I loved it all. I remember hoping he'd take me to a gig one day when I was older, but he didn't stick around long enough for that to happen. He did buy me my old guitar, though. It was the first birthday present I got from him after he left. His attempt to pretend everything was fine, I guess.

It came as a surprise. When Dad moved out his records and the player went with him, and even though I'd never really understood the point of it, it felt weird to listen to music digitally. That, and I couldn't listen to any of my favourite songs without being reminded that he'd abandoned us. And the more Mum sunk into her depression, the less time I felt I could spend listening to music.

Then came the guitar. I was God awful at first, and neither Mum nor Dad could afford lessons for me, but there was plenty of stuff online to help me teach myself. I remember the first time I learned a whole song. Mum was deep in one of her bouts of sadness, but I hauled the guitar into her bedroom and played for her.

Her reaction wasn't much, and I hadn't expected it to be, but I remember her smile clear as day and the words that followed.

"That was amazing, Seb."

Dad might have bought the guitar, but it was Mum who kept me playing.

It's Sunday evening and Aym's busy at her house, so I sit in the living room with my new guitar, pull up an app full of tabs, and choose a song I've never played before. It's tricky at first, my fingers falling over each other in unfamiliar patterns, but it's not long before I nail the first verse. I throw in some vocals, too. I've never been that confident about my singing voice, and until recently no one else had ever heard me sing. But a couple of months back, Aym came over while I was practicing and heard me. I went bright red when I realised she'd been listening, but then she hit me with a thousand compliments and perked me up. Since then, I've gotten more open to the idea that maybe I don't sound so bad. I open up my phone's voice recorder and record myself playing and singing the first verse.

That's when the knocking starts.

It comes fast and heavy, someone pounding on the door like they're trying to break it down. A gruff voice shouts, "Jane! Open up!"

I almost drop my guitar, only just managing to steady it before it crashes into the floor. I rest it down and stand up slowly, trying not to make any noise.

"I know you're in there!" comes the voice again. It's deep and gravelly, and the sheer sound of it makes me go cold. I don't know who it is, but I'm sure as hell they're bad news. "I can see the light, it's no good hiding."

Shit.

He pounds on the door again and I shift slightly so that I can see it down the hall. The hinges are shaking, already pretty weak. If he carries on, he could easily break the whole thing down.

"She's not here!" I shout.

The pounding stops and I move down the hall, closer to the door but keeping it closed.

"She's not here." I repeat, quieter this time, my voice a lot shakier than I'd like it to be. "Who are you?"

The man is silent for a moment, so I take the opportunity to take a glance through the peephole. His face does nothing to make me feel better. His skin is sallow and tight, as if being pinched from behind, and he has wide, dark, bloodshot eyes and grey-brown, receding hair. His nose is flaring and a vein on his forehead looks fit to burst. A filthy looking trench coat hangs off his lanky frame.

"You must be her son," he says, eyes darting to the peephole as if he can see me too.

I stumble back.

"Seb, isn't it?" he asks.

I'm shaking. I clench my fist and grit my teeth to try and stop. How does he know who I am? How does he know Mum? I've never seen him before.

"Where is your mum, Seb?" he asks.

I take a breath. I've got no reason to trust this guy and I'm definitely not going to tell him where Mum is. "She's not here and she won't be for a while."

Silence.

"Well," he says. His voice has that painful edge to it that only comes from years of smoking. "When you see her, let her know Dan called and that she's late with her payment."

At that, I can't resist. I open the door, but I keep the chain on, so it only opens a crack. I face him but keep myself primed to slam the door if he attempts to dash forward.

"What payment?" I ask.

He smiles–if the rancid sight can even be called that–revealing two rows of yellow, cracked teeth. I can smell the stench of smoke and booze from here.

"She'll know what I mean," he says.

And with that, he leaves, turning away with a smirk and walking down the darkening street. I don't notice the cold sweat that covers me until I close the door.

"And he said his name was Dan?" Aym says down the phone.

"Yeah."

"Nothing else? No surname, no–"

"Nothing."

I'm on the sofa, legs hiked up against my chest with one arm wrapped around them while the other holds my phone. The curtains are drawn tightly closed and only the dim lamp on the table is on. I keep glancing down the hall at the front door, flinching whenever I hear the slightest noise from outside.

"Maybe he's just a friend," Aym says, but I can tell from her voice she doesn't believe what she's saying.

"He's not a friend, Aym. I don't know what he is, but it can't be good can it? He's expecting money! She doesn't have any money! Not after..." I look at the guitar, glowing orange as it reflects the lamplight.

Mum looked at me strangely when she gave me the guitar. She wouldn't answer me properly when I asked how she afforded it. She left the room before I had a chance to question further. What if she hadn't just been saving up her benefits? What if she got the money from somewhere else?

I shake my head. "This isn't good, Aym. This could be some proper messed up shit."

"Like what?"

"I don't know, drugs? Something illegal. You didn't see this guy, Aym, he was...I don't know, he was dodgy. Proper weird." I run a hand through my hair, breathing quickly, mind racing. "I don't know what to do."

"Take a moment, breathe slowly, and calm down, okay?"

I hear a bottle smash outside. How close was it? Down the street? Outside my door? I can't tell.

"Seb?"

"Yeah?"

"Listen to me. Whoever he was, he's gone now. Yes?"

I gulp. There's chatter outside, but it's distant and sounds like the kids from four doors down. "Yes."

"Good. So, you don't need to worry right now, do you? We'll figure this out, but tonight you just need to rest. You can go see your Mum tomorrow and find out who Dan is. Okay?"

I nod, forgetting Aym can't see me through the phone.

"Seb?"

"Yeah. Okay. Good plan."

"Good. I'll see you tomorrow. Call me if you need anything."

"Bye."

Aym hangs up and I rest my phone down, glancing at the time. Eight. Too early to sleep, not that I think I'll be able to sleep at all tonight. Theories keep running through my head, about why Mum owes money to Dan. And I keep picturing his face. His pasty skin. His broken teeth. His dark, bloodshot eyes.

I head upstairs, but instead of my bedroom, I go into Mum's. I haven't been back in here since finding her the other night. The curtains are still drawn, the bed is still an unmade mess, and dirty clothes litter the floor. Of all the rooms in the house, this one makes me feel the most uneasy. Just stepping inside, it feels like the air is thicker. With every movement, I'm wading through years of sadness, or perhaps it's guilt because of what I'm about to do.

I pull the duvet and pillows from the bed and start patting down the surface of the mattress, even lifting it up and checking underneath. Finding nothing, I feel my way through the pillowcases and duvet cover. Then, I check the drawers, disgusted with myself as I sift through the underwear. I can't leave anything unchecked. I need to know if she's hiding something. Anything that might explain who Dan is.

But there's nothing. Not in the drawers. Not in the wardrobe. Not hidden on a shelf or under any covers. Not even tucked away inside a photo frame.

I don't know how to feel. It should be a good thing, but somehow finding nothing seems worse. If I'd found drugs, at least I'd know how Mum's been getting money and why Dan wants some. It could still be about drugs but what if it's not? What if it's even worse?

I shake my head. Whatever's going on, I'm going to have to wait to ask Mum in person tomorrow.

ELEVEN

Elliot

By the time I wake up on Monday morning, Mum and Dad have already gone to work, which makes it easier to relax. Ever since my Glimpse, every moment I've spent with them feels like a ticking time bomb, quickly approaching an explosion where they'll find out I'm not straight. I didn't tell them I had a Glimpse–the beauty of the Glimpses only being offered to those over sixteen is you don't need your parents' permission–but I know they can sense something is up.

Four years ago, Mum, Dad, Simon, and I were at Grandma's eightieth birthday party. Everyone from Dad's side of the family was there–aunts, uncles, cousins, second cousins, first cousins twice removed. Dad's side has always been close-knit, even though most of them live down south. There was a moment at the party that's always stuck with me, and I guess I didn't really know why until now, but it was when Simon went inside to get some food.

Everyone else stood in Grandma's large garden, chatting with glasses of champagne, gossiping or admiring the rose bushes that were Grandma's pride and joy. And then out came the cake. It was a huge, intricately decorated thing with the number eighty iced onto the top. People gathered round as it was placed on the table, but Simon was still inside.

"Come out, Simon!" Mum called back to the house.

And then, in his exaggerated poshness, Uncle Andrew said, "But not in the modern parlance." Which, in his obnoxiously wordy way, was basically him saying 'don't come out of the closet.' As if not being straight is something modern.

Everyone, save for me and a few of the other kids, laughed. I was twelve at the time, but I understood Andrew's meaning well enough. I didn't understand why everyone thought it was funny, though. And I'll never forget that my parents laughed along. Or what Mum said in response.

"Oh, no. We wouldn't want that."

I've always known that my parents, my whole family in general, are a bit stuck in the past. But that moment made it clearer than anything else. It doesn't matter that same-sex marriage has been legal for a decade now–people still think being queer is wrong. Or weird. Or disgusting.

I've seen the way people have treated Seb at school. And the way they still throw the word *gay* around as an insult. Hatred and bigotry are relentless; they don't just go away with time. Even my parents have it ingrained within them. So how am I supposed to deal with being part of a group that's hated like that? How am I ever going to be my real self around my family?

When I get downstairs, there's a note waiting for me on the fridge, pinned down by a magnet. It's from Mum, asking me to go shopping for her while she's at work. I pull it from the fridge and pocket it, accidentally knocking another magnet and sending a photo drifting to the floor. I pick it up. It's a picture of me, Mum, Dad, and Simon on the day Simon moved to uni. I'm holding the camera, arm outstretched to fit us all in while the other three have arms full of boxes. I caught the exact moment a box fell off Dad's pile, so everyone's expression is one of pre-emptive horror.

In the photo, Simon looks a lot like I do now. My hair was shorter back then, while his was longer. We've basically swapped since he's gone to uni, so now I have the ginger curls he's sporting in the picture. He's also changed quite a bit since then. When he visited last Christmas, I was taken aback by the amount of muscle he'd gained. And just as taken aback by the girlfriend he had in tow. She was absolutely stunning; long, dark hair, brown skin, and hazel eyes. Mum and Dad welcomed her with open arms.

Christmas was basically all about Simon and Alyssa from then. He'd had a girlfriend before, briefly in high school, but this one was different. It was obvious Mum and Dad thought they were meeting their future daughter-in-law. To be fair, they first met at university themselves, so that's their blueprint for what all relationships must be like. They probably expect it of me too. And maybe it will happen...it just might not be a *girl* that I end up with.

Once the photo's stuck back in place, I pour myself a bowl of cereal, sink into a dining room chair, and pull out my phone. I open Instagram and am immediately faced with Seb's profile. I've been spending a lot of time staring at his profile picture over the past couple of days. His privacy settings are all on, so that picture is all there is to see other than his barebones bio (guitar player, 16). He's playing his guitar in the picture, fingers pressed against the strings, fringe hanging from his head as he looks down slightly. He's wearing an oversized grey t-shirt, and there's this hint of a smile on his face that brings my Glimpse to mind every time I see it.

I've been dreaming about the Glimpse every night, replaying it on a loop in my mind and waking up with a racing heart...and sometimes something else, hidden by my covers. It's strange, until the Glimpse, I'd barely even noticed Seb. I knew who he was, I knew his name, I knew his face, and I knew he was gay. But that's all. That's everything. I keep thinking back, wondering if I ever found him attractive. It's hard to tell since I was convinced I was straight. Maybe I filed away any crushes on guys to the very back of my mind. Now, though? I can't deny there's something about Seb that intrigues me. He's...cute? Handsome? It helps that I've seen him so up close in my Glimpse. Now, my memories of him aren't just far off glances. I've seen (and felt) his soft lips, his sharp jaw line, his blue eyes. I know what it's like to run my fingers through his hair. I've seen what he looks like without a shirt, and without...other things...as well. These feelings excite me and terrify me at the same time. But I know, without a doubt, that the Glimpse will come true whether I try to avoid it or not. And I also know that once it's come true, there's no turning back.

"Morning, Elliot," Paul says when I enter the grocery shop. He gives me a friendly wave from behind the counter.

Paul owns the shop and is an old family friend who knew Mum at school. Apparently, they were boyfriend and girlfriend at some point, though I've always been surprised by that since he looks so different to Dad–much darker hair, and a whole lot larger around the waist. Maybe he looked different as a kid.

"Morning, Paul."

"Not at school today?"

"No. Exams finished last week." I grab a basket and head down the nearest aisle.

"Oh, I see. Did they go well?"

I'm not even within view of him anymore, but I know that won't stop him from chatting. Trips to the shop with Mum and Dad (but especially Mum) always take way longer than they need to thanks to Paul's never-ending conversations.

"I think so," I say, grabbing a multipack of crisps.

"Sixth form next, I take it?"

"Mhm."

"And then you'll be off to university like Simon."

"Yep." I roll my eyes, glad of the shelves hiding me.

"You know, it seems only yesterday you and your brother were in here as toddlers..."

I tune out. Once he's set off down memory lane, Paul will keep himself talking for ages. No need for me to make any comments. I grab the rest of what I need and bring it to the counter. Paul scans the items, still twittering on the whole time, and I just nod along. That is, until I hear the door open and turn to see who's just come in.

It's Seb.

And suddenly, I wouldn't be able to hear Paul even if I wanted to because all I can hear is my own thumping pulse. Seb keeps his eyes down and fringe over his face as he walks off down an aisle. I shouldn't be shocked by his presence–now that I've seen us together in my Glimpse, we're bound to cross paths at some point.

"Elliot?"

I turn back to Paul, who is looking at me with a raised eyebrow.

"Are you okay?"

"Um...yes. Sorry. I was just...distracted."

He hands me my bag of shopping. "That's £25.72, please."

I pass my phone over the scanner to pay, say thanks, and head to the door. My face feels hot, and I'm biting my lip, all while my pulse continues to fill my ears. As I open the door, I glance back and spot Seb taking a bouquet of flowers to the counter. I wonder what they're for. Is he going on a date? Is he even single? Is that any of my business?

Outside, I take a moment to breathe, in through the nose, out through the mouth, just standing there to the side of the door. If I'm right, and we're guaranteed to keep bumping into each other, I'm going to need to learn to cope with this feeling. I know what the solution is, of course. I should talk to him. Just say hi. That's all it would take. Right? And what if he's had a Glimpse too? What if he saw me in his? What if every time I've looked away from him, he's looked right at me, feeling exactly the same way I do?

I shake my head. This is too much. All of it. It was too much for me the other day, with Callum in the park. It was too much in the Glimpse itself. And it was too much when he walked in on me crying at Harvey's party. I should just go home.

I turn, but it's already too late as the shop door swings open and I walk straight into Seb, colliding head on, sending my shopping and his flowers all over the pavement.

MEANWHILE

Agent Sigma

I've been waiting for this moment for a long time. And now, finally, here I am. My days of recruiting, of handing out flyers, and seeking out the most passionate of Anti-Fates, are over. It's time to be part of something far greater.

The rusted metal door slides open with a clunk. A short man, lower half of his face covered by a bandana, faces me from the other side. He jerks his head to the side, indicating that I should follow him, and leads me into the dark corridor. The door closes behind me under its own weight and I steady my nerves. There's no turning back now.

Bare brick walls surround me on either side and a damp smell fills my nose. I swallow, fighting back the urge to cough. The short man turns a corner, leading me into a wide room. Large electric lights are set up around the perimeter, their wires trailing across the dust-coated floor to a generator in the corner. A pair of moths fly in from a hole in the ceiling, dancing as they approach the brightness. In the centre, sat on tattered sofas and stained desk chairs, is the group I'm here to see.

I don't recognise any of them–anonymity is rather important to the cause; no one even uses their names in here–but they all watch me with unrelenting eyes as I find the one unoccupied chair. I run a hand through my dark blond hair, smoothing it down.

"Welcome," comes a familiar voice from a dark corner of the room, "our newest member." The speaker steps out into the light: a man in his fifties, greying hair set atop an angular face. His cold eyes are framed by round glasses, and he wears a sombre expression. Though I've never seen him before, we have spoken many times. It was he who invited me here.

"Thank you," I say, nodding at him.

I notice a few people (at least those whose mouths aren't hidden by masks) around the room smirk, and I'm suddenly very aware of the fact I don't know any of this group's customs. Was I not supposed to say thank you? Was I supposed to just sit in silence as everyone else is? I suppose when everyone keeps their identity a secret, there's little point in introductions.

The Instructor, as he is known, drags a desk chair along with him and sits down. A woman to his right passes him a bulky laptop which he opens and spins round so the screen faces us. It displays the image I have come to know intimately over the past few months. The wide-open eye with the plus sign for its pupil.

"Now," The Instructor says, voice deep, soothing, almost hypnotic, "to business." He taps the keyboard and the screen changes, now displaying an image of the Prime Minister. Maria McBride in one of her usual sleek pantsuits. "Investigations by our agents within parliament are continuing. Believe me when I say their findings are shaping up to be quite revealing."

Quiet laughter spreads among the others, and I add a couple of fake laughs of my own, unsure what joke I've missed out on.

"But more interesting than that," he continues, "is the discovery by one of our moles within GlimpseTech HQ itself." Another click and a map of the UK fills the screen. "It has come to our attention that the centre of operations at GlimpseTech is not the headquarters in London as the public has been led to believe."

Others in the group glance at each other, shocked by this revelation, but I don't find anything about GlimpseTech surprising anymore. Anyone out there who still trusts that company is a fool.

"The true centre," The Instructor says, drawing everyone's attention back to the screen, "is here." He points at the map, where a red dot has appeared halfway between Leeds and Manchester. "Millfield. An unremarkable town where GlimpseTech erected a new building a few years ago. The first and only GlimpseTech not located in a city. Now we know why. Central command was transferred there upon the building's completion."

I stare at the screen. Millfield? My hometown. I was there just days ago, recruiting at a protest. It was an interesting one. On my way there, I'd been reading posts on GlimpseNet –a habit I've found myself obsessing over lately, much to my own dismay. There was a post from a woman named Eliza that had caught my eye. Her Glimpse showed her the very protest I was on my way to and described a man with a stack of flyers, one of which had been placed on her windscreen. It wouldn't have been memorable, were it not for the fact that I found myself bringing the Glimpse to fruition.

The moment I saw her face through her car window, I knew it must have been Eliza. I found myself grinning as it dawned on me that I was the man she'd described in her GlimpseNet post. It was yet more confirmation that I'm right about GlimpseTech. That they steal our free will and will be the downfall of society if no one stops them.

"If we are to take GlimpseTech down," The Instructor says, "this is where we need to search. We are going to need people on the inside, and for that, I need volunteers."

I barely give it a moment's thought. Almost by instinct, I raise my hand. This is what everything has been building up to. The protesting. The recruiting. The mindless lacky work. It's all been for this. To rise up. To be part of something greater. To save humanity.

To prevent the Last Day.

PART TWO

BELIEVING

GlimpseNet Post #5971G6

Subject: Hassan Fawaz

Date Glimpsed: 25th June

Verification Status: Verified

I was on the cobbled road behind my sister's business, looking at this graffiti some idiot Ani-Fate must have sprayed on the wall. It said, 'RESTORE FREE WILL'. The usual nonsense. The O looked weird, though. Like an eye. Then this man walked up next to me. Blond. Late twenties at a guess. He looked at the graffiti, then at me.

"You don't look like you approve," he said.

"Of vandalism?"

"Of the message."

I didn't know what to say to that, but he carried on.

"It's not how I'd have got it across, but I can't say I'm unhappy with the message spreading." He pulled out his phone and took a photo of the wall.

"Right…" I turned to leave, but he grabbed me by the shoulder.

He rolled his eyes. "You still flinch, even when you know what's coming. How can you not agree?"

"With what?"

"With this!" He pointed at the graffiti. "Can't you see what we've lost? These words, from me, from you, you know what's coming and yet you say them anyway!" He looked back at his phone and started tapping on the screen, then held it up in front of me.

He was showing me GlimpseNet. Specifically, this very post I'm currently typing. The conversation we had just had, written out on the screen. His eyes were manic, like he thought he'd unveiled some great truth. But I wasn't shocked.

"I think you should go home," I said. And then I left.

Seb

"Shit!" I yell as I stumble backwards, dropping the flowers to the floor and bringing my other hand to my throbbing face.

"Oh my God, I'm so sorry!" someone in front of me says. My eyes are jammed shut from the pain "Are you hurt?"

I take a moment to breathe, clutching my nose. The pain fades a little, but something hot and wet is trickling down my hand. I blink my eyes open and hold my hand in front of me. It's covered in blood.

"Shit," I say again.

"Oh God oh God oh God." There's a boy in front of me, his face filled with horror. Anyone would think he'd just seen a person with their face half ripped off. I can't look that bad. "I'm so sorry, I didn't mean to–I didn't see–I just stepped forward and–and now you're bleeding!"

I almost laugh, but instead pinch the bridge of my nose. "Yep, you're not wrong there."

The boy frantically searches his pockets and pulls out a wad of tissues. "Here," he says, stepping forward, looking less horrified and more...nervous?

I take the tissues and wipe away the blood. The flow is already stopping, so I guess it's not broken, thank God. It wouldn't have been great to show up to the hospital as both a visitor and a patient.

"Sorry," the boy says again.

"You say that a lot."

"S-" He catches himself and stares at his feet, like he's suddenly too scared to look directly at me.

It's only now, when the pain is mostly gone and the boy's become super timid that I finally recognise him.

"Hey," I say, "I saw you the other night, didn't I? At the party? You were..." I stop myself, remembering exactly how I found him: crying alone in the bedroom. Maybe not the best thing to bring up. Although now that I think about it, I had a bleeding nose then too.

He nods, no longer looking at his feet but still not making eye contact.

"Do you, er, want help with that?" I ask, pointing down at the pavement, where his groceries have fallen out of their bag.

"Oh. No, it's okay, thanks." He starts gathering up the mess.

I pick up my flowers, which have thankfully only lost a couple of petals here and there. "I'm Seb, by the way."

"I know," the boy says, standing up with his refilled bag. He goes bright red as soon as he catches my eyes. What the hell is up with this guy? "We go to school together. *Went to*, I mean."

"Yeah." I nod. "I know. I'll be honest though, mate, I never actually caught your name."

"Oh." He goes red again and scratches his cute ginger curls. "It's Elliot. I'm Elliot. Dove. Elliot Dove. That's, er –"

"Your name?"

"Yeah."

I can't help but laugh this time. "Cool."

His eyes (a lovely shade of hazel from the brief moments I've seen them) return to his feet once again. There's a silence between us that's getting way too uncomfortable for my liking.

"Well, Elliot Dove," I say, shaking the bunch of flowers, "I'd best be off. See you around."

"Bye," he mutters.

I walk off with a grin. What a weird guy. Cute, sure, but weird.

Mum beams at me from her bed when I enter her ward, but it looks false. She's putting on a front for me. Pretending she's happier than she is. I can't imagine anyone could feel very happy here. Their joy would sapped away by the beige walls and green curtains.

"Hi, Mum."

"What happened to your nose?"

"Nothing, just bumped it." I take a seat beside her and hold out the flowers. "I got you these."

She takes them, smells them, and says thank you. A series of perfect movements, acted out as if there's a camera on her. A nurse watches from nearby but loses interest quickly.

"How've you been?" I ask. "Are they treating you well?"

"Mhm. I've been good," she says in the same fake way she has every time I've visited. I'm sure they are treating her fine, but I know she isn't 'good.'

She places the flowers on her bedside table, and I pick at the foam in the damaged seat. Now's my chance to ask the question I've been dreading. I check behind me to make sure no one's close enough to overhear.

"Mum?" I say, already having to hide how much I'm shaking, "Who is Dan?"

She tenses instantly. Her eyes go wide and what little colour she had drains from her face. "Dan?"

"He came to the house yesterday," I look around again. The nurse is definitely gone. In a whisper, I add, "He was asking for money."

Mum bites her lip and closes her eyes. She's shutting down. Hiding away. But I can't let her, not now.

"I need you to tell me what's going on." I keep my voice low. "Are you...are you dealing?"

Her eyes open at that. "No," she says, and unlike everything else she's said today it sounds sincere. "I'm not a drug dealer, Seb. I'd never do that."

I breathe a sigh of relief, but I don't let myself relax too much. Because that means something else is going on.

"Then what, Mum? Why does he want money from you?"

She won't look at me. The second person to do that today. I can take it from a random guy from school, but not from her.

"Mum!"

"Everything okay?" comes the voice of a nurse who must have teleported behind me.

"Everything's fine," I say, trying my best to hide the bitterness in my voice.

Mum sends the nurse a fake smile and that does the trick. We're alone again.

"Tell me what's going on," I whisper. "*Please.*"

Mum hesitates, but eventually she looks at me. "I work for him."

"Since when?"

Mum grips her blanket, rubbing the fabric between her fingers like her life depends on it. "Since a while back."

"How come I never noticed?"

"It happens while you're at school."

I let out a huff. God knows how long she's been hiding this from me. "And what is the work?"

"Stuff."

I grit my teeth. "What stuff?"

"Ssh."

I take another breath. I hadn't realised I was getting louder. It's hard not to when I'm getting nothing out of her.

"He came to our house, Mum. He banged on the door demanding money and I didn't know what was going on. You need to tell me what he has on you."

Her eyes start to glisten and tears fall as she nods. This surprises me. I'm used to her being sad, but usually it's the empty, silent type. There aren't normally tears. In fact, I can't remember the last time I saw her cry.

I reach out a hand and place it on hers. "Mum?"

"Clients call him. Men. Lonely, desperate men. They find him and he sends them to me and I...I..."

"You're a prostitute." It falls out of my mouth without me even thinking. And the tears she cries in response are enough confirmation for me.

I leave without saying goodbye.

Smash. Tear. Throw. Rip. Break. Punch. Flip. Kick.

The living room wasn't tidy before, but now it's unrecognisable. Torn papers, smashed plates, an overturned coffee table, cushions ripped to shreds. I sit in the centre of it all. The carnage. Head in my hands. Not knowing whether to cry or scream.

"Right," says Aym from the doorway where she's watched it all unfold. "Now that you've got that out of your system, do you want to talk?"

"No." My voice is muffled by my hands.

"Well too bad." I hear her stumble through the wreckage and plant herself right in front of me. "Put your hands down, Seb."

I do as she says, as if she's suddenly become my mother. She's perched on a mound of ripped-up cushion.

"Tell me what happened."

So, I do. I tell her exactly how my meeting with Mum went. Right down to the last revelation. "She's a prostitute."

"Right..." Aym looks around the room. "And that's why you've done this?" She says it like it's a ridiculous reaction. Like I'm not justified in being angry.

"Did you not hear me? My mum is a prostitute. Dan sends men to this house while I'm at school and she–"

"Yes, I know how it works, Seb."

"And you don't think I should be angry about that? It's fucking disgusting!"

Aym puts a hand over my mouth. Like, full on, actually takes her own hand and forces it over my mouth to stop me speaking.

I push it away, more forcefully than I've ever touched her before. "What the fuck are you doing?"

Aym laughs.

"It's not funny!"

"No, Seb. It's not funny. But I'm not just gonna sit here and listen to you call sex work disgusting."

"But, it–"

"No. No buts. Your mum is in a crap situation, Seb, no one's denying that. And from the way you spoke about this Dan guy, it sounds like he's a piece of shit. But for you to just abandon your mum after she told you something she's clearly ashamed of and then trash your house because you're angry with her? That's not okay. And you are not gonna call sex workers disgusting. It's her decision. And it's a lot of other people across the world's decision too. It's not for you to judge."

I still feel angry. I still feel like tearing my whole house apart. Every part of me is tense and my heart is beating overtime. But Aym's words keep me still. Keep me thinking instead of punching. The thought of my mum in this house while I'm at school, working for these men–for Dan–it makes me feel ill. But I know why she did it. To buy food. To pay rent. To buy me that guitar. It's all been for me.

"Understood?" Aym says, stone-faced.

I nod.

"Good. Now let's clean this place up."

Elliot

I ring the bell again. A cool breeze passes against my back, and I pull my coat tighter. I might be making a huge mistake coming here, but it's either talk to someone or keep torturing myself alone. The door swings open to reveal Callum, wearing loose fitting clothes and pushing his damp hair off his forehead.

"Oh, hey," he says.

"Sorry, I should have asked if I could come over. Is this a bad time?"

"Nah, I just got out of the shower. Come in."

I follow Callum through to the living room. I've always liked it at Callum's house–somehow spacious and cosy at the same time. The walls are lined with bookcases and a large TV stands in the corner, with two red sofas angled towards it. I sink into one of them instantly. They're unbelievably soft.

"Are your parents home?"

"No. They're at a friend's. Want a drink?" He wanders over to the kitchen.

"Sure, thanks."

He comes back with a can of coke for each of us, throws one to me, then sits on the other sofa.

"So, what's up?"

I crack open the can and take a sip before starting. It's too late to turn back now. "I had my Glimpse."

Callum sits bolt upright at that. If he wasn't paying attention before, he certainly is now. "You what?"

"Last week, I had my Glimpse."

"Last week? Was that before we met up in the park?"

I nod.

"What did you see?"

I'm suddenly very aware of the cold can against my skin. Tiny droplets of condensation drip down my fingers. I bite my lip. I could lie. I could run away and never tell him what I saw. But I've already told him I'm not straight. The hardest step is over with, right?

"El?"

"I saw myself having sex."

There's a silence that seems to last both a lifetime and no time at all. I feel like I'm falling into an abyss but also like I'm being scrutinised under a microscope. Absent yet exposed.

I look at Callum. I can see the questions primed on his lips. But he restrains himself. He doesn't pry. He waits for me to say what I want to say.

"I saw myself having sex with Sebastian Glass."

Again, the silence. I can hear the fizzing from the can in my hand.

"Sebastian Glass?" Callum says. "Seb? From school?"

"Yeah."

The fizzing continues, as though I'm hearing Callum's mind. Each bubble a question, too many for him to choose between. I know the feeling. We sit in silence for a moment longer, until Callum says, "This is why you came out, isn't it?"

I nod again. "I started thinking I might not be straight after the party, and I thought maybe the Glimpse would help. And, well, I don't know if it helped, but it definitely cleared some stuff up."

"You can say that again."

I don't know whether to laugh or cry.

"And...in the Glimpse..." Callum continues, "were you...happy?"

There are many things I'm unsure about when it comes to my sexuality; a thousand questions I've asked myself over and over again. I've imagined worst-case scenarios for what could happen if I come out to my family. I've cried myself to sleep and debated my next steps in my dreams. But the answer to Callum's question comes easily because it's completely undeniable.

"Yes," I say. "Happier than I've ever felt. And I don't just mean because we were...you know..."

Callum's lip curls into a smirk. "Having sex?"

"Yeah." I think my face is red more often than white these days. "It was more than that." That incredible, overwhelming feeling has been lingering ever since I had the Glimpse. And I think I've finally found the word to describe it. "It was like...I felt...love? Maybe? I don't know. It's stupid."

"It's not stupid." His eyes suddenly widen. "Wait, that's why you ran off the other day, isn't it? In the park? Seb and his friend were walking past."

"Yeah." I take another swig of the can and put it down on a side table, wiping the condensation off my fingers.

Callum lets out a huge sigh. "Well, no wonder you've been so off lately. That's a lot to handle. Thanks for telling me, man. I'm glad you trust me like that."

"You're my best friend."

The sweet smile he sends me reminds me of my more-than-friendship feelings for him. But it does something else, too. That pang in my chest, that longing for Callum, is changing. The smile on his face doesn't bring me joy because I fancy him. It brings me joy because it's a reminder that he is still my friend, even after everything. And I wonder whether that pang of longing might shift over to Seb. Is that how these things work?

"So," Callum says, getting up off his sofa and joining me on mine, "the question now, is: how do we get Seb to fall in love with you?"

If I still had coke in my mouth, I'm sure I would have spat it out. "Are you serious?"

"Dude, you two are *literally* meant to be!"

"*That's* what you got from what I just told you?"

Callum laughs. "Oh, I'm sorry, were you not the one who said your Glimpse was the 'happiest you've ever felt'? I think you were."

I roll my eyes. "Okay but that doesn't mean we need to force it to happen. It's gonna

happen no matter what."

"So, you're just gonna run away from Seb whenever you see him and just *assume* you'll end up in bed together?"

"Actually...we were in a tent..."

"I'm sorry, what?!"

At that, I burst out laughing and so does Callum. Two friends, laughing about sex. The most normal I've felt in days.

When I get back home, my thumb is hovering over the follow request button on Seb's Instagram account. It was Callum's idea that I should follow him. I told him how I bumped into Seb outside the shop and how we saw each other briefly at Harvey's party. According to Callum, that's enough of a reason to follow him. I'm not so sure.

I put my phone away and join my parents for tea. The news is on, as it always seems to be these days, and yet again it's all about the protests. Mum and Dad roll their eyes at every mention of it. In fact, at one point Dad almost chokes on his food while laughing at a reporter showing sympathy towards the Anti-Fates.

I can't help but wonder if they'd have this sort of reaction if I came out. Would they snort derisively at the notion of me drifting from the norm? Of being anything other than the perfect straight boy like my brother has always been? Perhaps they'd say it's just a phase, or that I can't possibly know how I really feel at my age.

The thing is...if I am bi, then I could still end up living out the life my parents expect of me. I could still fall in love with a girl. I could still marry a woman. I could still have children the 'traditional' way. But it's like Callum pointed out: I was happier in my Glimpse than I've ever felt in my life. And even though I could have that 'traditional' life, I still wouldn't be straight. I want my parents to accept *all* of me. Without conditions. How can that not be worth pursuing?

While Mum and Dad are distracted by the TV, I pull my phone out of my pocket and bring up Seb's Instagram again.

This time, I hit follow.

FOURTEEN

Seb

I'm back in the hospital first thing the next morning. This time, it's not flowers I carry with me but guilt. Mum barely even acknowledges me when I sit down next to her. Her mouth is drawn into a tight, flat line, head turned away from me. She's ashamed, and it's my fault.

"Mum, I'm sorry."

Nothing.

"I was an idiot yesterday. I shouldn't have reacted the way I did. I'm sorry."

On the opposite side of her, atop the bedside table, are the flowers I got her. They're drooping already.

"Mum?"

Her hands are resting on her lap, over the cover of her bed. I reach out and hold one.

"Mum?"

"I'm sorry too," she says, finally turning to me. She looks tired and paler than ever.

"Don't be. You didn't do anything wrong."

"I should have told you sooner."

I shake my head and there's a thick moment of silence, save for the constant background noise that's impossible to escape in a hospital.

"There's £100 under the cutlery tray in the kitchen drawer," Mum says suddenly.

"What?"

"That should be enough for Dan." She meets my eyes. "And then I'm done with him. That'll be the end of it."

I want to ask more. I want to know if I can trust her. But the look in her eyes is focused. A moment of clarity in the fog that usually surrounds her. I can't ignore that. After how I treated her, the least I can do is listen.

"If he comes back, give him the £100."

I grip her hand tighter, telling her without words that I'll never let her down or abandon her again. "I will."

On my way home, I notice a follow request on my Instagram from Elliot. It's pretty weird. I mean, I barely know the guy. He seemed nice and everything, but he wasn't much of a talker. I ignore it, putting my phone away. I have more important things to worry about right now, like finding this money.

Once inside, I head straight for the kitchen drawer. The money is right where Mum said it would be, tucked beneath the cutlery tray, somewhere I'd never think to look. I rifle through the notes, counting them, making sure there's exactly the right amount.

£100. It's all there. I breathe a sigh of relief.

It's a waiting game now, I suppose, until Dan turns up again. My whole life is made up of waiting games these days. Waiting for school to finally end. Waiting for Dad to get in touch. Waiting for Mum to have a moment of happiness. Waiting for her to recover in the hospital. Waiting for my exam results to find out what the hell happens next.

I did the same as basically everyone else in my year when planning what to do after school: apply for the local sixth form. It was a weird process, since they basically give offers to everyone anyway, as long as you live locally. They made us write a personal statement–a page of text about what we want to do with our lives and why applying to sixth form is the best decision for us. I filled mine with utter bullshit.

I don't know what I want to do with my life. I've never known. Sixth form will just be another way to bide my time until I get thrown out into the real world. Or, at least, it will be if I get in. And from how I feel the exams went, I doubt that's going to happen.

Hours later, I'm sat strumming my guitar, singing the new song I've been learning. It seems the universe is out to get me because, just like the other night, my playing is brought to an abrupt stop, but not by knocking at the door this time.

With a crash that makes me flinch so hard I almost sever my finger on the B string, a small object comes flying through the living room window, bursting through the curtains, shards of glass spiralling in its wake. I don't have the chance to register what's happened when I hear the sound of a car engine flare up outside and quickly fade away as the car makes a quick escape.

On the floor, surrounded by broken glass, is a rock with a piece of paper bound to it with rubber bands. I remind myself to breathe before I lay down my guitar and walk carefully to the rock, avoiding the glass. There's a ringing in my ears. My hand shakes as I reach out to grab it.

I unfurl the paper, finding a note scrawled on it in block capitals, aggressively scribbled as though by a child.

£300 BY FRIDAY
NO EXCEPTIONS
I WILL BE BACK

Time passes in a blur, like I'm never quite sure if I'm here or floating above my body in a trance. I clear the glass and cover the broken part of the window with cardboard and tape, all without ever truly feeling present. I can't say how long it takes, only that when I'm finished my stomach is groaning with hunger and there's not a hint of natural light coming in.

Dan's note sits on the coffee table. Taunting me. Begging to be noticed.

But I don't think about it.

I can't.

Because I don't know what to do about it. I don't know how to handle it.

£300 is money I don't have. Money Mum doesn't have. There's the £100 she had hidden, and about £50 left for food before she next gets paid. But Dan wants £300 by Friday. That's three days away. How the hell am I supposed to find that much money by then?

I should tell Mum. She should know what's happening. But after how she looked today...how worn out, how pale...what would this do to her? How would she react? I don't know if I can risk that.

I could call the police but they'll take me away, place me in a home or something, since I lied about staying with my dad.

I do the only other thing I can think of and call Aym. She'll know what to do. She always does. Always.

But she doesn't answer.

I pace the living room a thousand times. I walk up the stairs only to walk back down moments later. I clean. I tidy. I hold my guitar, consider playing it, then put it away. And then again. And again.

Until I get a text from Aym: **Sorry I didn't answer, been busy packing. You okay?**

Packing. Of course. In all the chaos of the last week, I'd completely forgotten about Aym's retreat. She told me about it weeks ago–a creative retreat for underprivileged artists, paid for by the college she has a place at. I check the date on my phone and the memory comes flooding back. It's tomorrow. She's going tomorrow.

I'm fine, I text back in reply. **Hope you get there safe.**

I collapse onto the sofa, and despite the house being tidier than ever I feel like it's crumbling down around me. Like the cracks of the broken window have spread into the walls and foundations, trapping me in a pile of rubble. Leaving me to suffocate.

£300. Three days to get it. Mum still in hospital. Aym away for days. What the fuck am I supposed to do?

Elliot

One thing I didn't plan on becoming once school ended was a servant for my mum. But here I am, traipsing all around town, struggling with bags full of crap she's asked me to pick up. The heaviest bag is so full of books I'm worried the straps might snap off. I mean, seriously–has she not heard of delivery? It's not like she can't afford the charge.

I make my way down a cobbled road, taking a shortcut to the bus station. Town isn't so far away from home that I couldn't walk back, but there's no way I'm carrying these bags all that way. There's graffiti on a wall nearby, half cleaned away but still clear enough to make out the words: RESTORE FREE WILL. I pause for a moment to look at it, noticing something odd about the O in 'restore'. It's not really an O, but at eye, wide open with a plus symbol for a pupil.

A girl barges past me, giggling as she runs along the cobbles, and I almost drop my bags.

"Sorry!" calls a man from behind me. "Emily! EMILY, STOP! You just hit that boy!" He runs after the girl, shooting me an apologetic look.

"It's fine," I say, but he's already gone. Seems I'm getting good at bumping into people recently.

When I reach the end of the road, I hear the distant sound of music. It's just a single instrument–a guitar–and there's a voice, but it's too quiet to make out properly. The bus station is to my right, but the music is coming from my left, somewhere near the park.

Usually, I ignore buskers, but for some reason the sound of this one makes me hesitate. Though I'm desperate to relieve my hands of the weighty bags, I find myself turning towards the music, lured by intrigue.

I let my ears guide me, turning a corner towards the edge of the park, the music becoming clearer with each step. I can hear the voice properly now.

Male. Young, I think. And there's a sort of raspy edge to it. An edge that makes the hairs on the back of my neck stand on end, as if the voice runs through me, igniting every cell.

I follow the curved edge of the park, keeping the iron fence to my right, until I reach the entrance gate. And there, strumming a gorgeous, rosewood guitar, case open on the ground at his feet, is Seb. And the voice, that beautiful voice, is coming from him.

I watch, frozen to the spot, as people pass him by. Families, groups of friends, and lone shoppers hurry past without giving him so much as a glance. Every so often one will pause for a moment, throw a few coins into his guitar case, and move on. But Seb doesn't seem to notice. He's not looking around at the non-existent crowd, no, he's in his own world. His eyes are closed, his face a tight ball of concentration, like he's scared of getting the song wrong. But he doesn't slip up. His right-hand strums while the fingers of his left move about the strings, switching between chords effortlessly. His face might not agree, but it looks like playing music comes as naturally to Seb as breathing.

The longer the song goes on, the more he seems to relax. With his eyes closed, I don't feel the awkwardness that I did when we met at the shop, so I don't look away. Instead, I see him more clearly than ever before. He has a small scar above his right eyebrow. A dimple that forms in his cheek when he hits a certain note. A watch on his wrist that doesn't seem to fit with the rest of his look.

He transitions into the bridge, voice rising, soul ascending. His face, now lost in the music, reminds me of how he looked at me in the Glimpse, and I feel my breath catch. The closer he gets to the final chorus, the harder he makes each strum, pouring his entire being into the song.

And it works. God, does it work. He sounds incredible. He looks incredible.

But no one else seems to care.

Seb finishes his song with a final strum, then takes a moment to breathe. The first place he looks is the case, with its pitifully small number of coins, then he looks up. At the people walking past. The people who won't stop for him.

Then he looks at me.

For a moment, neither of us say anything. We just stare. Each taking the other in. It's like a silent conversation passes between us.

Are you the boy from outside the shop?

Yes, and you're the one who walked in on me crying at the party.

Elliot, right?

Yes. And you're Seb.

I think about my conversation with Callum the other day and the fact that Seb still hasn't accepted my follow request on Instagram. Not that I've been checking.

Is this another chance the universe is throwing at me? Are these meetings going to keep happening until I have a proper conversation with him? Until we finally set in motion the chain of events that will lead to me and Seb being in that tent together? Is that how the Glimpses really work?

"Hey," says Seb, still a little breathless from his performance.

"Hey." Well, here goes nothing. I step forward, removing the awkward distance between us. "That was amazing. I didn't know you could sing." My eyes flash to the guitar hanging from his body. It gleams in the sunlight. A perfect, untarnished surface. "Or play."

"Thanks."

"I'm surprised you never did any of the school talent shows. You'd have won, for sure."

He shrugs, and his shirt lifts up a little to expose his skin, but it's blocked by the guitar. Not that I was looking.

"I don't really like performing in front of people," he says.

I raise an eyebrow and look around.

"This is different. I did this for..." He trails off, but his quick glance at the coins in his case finishes the sentence for him.

I suddenly become very aware of the cash in my pocket and feel my cheeks flush.

"Anyway, it's been a waste of time," he says, hands ready to take the guitar off his shoulder.

"No, wait." I reach into my pocket and pull out a fiver. "Here." I toss it towards the case, but a gust of wind knocks it off course and before either of us can react it's already flying down the street.

Seb stares, open mouthed, a laugh primed on his face.

"Shit," I say. "Wait, I've got another, let me just..." I reach into my pocket again.

"Don't be stupid." He grabs the coins from the case and pockets them. "It's fine. I don't need your money." He takes off the guitar and sets it down in the case with the delicacy of a parent holding their baby.

"No, you were really good, I want to–"

"It's fine." He rises back up with the case in hand.

For a second, his eyes catch the sun in such a way that I'm reminded of the ocean on my family holiday to Greece last year. They have the same sparkle. The same depth. I could look into them all day.

"Then at least let me help you find a better spot," I say.

"Huh?"

"You've chosen the wrong end of the park. No one uses these gates to go in, because from here they're all heading home." I point at the hordes of people walking speedily past us. "See? If you go to the other end, that's where people who are planning on staying in the park come in. They'll actually listen to you."

Seb scrunches up his face. "I'm not sure."

"Come on, I'll walk you there."

He still looks uncertain, but he nods and swings the case over his shoulder. And suddenly I'm walking through the park with Sebastian Glass. And I have no idea what to say.

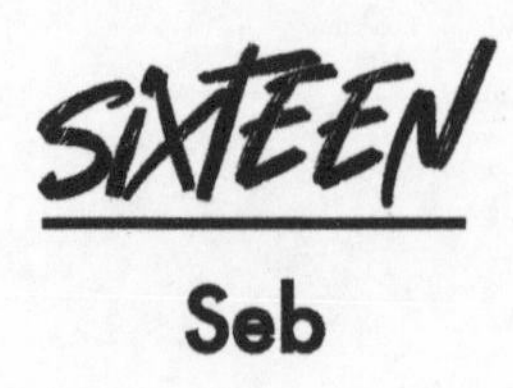

Seb

Well, this isn't exactly how I thought my day would play out. I didn't expect busking to help much. I mean, I need to find at least £200, and there's no way I'll make that by playing music to strangers. I might be alright on the guitar, maybe even at singing, but people just aren't that generous. Even so, it was the only thing I could think to do. I barely slept last night, spending every moment debating whether I should tell Mum what happened, or thinking of ways to make money. When I finally did get to sleep, I had a nightmare about Dan breaking into the house with an axe and murdering me. So, you know, all in all it was a fun night.

In any case, I thought maybe I'd make more money busking than I have. I haven't counted them properly, but the coins in my pocket can't add up to more than a few quid at most. Hopefully Elliot's right about the other end of the park.

He's a strange one, this boy. One minute he's saying more to me than he ever has before, and the next he's completely silent. We're walking through the park, sun bouncing off the curls of his hair, a fire alive and warm on his head. Yet the rest of him is cold and frosty.

I clear my throat to break the tension. His dark eyes flash my way.

"You know," I say, "for someone who never said a word to me when we were at school, you sure are showing up a lot recently."

He laughs, but it sounds forced.

"You're not stalking me, are you?"

"What? No! I just heard you singing and thought you sounded good and..."

I can't help but laugh. "Woah there, calm down. I was joking."

"Oh." He fiddles with his shopping bags. "Sorry."

"Want a hand with those?" I nod at the heaviest looking bag. The straps are primed to snap.

"Oh, er, sure. Thanks."

I take a couple off him, and immediately he loosens up.

"I like your watch," he says.

"Thanks. It was a birthday present." An expensive birthday present. It hasn't escaped my notice that it'd probably be worth something to Dan. And I'm sure Aym would understand if I gave it to him.

"Your sixteenth?"

"Yeah. Same day as prom."

"Oh. I didn't know."

I smirk. "Why would you?"

"Fair point."

We pass the pond, where families are throwing bread to the ducks. A group of teenagers fresh out of school, with their ties halfway off and shirts untucked, are on the other side, tormenting a pigeon.

"I didn't see you at prom," Elliot says.

"That's because I didn't go. I don't exactly have friends in our year I could have gone with." As if I'd even want to be around those homophobic assholes.

"I know the feeling."

I raise an eyebrow at that. While I didn't know Elliot personally, I saw him around school, and he was always with friends. "Aren't you mates with that guy, Callum?"

"Yeah, but he's usually with his girlfriend these days."

"That sucks."

He mumbles an agreement, then comes to a stop. "Here we are."

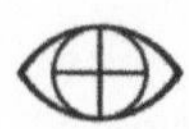

Elliot's right. While there are fewer people at this end of the park, they are willing to stop and listen for a lot longer than anyone did at the entrance. In fact, by the end of my first song a small crowd has started to form. And plenty of people have thrown money in my case.

Elliot stands off to the side, bags resting at his feet, and he smiles all the way through each song, clapping every time I finish. He might be a bit odd, but I can't deny he's a good hype man. The longer he keeps watching me, the longer others do too. And the best thing is, he actually seems to be enjoying it.

I find myself keeping my eyes open a lot more while I sing. Sometimes, I look at different people in the crowd, but I'm always drawn back to Elliot. His cute smile. His pink face. The freckles that cover his nose and cheeks. Those big, hazel eyes. That fiery hair. His energy fuels me. His cheers keep me going. And when the crowd eventually dies down, he's still there, just as eager to listen as he was at the start.

"I think that's enough," I say, pulling the guitar off my shoulder and collecting the money–a whole lot more than I made earlier. There are even some notes in there.

"You were amazing," Elliot says. "I mean it."

"Thanks." My mouth hurts, and I realise it's because I'm smiling so hard.

He picks up his bags again. "I, er, I'd best be going. Mum'll be wondering why I'm still out."

"Yeah, I should get home too. I'll see you around, though?"

He nods.

"Tell you what," I add, pulling out my phone. I open up Instagram and find my follow requests. There's Elliot, the only one I haven't responded to. Until now. "There. Chat to me on Insta."

He smiles even wider than he did during my performance, which I can't help but laugh at.

"See you later, Elliot."

SEVENTEEN

Elliot

I go to bed way earlier than usual, curling up with my blanket over my knees and my phone in my hands. Seb's Instagram is open on my screen. I scroll through the photos, reading each and every caption. I want to know more about him. I want to know who he is. What he likes. Who he hangs out with. I want to *know* him.

I'm surprised (and a little annoyed) to find no videos of him playing guitar or singing. After his performance in the park, I just want to listen to him play on an endless loop. Most of his recent photos are with the girl I saw him with in the park when I came out to Callum. She's tagged as **@AymForTheBest** and she's the only person to comment on all of Seb's posts.

There's a picture from Harvey's party with her. A selfie of the two of them, tongues out, looking all the way drunk, the background a blur behind them. I wonder where I was when the photo was taken. Was I hiding in the bedroom upstairs? It must have been before I left because Seb doesn't have a bloody nose.

I scroll further, all the way to last year, where I find a post about GlimpseTech. The image is a screenshot of a news article about two children whose mother killed herself after seeing nothing in her Glimpse.

Horrific, reads Seb's caption. **GlimpseTech should answer for this**.

There's a comment from **@Carl_Thomas** disagreeing and a whole back and forth between them. It's pretty clear Seb doesn't believe there's anything good about GlimpseTech and that the world would be a better place without it.

I spot Carl in comments here and there. I press his name, opening his profile, and I immediately recognise him as the boy Seb was dating last year. He was also the boy Callum spoke to at Harvey's party, who, despite my drunken haze that night, I remember saying he was no longer with Seb.

It shouldn't, but the knowledge that Seb is single makes my heart leap just a little.

I keep scrolling, and eventually stop at a very early image of Seb holding a guitar. It's not the same one I saw him playing today. It's far older, far more scuffed. It was posted three years ago, and Seb looks so young. His face is chubbier, and his hair is longer, but he still has the same pale blue eyes and cheeky grin.

I move my thumb to keep scrolling, but accidentally hit the 'like' button on the photo.

Shit.

Shit shit shit.

I unlike it immediately, heart pounding in my chest, face hot enough to melt an igloo.

Maybe he didn't see. Maybe he has his notifications turned off. Maybe–

A message flashes on screen. A message from Seb.

Shit shit shit shit shit.

You know, he says, **liking my old photos isn't the best way to stop me thinking you're stalking me.**

I'm dead. I'm actually dead. My heart has stopped beating and I am clinically deceased. There's no recovering from this. None at–

Not gonna lie, I've been looking at your old posts too.

Thank God for that. The tension falls out of me with one, huge sigh. For a moment I thought I'd found proof that Glimpses don't always come true. I take a moment, breathe again, then start typing my reply.

You caught me, I say. **I almost had a panic attack just then.**

Happens to the best of us!

My fingers hover over the keyboard. What do I say now?

Typing...

Looks like I don't need to say anything.

Hope you got that shopping home safe.

I did, thanks. Same to you with your guitar!

Hahaha. I managed fine enough. You were so right about that spot in the park, btw, I made like £20! Thanks for the help!

Nice one! And it was no problem, really. I only found you a spot, you're the one who actually performed. (Which, again, I need to remind you was INCREDIBLE).

He sends a GIF of a panda flopping its hand with the caption 'STOP IT.'

I bite my lip as I type: **I will not!**

Is this flirting? Is that what this is? Feeling all giddy while I message someone I...someone I...

Honestly, texts Seb, **where were you during high school? I could have done with your stanning. You might have upped my street cred.**

You did *not* just unironically use the phrases 'stanning' and 'street cred'!

Correct. I did not. That, my friend, was called humour.

I bite back a laugh and glance at my bedroom door, somehow worried that my parents can hear my thoughts through the wood. I feel like whenever I talk to Seb, I start out super tense and then relax as we go on. And the more we text, the more I feel like I can let go. The more I can let my guard down.

Weird, I type, **because I'm not hearing any laughter.**

Oh, please. As if you're not rolling on the floor at my comic genius.

You can say it as much as you want, it doesn't make it true.

Suuuuuuure.

And anyway, if you think *I'd* be able to give you street cred then you've severely misjudged me!

I'm sorry... He attaches a photo from my page with Callum and Nikita sitting in the park. **Is this not *the* Nikita? You CANNOT tell me you don't have street cred when you're friends with her.**

It would be a strong case, if it wasn't for the fact I'm very much a tag-along when it comes to her group of friends.

Ha! I text back. **You should've seen me at prom. Her friends barely even looked at me. If anything, I bring down her 'street cred.'**

Typing...

Typing...

Typing...

Ah. Fair enough.

I wait for him to say something else, but he doesn't. He leaves it at that. And the flow of conversation has just stopped. I pause for a moment, unsure if I should dig deeper about something that's been weighing on my mind, especially after seeing his old post about GlimpseTech. I know that Seb has just had his sixteenth birthday, but I have no idea if he's had his Glimpse. And if he has, he's made no implication that he saw me in his. Not that there's any reason he would. I mean, even if we're...together...in the future, the Glimpses take you to a completely random moment. And I'm not going to be with him every moment of every day.

But still...if he has seen his Glimpse...maybe it would tell me something about my own future. Whether the night in the tent is just a fling, or something more.

Hey, I type, **can I ask you something?**

Shoot.

Have you had a Glimpse?

Typing...

Typing...

No. Why? Have you?

No, I reply way too quickly. I hit send before I had a chance to think, before I could construct a proper answer. Guess I'm stuck with this now. **I haven't, but I was thinking about it and I know you just turned sixteen so I thought I'd ask you.**

I see. Well, I haven't. And I never will, to be honest.

Why not?

Reasons.

Fair. I'm being risky enough with my questions. I'm not about to pry further.

Anyway, if you believe the rumours, they'll be pointless pretty soon.

Because of the Last Day?

Yeah.

Do you believe in it?

Idk. Maybe. I don't think it's the end of the world.

No?

No. I think it's something else. Maybe something good.

That surprises me. Glimpse sceptics tend to think the worst about the Last Day. It's the main reason a lot of people join the Anti-Fates–they think GlimpseTech is going to bring about the apocalypse. I've never been sure, myself, but I like what Seb is saying. That maybe it could be something good.

Anyway, Elliot, I've got shit to do. Been nice talking to you, though!

I want to smile at his compliment, but I can't help thinking I've said something wrong. 'Got shit to do' is just code for 'I'm done talking to you now.' Still, I send a reply. **Yeah, you too.**

Goodnight!

Goodnight.

EIGHTEEN

Seb

I got more sleep last night than the past week combined. Chatting with Elliot gave me a nice distraction from worrying about Mum and Dan and the money, but it's back to reality when I wake up. Downstairs, I count my earnings from yesterday's busking for the billionth time. It's all laid out on the table–coins, notes, a couple of random bits of paper (thank you, oh great and kind person who threw those in the case).

£17.63. On top of the £100 from Mum and the £50 left for food shopping, that's £167.63. And that's only if I don't buy any food, which is getting harder not to do the more the fridge and cupboards empty. All that's left in the house are a few slices of almost-mouldy bread, some butter, and a few old tins of who-knows-what.

My stomach groans at the thought.

I could call Dad. I *should* call Dad.

That's when I remember the envelope.

I run upstairs and sift through my pile of unwashed clothes on the floor. There, beneath them all, is the red envelope. It's slightly crumpled but still unopened. The card inside still unread. I lift it up, feeling its thickness–too fat to just be a card. There has to be something else inside it. Something like money. I take a deep breath and tear it open.

The card is simple and cheap looking, just some silver lettering saying *Happy 16th* on the front. But it's what's inside that matters. I open the card, and like a gift from heaven itself, a wad of notes falls out, right onto the pile of clothes. Suddenly, I've never loved Dad more.

But the feeling doesn't last long.

Because it's a wad of fivers. Three fivers.

£15.

That's what I'm worth to him.

That's all he gives me in return for abandoning me forever.

Fifteen. Fucking. Pounds.

I count everything up again. And again. Hoping something will change. Praying I've miscounted. But I haven't. I never have.

£182.63.

£117.37 less than I need. For a man who throws rocks through windows, who exploits sex workers, and who won't be lenient.

I slam my hand on the table, making the coins bounce. A jolt of pain travels up my arm. What else am I supposed to do? What the fuck else can I do? AND CAN MY STOMACH STOP GROWLING FOR JUST ONE GOD DAMN MINUTE?

I don't even notice that I'm crying until my face is soaked, my throat is dry, and my head is aching. The tears won't stop. They won't fucking stop.

And I'm tired.

So tired.

Of everything.

I get up slowly and make my way to the sofa, eyes half closed.

I want everything to stop.

I want the world to stop spinning and for Dan to disappear and for Mum to be better.

And even though I've only been awake for less than an hour, I just want to sleep.

I wake up on the sofa, under one of Mum's tattered old blankets. My mind is a blur. Daylight is still streaming in from outside, bouncing off the table and the coins that are scattered across it. I look at my watch. The expensive, golden watch. And I don't even register the time.

I take it off, quicker than I opened the envelope, and in one movement I run over to the table and set the watch down beside the money. It has to be worth something. Maybe even the whole amount.

In my head, I picture Aym giving me the watch. Something that was meant to be hers. A pang of guilt stabs in my chest as I rub my naked wrist and stare at the watch. I brush the guilt away. If anyone would understand this decision, it would be Aym. No way would she hold it against me.

And then I think of my other expensive birthday present. Worth even more than the watch. More than I've ever seen in cash.

But I can't lose that.

I can't.

Can I?

My stomach groans again and I realise I'm going to have to find food somehow. Even if I manage to go the rest of today without it, I can't last till Mum's next allowance comes in.

There's no way.

I've never shoplifted before. Not even a packet of sweets as a kid, though I certainly felt tempted to. But I've seen it attempted plenty of times, even successfully. The kids on my street have a bit of a reputation for it, so I know the closest shop is already prepared. It'd be way too risky to try there.

The shops in the posh village, though? A shop I've been to before and won't look suspicious in? That's my safest bet. I put on my baggiest coat and head up to the village, leaving the litter strewn streets and sad looking houses behind as I cross the main road. My mouth is dry, and I feel like I'm shaking with every step. This is a bad idea, the worst I've maybe ever had, but what choice is there? It's not my fault that my life has come to this, while the rich fucks in the village never have to worry about having food to eat. Still, it hurts to know I'm becoming yet another statistic. One more kid from the rough part of town turning to crime to survive.

There's a chime as I open the shop door and the owner smiles at me from behind his counter. Guilt erupts inside me. I look to the left, towards the aisle where I found Mum's flowers just days ago. Flowers which I bought with money I should have saved.

"Are you okay?" calls the shop owner.

I've been stood still for a suspiciously long time. "Yeah," I say. "I'm fine." I send him a smile in the hope that'll make him ignore me, and I start walking down one of the aisles. Solidly out of his eyeline.

The smell of freshly baked bread washes over me, sending my growling stomach into overdrive. My eyes scan the shelves. So much choice. Too much. I didn't plan what I'm going to steal, which I now realise was completely stupid. I could've been in and out in a flash. But now I'm just overwhelmed. And so, so hungry.

I hear the door chime again and the owner greets the new customer. A distraction. A chance. I grab the nearest thing–a pot noodle–and bury it inside my coat.

"How's your mum?" the owner says.

A longer distraction. I grab a pack of crumpets.

"She's good, thanks," the customer says. "Still sending me out to do shopping for her."

Three packets of crisps into my pockets.

"Ah, well tell her I said hello."

Biscuits. In my hand. Almost in my coat.

"Will do."

Wait, I know that voice.

There's the sound of movement and, in a panic, I shove the biscuits into an inner pocket. Or at least I try. They won't fit. I have to keep my hand around them to stop them from falling out. From exposing me. And I don't have time to readjust because Elliot has just appeared at the top of the aisle.

"Oh!" he says, pausing with his hand halfway to the shelf when he sees me. "Seb! Hey. Didn't expect to see you here."

Now my hand really is shaking. It takes all my effort to keep it still. Beads of sweat start to form on the back of my neck.

"Hey," I say, trying to keep any hint of guilt out of my voice. "H-how are you?"

"I'm good, thanks. Just doing some shopping for my mum." He holds up a basket and grins in a way I'd usually think is cute but right now just makes me want to run and hide. "You?"

"Yeah, I'm good too. Just...you know...browsing."

Keep calm. Keep calm. Keep calm.

"Cool," he says, eyes flashing to my arm, the one halfway inside my coat. How long until he realises the reason?

I fake a smile. The sweat continues to cover my neck and I can practically hear my heartbeat in my head. I need to get out. I need to leave, quickly, without looking suspicious. But that's impossible with a hand shoved in my coat. My coat which seems heavier and heavier, keeping me rooted to the spot.

"Are you sure you're okay?" Elliot says. "You look like you're going to be sick."

"I'm fine." I say it way too fast.

His eyes flash to my arm again for less than a second.

I can't wait any longer. If I don't do something now, it'll be too late. I try to move the biscuits around, forcing them to fit in the pocket, without it looking obvious to Elliot. A few of the biscuits snap in my grip, making them easier to force into the pocket. It's enough to give me a chance.

"Anyway," I say, bringing my hand out from under my coat. "I don't think they've got what I need here. I'd best be off."

I step forwards, ready to leave the shop. Ready to run home and never come back. But I barely move an inch before the biscuits fall out of my coat and onto the floor.

There's a moment where all I can do is stare at Elliot while he stares back at me. Realisation dawns on his face. Followed swiftly by the most judgemental look I've ever seen.

Someone clears their throat behind me, and with a feeling of dread, I turn and face the shop owner. His brow is furrowed, and his arms are crossed over his large stomach.

"Young man," he says. "I think you need to empty out your pockets."

NINETEEN

Elliot

I can't believe what I'm seeing. Seb, the boy I saw in my Glimpse, the boy I'm supposed to...feel *something* for, the boy I'm supposed to get closer to than I've ever been with anyone in my life, is a thief. A shoplifter. A criminal. Stealing from an innocent man like Paul. Is this who Seb really is? Is this the sort of person I want to end up with?

I watch as he empties his pockets, revealing all the stuff he's swiped from the shelves, while Paul berates him, shouting with abject rage. From Seb, all I hear is quiet apologies, weak against Paul's yelling.

"Sorry," he says again and again. There's a crack in his voice that can only come from crying.

"You're a good-for-nothing, lowlife, filthy little–"

"Hey!" I say it without thinking. An instinctive reaction.

Paul looks at me in shock, his insults waiting desperately in his mouth.

"Shouting at him isn't going to help," I say. Because it's true. Even though he's done this shitty thing, hurling insults at him isn't going to make anything better.

"Are you actually defending him?" Paul asks. "I'd expect better from you, Elliot."

"I'm not defending him." Am I? I know what's going to happen between me and Seb, and that means he can't be a bad person. Surely. Even if he's done this one bad thing. "I just... I know him, Paul. He's from my year at school. And I believe him when he says he's sorry."

Paul almost laughs. "So, I'm supposed to just forget about it, am I?"

"I'm not saying that." I don't really know what I'm saying. Part of me thinks Seb deserves to hear everything Paul was shouting at him, but there's another, and I guess stronger, part of me that doesn't want him to get hurt. "Can't you just, I don't know, ban him from the shop or something?"

I can feel Seb looking at me, but I don't meet his gaze.

"Please?" I add.

Paul rolls his eyes, then looks to Seb. "You'd better count yourself lucky that you had Elliot here to back you up. Now clear off. And you're not to come in here ever again. Is that understood?"

"Yes, sir," Seb mutters weakly.

Paul nods at me and we watch as Seb leaves the shop with his head low. A lump rises in my throat.

"I'll be back in a minute," I say to Paul.

Seb is already walking away when I get outside.

"Hey!" I shout after him. "Wait!"

He pauses and looks back, eyes red with tears.

I walk up to him, but I don't know what to say. I don't know what's stronger: my anger at what he did, or my sympathy. My mouth seems to decide for me.

"How could you do that?" I say. "Stealing? That's not who you are, Seb!"

Seb laughs, but it's a laugh that comes with tears. "Right, 'cause you know exactly who I am, don't you?"

"I thought I did." I say it without thinking. It's true...sort of, but it's not going to make sense to Seb.

"We've spoken to each other like three times! You don't know the first thing about me!"

"So, you're a criminal, are you? You're okay with that?"

"No, of course I'm not okay with it you fucking prick!"

I feel like I've been slapped across the face.

"If you knew me at all, you'd know exactly why I did what I did!"

I shake my head. None of this makes sense. The Seb in my Glimpse and the Seb who steals from shops are one and the same, but that doesn't feel right at all. "There's no excuse for stealing."

Now he really does laugh, and I see his sadness turn into pure anger. "Isn't there? None at all? How about the fact I've got no food in the house? Or the fact I have no money to buy any? Or that my mum is in hospital because she tried to kill herself? How about that? Is that a good enough excuse for you?"

All the words I could possibly say vanish from my mind. I forget everything. How to speak. How to move.

"But of course, those things would never cross your mind, would they?" His hands wave frantically about as he speaks, his body erupting with rage. "No, not rich boy Elliot, living in the posh village and never having to worry about money or food because it's always there whenever he needs it. Such a good reputation that all he has to do is say a few nice things to the shopkeeper and he can stop lowlifes like me from being arrested."

"I..."

"Fuck off, Elliot. Fuck off back to your perfect, privileged life."

He turns and walks away before I have a chance to answer. Not that I know what I'd say anyway. There are no words that can match the weight of what he said. No words at all.

"Here you are, darling," Mum says when she sets my food down in front of me.

She takes her seat beside Dad. All three of us at the dining table: the large, oak dining table in the dual aspect room. Photo frames hang on the unblemished, white walls. They contain pictures of me, of Simon, of all of us on holiday, of our grandparents with us, even one with the whole extended family. There's a painting, too. A heavily detailed landscape by my great-grandfather that was left to my dad in his will.

The meal on my plate seems to scream at me, repeating Seb's words. Telling me he has no food or money. Calling me privileged.

"I was thinking perhaps we could go to New York next summer," Mum says between mouthfuls. "What do you think?"

"Maybe," Dad says. "So long as things over there have cleared up by next year. Did you see how violent those protests turned yesterday?"

"Oh yes. That's the Americans for you though, isn't it? Always blowing things out of proportion. I'm sure that won't be a problem next year, though." She turns to me. "What do you think, Elliot? New York next summer? It's been a while since we visited."

"We haven't even had this year's holiday yet!"

I didn't mean it to come out quite so loud, but Mum and Dad both drop their forks and stare at me.

"Sorry," I add. "But isn't it a bit early to be planning another holiday."

"Well, why not?" Mum says. "The earlier the better I always say."

Seb's words run through my mind again and again. He has so little money that he resorted to stealing food, and yet here my parents are talking about booking next year's holiday. *Perfect, privileged life.*

"I'll call Simon after tea and see what he thinks," she adds. "He had his final exam this morning, you know? Did he tell you?"

He didn't need to, what with Mum mentioning it at every opportunity she's had. One step closer to her golden child coming home from one of the best universities in the world for summer, how could she not be excited? I wonder if Seb is even considering uni for his future. Can you even plan that far ahead when you don't know if you'll be able to eat tomorrow?

"It sounds like it went well," Mum carries on. "At least from what he told me, which wasn't a lot. You know how he is. Always underselling himself with an 'it went fine.' Just like you, Elliot." She smiles at me in the most patronising way she can, sending an unclimbable mountain of expectation with it.

"I'm not feeling well," I say, resting down my fork.

"Oh no," Mum says, "whatever's wrong?"

"Just my stomach," I say, making a pained face as I rub it. "I don't think I can eat anything else. Do you mind if I just go to bed?"

"Of course not, darling. Let me know if you need anything."

"Will do."

I head upstairs and my stomach really does start to hurt. But it's not from illness, it's from guilt as I realise just how much food I left behind. Food that Seb would do anything for.

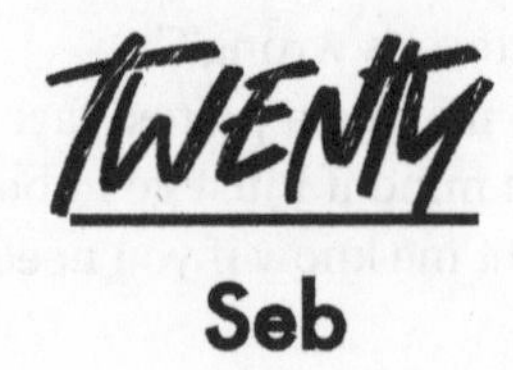

TWENTY

Seb

Sleep. Starve. Cry. Repeat.

Sleep.

Starve.

Cry.

Repeat.

Until it's too much.

Until I can't take it anymore.

The watch will be enough. It *has* to be enough. Enough to make up for the missing money. The amount owed grows by £10 when I just can't cope without food anymore. I cry with joy when I finally eat.

It's been a week now since Mum was taken to the hospital, and I haven't seen her in days. I can't see her. Not until this is all over and done with. Not until Dan takes his money and leaves us for good. I just have to get through today. I just need him to turn up, take what he wants, and go. Then I can face Mum again.

I haven't spoken to Aym either, at least no more than a few 'how are you?' texts and lies in response. She's having the time of her life on her retreat. I can't ruin that for her.

My phone is stacked with messages from Elliot. All different forms of an apology or admissions that I was right. Which I was. I meant every word of what I said to him, and I'd gladly say it again. I'll say it to anyone who judges me before they know me.

I read every message he sends, but I never reply. He doesn't deserve forgiveness. He doesn't even deserve the space he takes up in my brain. I hate that I'm thinking about him still. He's a dick. A privileged dick.

There's a knock on the door just after 6 PM, and I know it's Dan on the other side. It's not the aggressive knock of his that still stains my memories; I can just tell it's him. I grab the bag I've shoved all the money and the watch into and open the door.

And there he is. Sallow skinned and stinking of smoke, still wearing the filthy brown trench coat.

"You look like shit," he says. "Mummy still not home?" His voice feels like gravel against my ears.

I hold out the bag to him. I won't let him provoke me. I just want him gone.

"This the money, is it?"

I nod, and then I brace myself before saying, "Most of it."

His bloodshot eyes dart to mine in an instant. "*Most*?"

"I couldn't get you all the cash, but there's a watch in there that's worth plenty."

He's silent for a moment and I worry that he's about to punch me, but instead he says, "Is that so?" and peers behind me. "Well, I'd better check this watch and count the money before I leave. Can I come in?"

I want to say no, of course I do, but I know that would be a mistake. Dan looks like exactly the type of guy who wouldn't care about beating up a teenager. So, instead, I step aside and let him walk right past me. Into my house. Into *Mum's* house.

"Nice place," he says as he takes a seat on the sofa. He doesn't try to hide the sarcasm.

I watch silently from the edge of the room. The quicker he counts the money, the quicker he leaves.

"Let's see, then." He empties the contents of the bag onto the coffee table and gets to work, meticulously counting each note and coin. Then he takes the watch out of its box and turns it over in his hands, staring at it like an antiques dealer. "Nice," he says. "Looks like it's had some wear and tear though." He flashes me a smile, but it's not one of kindness.

I go cold.

He looks around the room, eventually settling his gaze on my guitar case. It leans against the wall, stupidly visible. My heart plummets. Why didn't I hide it?

"What's in there?"

"N-nothing, it's just..." I don't know why I even bother to lie.

"Just a guitar?"

He gets up and wanders over to it, each step a foot on my neck, choking me. He opens the case, and seeing him so close to the most beautiful thing I've ever owned is crushing. Then he touches it.

"NO!" I shout, stepping forward, driven by instinct alone.

He snaps up straight and looks right at me, freezing me with a glare. "What did you just say?"

"I don't...you can't...please..." I need to keep myself together. I can't break in front of him. I can't. But there's a lump in my throat and tears are already forming in my eyes. "The watch is enough," I say, voice cracking. "Please."

There's not a hint of sympathy on his face. Instead, he laughs a gravelly laugh, closes the guitar case and lifts it up. "The guitar is enough, you little shit."

That's the last thing he says to me before he gathers up the money and the watch. He shoves it all back in the bag and walks out of the house, taking the guitar with him, closing the door behind him, and never looking back. Not even once.

He's taken the one thing I had left, and now it's not just the cupboards or the kitchen or even the house that's empty. It's me. And I can't keep going anymore.

I fall apart.

TWENTY-ONE

Elliot

Callum's been busy with Nikita since she got back from holiday a few days ago, but I don't know who else to turn to. So, after an invite over text, I turn up at Callum's house and am met at the door by the bright-red-haired couple.

"Elliot!" shouts Nikita, opening her arms wide for a hug. "How've you been?"

I accept the hug and raise an eyebrow at Callum. I'd have much preferred to meet him here alone. "Um...well..."

"I haven't told her," Callum says.

"What?" Nikita says, releasing me. "Haven't told me what?"

"Didn't know if you wanted to do it yourself," Callum adds to me.

"Well, I guess I kind of have to, now," I say, rolling my eyes at Nikita's enthusiasm. "Can we sit down first?"

We all head into Callum's living room where he hands me a can of coke, as per tradition.

"So," I say, taking a breath in preparation and looking at Nikita, who is snuggled up against Callum on the other sofa. "Basically, turns out I'm bisexual." I'm surprised by how easily I say it. It's only the second time and yet it feels so much more natural.

"OH MY GOD, WHAT?" She almost jumps out of the chair, mouth wide with surprise.

"But I'm not, like, *out* out yet so please keep it quiet."

She nods enthusiastically. "Of course, I will! You can trust me."

I believe her. Even if we're nowhere near as close as me and Callum, I do consider Nikita a friend and I know Callum trusts her completely. And after how Callum reacted to me confessing everything, his trust is something I value without a shadow of a doubt.

"When did you realise?" Nikita asks.

"Well...that's the other thing..."

I notice Callum smile, and I don't know whether it's because he's so hooked on the whole me-and-Seb thing or because he knows I'm about to talk about sex.

"I had my Glimpse..."

"WHAT?"

"And I saw myself being...intimate...with a guy."

For the second time in my life, I tell someone all about my Glimpse. I tell her the same as I told Callum. That the guy was Seb. That I felt happier than I've ever felt in my life. And then I tell them both what's happened since and how badly I've fucked up.

"And he's not replying to you at all?" Callum asks when I finish my speech.

"Not at all. I don't know what to do."

"Well, it's obvious," Nikita says. And the look on her face tells us she's not joking.

"Is it?" I ask.

"You need to go to him."

"WHAT?" Both Callum and I say simultaneously.

"Go to him. Apologise in person. Classic rom-com trope."

"Not sure if you realise, Nikita," I say, "but we're not in a rom-com."

"And that is a bit of a creepy trope," says Callum. "Don't get me wrong, I'm fully here for Elliot and Seb to get together, but we don't want him to think he's a massive weirdo."

"Okay, okay," Nikita says, solidly talking to Callum now, "but hear me out... We know they end up together, no matter what, so what's the harm?"

"That's a fair point."

"I'm right here!" I shout, causing both of them to look at me. Finally.

"Sorry, El," Callum says.

"Look," I say, "even if I did want to go to him–which I don't, because it's a ridiculous idea–I don't even know where he lives."

The corners of Nikita's mouth twitch and I see her stifle a grin.

"What?" I ask.

"It just so happens," she says, "that my aunt lives on his road and my house is only a few streets away. So, I know exactly where he lives."

My heart leaps. Even though it's a terrible idea. Even though I can't go to him. I can't. That would be stupid. Wouldn't it?

Callum and Nikita both stare at me with eager eyes. It didn't take much for Callum to become hooked on the idea. I suppose that's what happens when you devote yourself to someone–it's easier to come round to their way of thinking. When you know someone that well, your minds hum in perfect harmony.

That's what I could have with Seb. If I try.

"There's no way he won't think I'm creepy if I do this," I say.

"Worst case scenario is he'll turn you away," Callum says. "It's like Nikita says, no matter what you do, the Glimpse is still gonna happen."

I don't know how I feel about that philosophy. It feels wrong to use the Glimpses as an excuse to get away with anything. But I do see their point. The worst thing that could happen is Seb turning me away, and if he does then that'll be my cue to stop trying to make something happen between us. If I even want that.

"This is all just happening too fast," I say, burying my face in my hands.

I hear movement, and soon enough the space on the sofa beside me sinks down and Callum's arm settles on my shoulders. I drop my hands and look at him, that face I was so close to kissing just over a week ago. Feelings that were purely one-sided, but feelings my Glimpse showed me I could share with someone else. Feelings that could turn into so much more if I let them.

"I know," Callum says. "It's a lot to take in."

I sigh. "If he turns me away, I'll go home and stop messaging him. I'm not going to chase after him. I messed up, and if he hates me, I understand."

Callum shakes his head. "He's not going to hate you. This will work."

"Okay." I take a deep breath and turn to Nikita. "What's his address?"

I've never stopped for long around where Seb lives, only ever spotting it in passing when heading to town. The sun has all but set now, turning the sky a deep purple, and a crescent moon hangs above the concrete hospital. I can't pretend not to notice the shift in surroundings when I cross from my village's side of the main road to Seb's. The houses get smaller and closer together, and there's far more litter. I hate myself for it, but when I see a gang of hooded guys smoking at the end of the street, I pull my coat a little tighter around me.

Seb's words come to mind again. *Perfect, privileged life.* Why would he forgive me when my sweaty palms are only proving his point? But maybe admitting how I feel in his neighbourhood is step one.

I turn a corner and steady the carrier bag that swings from my hands. Inside it are two large pizzas from a takeaway in the village. A gift. A peace offering. I don't really know. It might even come across as condescending, turning up to his house with food after what he told me, but how can I not?

When I reach Seb's house, I hesitate. Not only because I'm nervous (maybe even terrified) about how he'll react to seeing me, but also because of the shattered window, boarded up with cardboard. I'm worrying for my safety yet again, but my thoughts also turn to Seb. What happened here? Is he hurt? Did someone do this on purpose?

He was right: I really don't know anything about him. And yet, here I am, on his doorstep, thinking we're destined to be together. I feel insane.

Still, I knock on the door.

It opens a crack but almost instantly swings closed again.

"Wait!" I say, holding out my hand to stop it closing completely. "Seb...please..."

There's a beat of silence where nothing moves at all, then the door swings open slowly, revealing Seb. His reddened eyes have hefty bags beneath them, his dark hair is unkempt, there are patches of unshaved hair around his chin, and his loose grey shirt is super wrinkled and stained in multiple spots.

I want to reach out and hug him. I want to hold him close and ask him what's happened. I want to tell him I'm sorry, that I've never been sorrier in my life.

"Why are you here?" he asks, voice wearier than I've ever heard it.

"I... I wanted to talk to you. To say sorry."

He doesn't answer, but he doesn't close the door on me either.

"And..." I lift the bag and shrug my shoulders, fully aware of how weird this situation is. "I brought pizza."

He doesn't smile or give any expression except exhaustion, and for a while we remain silent and unmoving. But then he steps aside, keeping the door open. Inviting me in.

TWENTY-TWO

Seb

It's not that I want to talk to Elliot, or even see him for that matter. I just want *someone* here; and with Mum still in hospital and Aym still away I don't have many options. I'm exhausted and my head is throbbing from how much crying I've done. Plus, I'm hungry, and there's no way I'm turning down free pizza.

"How do you know where I live?" I ask, voice tired and croaky.

Elliot hesitates as he steps through the door. He stares at me, searching for approval that he's never going to get. "Nikita told me," he says.

I lead him through to the living room and watch as he looks around, taking in the place I call home, judging the state of it all.

"It's nice," he says when he spots me watching. "Cosy."

I know cosy is just a polite way of saying small, but I guess I can't hate him for trying. At least this is closer to the boy who helped me busk than the boy who shamed me for shoplifting. But I haven't forgotten what he said that day.

"Can I...?" he points at the sofa with his free hand.

I nod and he takes a seat, but he holds himself very stiffly, not leaning back, just perching on the edge. He's so awkward looking I almost laugh. Almost.

I sit down too but leave a gap between us. A gap he's trying to bridge. It won't work.

"I, er, didn't know what toppings you'd want," he says, taking the two huge pizza boxes out of the bag. I can already feel my mouth watering. "So, I got us both a margherita."

"Of course, you went with the most boring one." I don't know why I say it. I mean, I think he's a dick, but he is giving me this pizza for free.

He doesn't respond, just holds out a box to me.

I take it slowly, trying not to look too desperate, but once I open it and see the golden crust and melted cheese, I can't help shovelling a slice right into my mouth. Even if it is a boring topping. I hate that it tastes incredible.

Elliot starts eating his too, perched on the edge of the sofa. Neither of us look at each other. Or, at least, not when the other is looking. Not that I intentionally look at him. I mean, he's just a really loud eater and his lip smacking keeps pulling my attention. I'm not thinking about the way he looked at me when I was busking in the park. Or the way his hair glowed in the sunlight. Or how cute it is, the way he keeps thinking he's burnt his mouth on the pizza even though it's not that hot.

"I really am sorry," he says when he finishes another slice. "About what I said outside the shop. You were right, I don't know anything about you."

I keep eating.

"I'd like to learn, though. If you'll let me."

He's watching me. Those big, hazel eyes that demand to be met. But I won't look back at him. I won't.

"Why?" I say, eyes on the pizza. "Why do you want to know me? We didn't know each other all through high school and we were just fine."

"Were we?"

I look up at that. I can't help it. And there he is, all freckle-faced and ginger curls and chubby cheeks and–

"You said yourself you didn't really have any friends in our year," he says.

"Yeah, but I have friends." A lie. I have *a* friend. Singular.

"Right, sorry." He grabs another slice.

He really is trying; I can't deny that.

"I just think..." he starts, pizza slice in hand, "I think we missed a shot in school, you know. I think we could've been close."

He catches my gaze and shakes his head.

"I don't know," he says. "I'm being stupid, I'm sorry."

I can't tell what he wants or why he's here. The other day, in the park, it seemed like there was this...I don't know...connection? Some unspoken understanding between us. He doesn't know me at all, yet he tried so hard to help. Is that who he really is? Was what happened at the shop just a mistake?

I realise I don't know him at all either. I know he's friends with Callum, but that's pretty much it. I don't even know his sexuality. If he's gay, he's kept it quiet. Perhaps that's the connection I felt. Or feel. I don't know.

"No," I say. "I don't think you are." Is that true? I'm not sure, but it's my answer anyway. "You're a nice guy. You know, apart from..."

"Apart from my ignorant and privileged perspective?"

I laugh at that, almost choking on my pizza. It's the first time I've laughed in days.

"Yeah," I say. "Apart from that."

He smiles back, and for the tiniest sliver of a moment I forget about all my problems. Mum and Dan and the guitar and the money all vanish completely from my mind. So that it's only Elliot. Me and Elliot, smiling and laughing together. But it can't last.

"Seb," he says, "can I ask...what happened to the window?"

It's covered by the curtains, but from outside he must have seen my feeble attempt at covering up the damage, and his mention of it brings the moment it happened to the front of my mind. The rock, wrapped in the note. The desperate search for money that followed. I thought I was all cried out, but tears come back to my eyes.

"Shit," Elliot says, noticing, and half-rising from his seat, "sorry, Seb. Where are your tissues? I'll–"

"It's because of my mum," I say.

He pauses and sits back down.

And then I tell him everything. It pours out of me as freely as my tears, every word punctuated by sobs. The past few weeks of my life are laid out on display for him, and he takes it all in. He hears me. He listens. And when I'm done, he does the one thing I realise I've needed desperately for the whole of this week.

He hugs me.

I cry into his shoulder.

And it's like my emotions leave me and enter him.

Until we're even.

Until we reach a balance.

And it's then that I can sit back, and look into his eyes, and see the dawn of understanding in them.

And I know I've forgiven him.

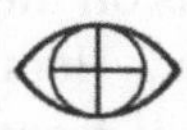

We stay quiet after that, each of us eating the rest of our pizza, but the gap between us no longer exists. I'm right next to him and he's no longer perching awkwardly; he's leaning back, fully embracing the sofa. Though I'm not pressed against him, I can feel the heat of his body. It's in every breath he exhales. In every moment his leg accidentally brushes against mine. And I find it comforting.

It's been a long time since I've sat this close, for this long with a boy. I'd almost forgotten the way it makes me feel. The comforting vulnerability. The way everything else in the world seems just a little bit less relevant.

The last time I felt this was with Carl, before he revealed his transphobia. The last good day I was with him in his room, cuddled up beneath the covers of his bed, our hands locked together. We'd had arguments before then, none quite strong enough to break us apart, and this moment came right after one of those.

He'd been angry about how much time I was spending with Aym, as if he should have been the only person I ever hung out with. As if I wasn't allowed friends. Maybe that's part of what stopped me making friends at school. While Carl was there, it was all about him, but even when he went to sixth form, he still had a grip over me. Texting me at every opportunity, checking what I was doing.

And I listened to him. I forgave him every damn time. I thought the moments we had together were worth the arguments, thinking the nights wrapped in each other's arms, watching movies in bed were enough to make up for all the moments we clashed. I sometimes worry about what might have happened if he hadn't said what he said to Aym. Would I still be with him? Would I have kept forgiving him? Would I have stayed stuck, not knowing there are better people out there?

Should I be so quick to forgive Elliot for what he's done?

I turn on the TV before we finish eating. It's on one of those channels that just plays quiz shows all day, but I don't pay attention; I just want some background noise.

"Mississippi!" Elliot shouts with a mouthful of pizza.

I almost choke on my own from the shock.

"Sorry," he says, swallowing. "I just knew the answer."

I laugh and watch as Elliot stares at the TV, giving every ounce of his attention to the presenter as he reads off the questions.

"Medusa... Flowers for Algernon... Hamilton!" He answers each question before the contestant even opens their mouth.

"Wow," I say. Only half sarcastically.

He blushes when he looks back at me.

"You're good at this."

He shrugs. "Mum used to test me and my brother on general knowledge growing up. Thought we could be child geniuses."

"She might've been right."

He chuckles. "Nah. My brother's the clever one, not me."

I raise my eyebrows and nod towards the TV screen.

He shakes his head. "Knowing a few fun facts doesn't make me clever."

"Sure." I shove him gently. "Is your brother at uni, then?"

"Yeah. Oxford."

I grit my teeth. "Impressive. Think you're gonna follow him?"

He shrugs. "That's what my parents want."

"And is that what you want?"

He doesn't answer, but his cheeks flush red again. Cheeks that I feel even more of an urge to run a hand across. It's always risky, feeling things like this about a boy. You never know if they're going to turn out to be straight. Maybe now's my chance to find out.

"You're cute when you blush," I say.

He looks at me as if I just confessed to a murder.

"Has no one ever said that to you before?"

His eyes shift downwards and he picks at his nails.

"I'll take that as a no." I stifle a laugh. "But you are. Super cute. Just so you know."

"I, er..." He continues to avoid looking at me, turning instead to the finished pizza boxes. I can hear the cogs turning in his brain. For a moment, he seems to consider answering me properly, but then he changes his mind with a subtle shake of his head. "I'd better go."

My heart sinks a little as he rises from the sofa.

"Are you sure?" I ask. "I don't mind you staying longer if you–"

"No, no. It's fine. I just have to... I need to..." He shakes his head again and heads to the door, but when he gets there, he stops.

This is on me. Flirting with a straight guy is such a rookie error. I open my mouth to apologise, but he remains completely still. I wish those spinning cogs could talk.

I stand behind him. Watching. Waiting. The TV is still blaring in the background, chimes and cheers sounding when the contestant gets their answer right.

Elliot's shoulders rise and fall–a huge breath before he turns around.

"Okay," he says. "I've never done this before, but..." It takes him a while, but his eyes settle on mine. "Seb, do you, er, do you...if you want to...I mean...if you think it'd be good...do you...want to, er..."

I step forward and put a hand on his shoulder, which somehow makes him both tense and relax. Maybe I wasn't wrong after all.

"Take a breath," I say.

He does. And then says, "Do you want to go on a date with me?"

I don't think I've smiled this wide in a long time. "Elliot Dove, I would love to go on a date with you."

MEANWHILE

Agent Sigma

I step into the GlimpseTech building with a perfectly rehearsed walk. Confident, but not overly; I need to look as though I belong. Getting the job was easy, thanks to the work of The Instructor. Now the rest is down to me. I'm wearing a plain, navy boiler suit: the perfect camouflage. As a cleaner, I'll have access to areas that others don't, and will be able to move unquestioned. For all intents and purposes, I am invisible. A silent ghost.

The workers at the front desk greet me with a smile, which I return. To the right stands Charlie Beckett, red in the face, dark hair all but withered away, wearing the same boiler suit as me. This is who I am to shadow all day. He'll show me the ropes, give me a tour of the building, and, though he is blissfully unaware, reveal the secrets that will jeopardise GlimpseTech's future.

"Nice to see you again, Jack," Charlie says, holding his hand out to me.

"And you," I shake his hand and suppress a smirk at the sound of that name. It's one of many lies on my job application. A necessary crime to keep me safe in the aftermath of what's to come.

Of course, I wouldn't have minded if The Instructor had used my real identity when finding me this job. My safety hasn't mattered to me for a long time. I'll go to hell and back for this cause, and if the plan succeeds, I don't see a place for myself in the new world, not when everything I ever cared about is already lost.

It's hard not to feel sick walking the corridors of GlimpseTech. This building didn't exist when I was a child, but it's identical to the one I visited all those years ago in Manchester. It has the same broken-shards-of-glass-like structure, the same unsettling gleam to every surface, even the same layout of Glimpse rooms. When Charlie opens the door to one of those, I'm thrown right back to the last time I saw a Glimpse machine up close.

I hadn't gone to have my own Glimpse, I was only fifteen, but my mum had taken me along as she had hers. I still remember the calming voice of the doctor and how it was drowned out by the whirring of the machine. That incessant whirring still haunts me in my dreams almost every night, always a precursor for something far worse to come: my mum's agonising scream as she tore the Glimpse device from her head.

Whatever horrific sight they made her endure changed her. It sapped any joy she had ever felt and left her forever on edge. Mum never told me what she saw in her Glimpse, but it was enough to scare me away from ever having my own.

Despite her silence, I came to learn what she'd seen four years later. I'd come home from university, for a mid-semester break, ready to embrace my family and tell them all about my course and the new friends I'd made. But fate had other plans.

I knew something was wrong as soon as I reached the front door. It was unlocked and swinging on its hinges in the cool night breeze. Inside, there was an eerie quiet and a smell that I've never forgotten. There, in the living room, on a night that was supposed to be full of joy and laughter, were the bodies of my parents, throats slit, blood coating the carpet around them.

"Ever been hooked up to one of these?" Charlie asks, snapping me back to the present.

The Glimpse machine glistens, taunting me. It doesn't need to be switched on for me to hear the whirring in my head.

"Never," I say truthfully.

"Bit of a sceptic, eh?"

I grit my teeth. "Something like that."

Charlie studies me, but I don't let my face betray anything.

"You should try it," he says. "My Glimpse wasn't much to look at, but my son met his wife because of his."

"How lovely." I'm not sure how believable my tone is. I couldn't care less about his son's love story, and I certainly don't want to hear the details. Whether a Glimpse shows a person something good or something bad, it's still robbing them of their free will. When my work is done, there won't be any happy couples thanking GlimpseTech for bringing them together.

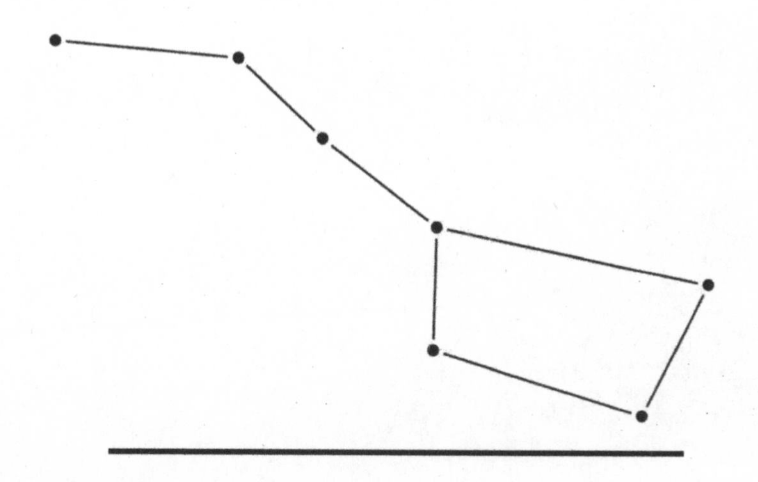

PART THREE

FALLING

GlimpseNet Post #1021H5

Subject: Anonymous

Date Glimpsed: 7th July

Verification Status: Verified

I was on my way to play golf at my local club. As I retrieved my golf clubs from the boot of my car, I received a text from a friend who I haven't seen in a very long time. He asked if I'd be free to speak in person, and I knew quite clearly what it was he wanted to speak about (something I won't be sharing here). I hesitated with my reply, not sure if I was ready to confront him after so long, but then I saw two boys enter the pine forest that surrounds the golf course. They looked the same age my friend and I were when we last saw each other. As they fell out of view behind the trees, I wondered if maybe they were doing exactly what I used to do with my friend. Things we didn't want the world to see for fear of judgement.

I looked back at my phone and pressed the call button.

.

TWENTY-THREE

Elliot

So, about this date you asked me on...

I was wondering when you'd bring that up.

Is that a polite way of saying you want to cancel?

No! Definitely not! I've just not thought of what we can do yet. But I will! I promise.

Dinner, I message an hour later. **Wednesday, 7 PM, Gusto in town. I'll pay.**

Are you sure? I don't want you to pay for me.

It's fine! Really. I want to. I'm the one who asked you out, so I should pay.

Typing...

Typing...

Okay.

I've had almost an entire week to plan for this, but here I am, less than an hour before I need to set off, convinced every shirt I own is the most disgusting thing on the planet. I can't possibly go on this date wearing any of them.

"Show me the blue one again," Callum says, his face filling my phone screen.

"Which blue one?" I set the phone down, propping it against a wall so that Callum can still see me.

"The plain one."

"This?" I hold up the shirt to the camera. It's pale blue, with short sleeves, buttons and a collar.

"Yeah. Maybe with the tan pants?"

"The *tan* pants?" Nikita says, voice a little less clear. She's with Callum, but off screen. "No way. Go with the maroon ones."

"Are you having a laugh?" says Callum "The maroon ones are awful."

I drop the shirt, so my anxiety-riddled face is clearly in shot. "You're not doing anything to calm me down here, guys," I say, wishing there was a way to turn off my sweat glands.

"Hey!" says Callum, "If it weren't for me, you wouldn't even have a place to go for your date." It's true. I could (and probably should) have asked Seb what he wanted to do since he's had an entire relationship before, but I didn't want to embarrass myself. So, I asked Callum for date ideas instead.

"Right," Nikita says, "give me the phone."

There's the sound of a struggle as Callum falls out of shot and the image gets all shaky, but then Nikita's face appears.

"As someone who actually finds guys attractive..." She says the last word with menace and looks off screen. I know full well she's shooting daggers at Callum. "I think I'm a little more qualified than my boyfriend to tell you what looks good."

"Whatever," calls Callum's distant voice.

"Now, try on the blue shirt and maroon pants and we'll see what we're working with."

I do as she says, going off camera to change clothes (and reapply deodorant–though I'm not telling them that bit).

I haven't seen Seb since the night at his house and I've been absolutely dreading the date ever since. It's not that I don't want to go–the way my heart fluttered when he called me cute is something I'm desperate to feel again–but I'm more nervous than I have been for anything in my life. And yes, I know it's natural to feel like this; Callum's given me approximately one hundred pep talks where he recounted just how scared he was for his first date with Nikita. I just didn't know it would be this bad.

I move back in shot once I've changed.

"Yep," Nikita says, "that's the one."

"Are you sure?"

"Positive."

"I don't need a blazer or a tie or–"

"El!" Callum nudges his way back onto the screen. "It's a date, not a job interview. Nikita's right, you look great. Just calm down and be yourself and it'll be fine."

"But what if–"

"It'll be fine!"

At my front door, I take a deep breath. I'm about to head out to my first ever date. The butterflies in my stomach are taking up so much room I wonder if I'll be able to eat anything at Gusto. I fidget with my shirt, trying to avoid making creases and worrying that it doesn't quite fit right. I've never felt this self-conscious about how I look before. Is this going to happen every time I meet Seb now? Will I lose hours trying to get my hair to sit right? Agonise all day about what shirt to wear?

Or maybe that's just how it starts. Maybe the closer you get to someone, the less you care about all of that. I guess the goal is for someone to like you for you, not for what you wear or how you look. But what do I know?

"Who's the lucky girl?" Dad says from behind me. He's standing in the living room doorway, smirking. I can see Mum over his shoulder with the exact same expression.

I haven't told them the truth about tonight. They don't even know Seb exists. As far as they're concerned, I'm just hanging with Callum. Or, at least, that's what I told them I'd be doing. It seems they didn't believe me.

"No point trying to lie, son," Dad says. "We heard you on the phone to Callum."

My heart plummets.

He looks me up and down. "No one puts that much effort into how they look unless it's for a date."

They can't know. I'm not ready for them to know.

"So," Mum says, squeezing past Dad and looking far too excited. "Who is she? Do we know her?"

"I..."

"Is it that Jessica girl you always used to talk about?"

Dad laughs. "That was years ago. It must be someone else. Right, El?"

"It's..."

"Is it one of Nikita's friends?" Mum says. "They're all very pretty."

"She's called Sarah." I say it so fast it almost sounds like just one word. I don't even know where it came from. I don't know a Sarah. I've *never* known a Sarah. But I can't tell them the truth. Not yet.

Mum and Dad look just like they did the day Simon brought Alyssa home. Like they're picturing me at the alter on my wedding day and already picking out outfits for their grandchildren.

"What's she like?" Mum asks.

"Whereabouts does she live?" Dad asks.

"Is she in your year?"

"Does she do well at school?"

"What are her parents' jobs?"

"How long have you been dating?"

"Are you being safe?"

"STOP!" I shout. I'm standing up against the front door, every one of their questions an arrow pinning me against the wood. "It's our first date, okay? You don't need to worry."

They deflate a little as they exhale their excitement.

"Can I go now?" I ask, nodding at the door. "I'll be back before ten."

Mum and Dad exchange a glance–a silent conversation passing between them, one I'm sure will be repeated aloud once I'm gone.

"Okay," Mum says. "Be careful."

"Always am."

It takes everything in me not to slam the door when I leave.

Town is heaving when I get off the bus. A mass of evening-shoppers is clogging the footpaths, and I have to force my way through to get anywhere near the restaurant. There's a group of people in hi-vis jackets, too, working to clean up a cordoned off area where a building's windows have been smashed and its walls covered in Anti-Fate graffiti.

There have been multiple protests over the past week. They're becoming more and more frequent, more violent too. I dread to think what will happen if we reach the levels I've seen on the news. The big cities have been dealing with countless protests, some of which have turned into all-out riots. And all because of the Glimpses.

Some people blame Maria McBride, saying she stirred up the protestors with her calls for GlimpseTech to be exposed, and I'm inclined to agree. Especially after her last speech. We've had months of her telling us that she's going to launch an investigation into GlimpseTech, only for her to come on the news last night and say the investigations are complete and nothing suspicious has been uncovered.

"All is well," she said, "and I would like to ask the British public to stop their protests. I can assure you, GlimpseTech have done nothing wrong." All that's done is make people angrier and swept them into the arms of the Anti-Fates, joining their rage against GlimpseTech.

Maybe Seb would join them if he didn't have so much to deal with already. He certainly seems to hate GlimpseTech enough. I wonder how he'd feel if he knew the real reason I ever started talking to him. Best not to dwell on it now, I suppose.

I reach Gusto. It's a small building, nestled between two large office blocks, with an Italian flag draped over the doorway. Mum and Dad always come here on their wedding anniversary. Last time I visited was the day Simon got accepted into uni, a repeat of the exact same celebratory meal we had the day after he had his Glimpse.

I step inside, welcomed by the ring of a bell and a wave of scents that make my mouth water. It's always cosy in here, with the closely packed wooden tables, the walls decorated with a thousand framed family photos, and a low ceiling with dim lighting. It's like being welcomed home.

A waiter greets me. He's a short man with dark hair and a red towel draped over his shoulder.

"Table for Elliot Dove," I say.

"Right this way, sir."

He leads me to a small, round table in the corner with two chairs and pulls one out for me, smiling throughout.

"Thanks," I say, taking my seat.

And now, I wait.

TWENTY-FOUR

Seb

I check the time on my phone again, as if that's going to make me any less late.

"She'll be here soon, don't worry," the nurse says.

I'm in the lobby of the hospital, waiting for Mum. I got the call barely a couple of hours ago that she's being discharged, so now here I am, rocking on the balls of my feet and silently cursing myself for not getting changed first. No way will I have time now. I bet Elliot's already at the restaurant–he strikes me as the kind of person to always be early. I wonder what that's like.

"Here she is," the nurse says.

I was so busy staring at my phone I hadn't noticed the doors open, but Mum's here now: smiling at me with her arms wide as she approaches. I embrace her with a hug and relief floods through me. It feels good to be near her again. To have my mum back.

The nurse shares a few words with her about medication, and I listen intently. I need to know this information as much as she does, because it's me who'll need to remind her.

"All three tablets, once a day," the nurse repeats.

I say it over and over again in my head, etching the words into my skull. All three tablets. Once a day.

With a final smile, the nurse escorts us out. Leaving the hospital is like getting out of a pool–cold and shocking, but suddenly I'm free to move unobstructed. We cross the street together, me and Mum, side by side, and soon enough we're back home. I'm not sure what to say to her, whether or not I should tell her everything that happened with Dan. As long as she was telling the truth the other day, he should be out of our lives for good now, so maybe it's best to keep quiet. She doesn't need more trauma.

Well, that would work if it weren't for the broken window which she notices instantly.

"It was Dan," I say, seeing her face as she takes in the damage. "But it's fine. It's all sorted now. We just need new glass."

She nods and swallows down the words she was about to say.

I open the door and lead her into the living room. It's a lot tidier than when she was last here, and I think that has an impact on her. She smiles as she looks around and thanks me before sitting down.

I check my phone again and see a text from Elliot: **I'm here, just so you know. Got our table ready.**

"What's wrong?" Mum asks.

"Nothing..."

She raises an eyebrow.

"It's just... I'm meant to be going out to eat...with a friend."

"With Aym?"

I hesitate, unsure whether I should tell her about Elliot. It's nice to have something exciting just for myself. "Yeah," I say.

"You should go!"

I shake my head. "I really don't mind cancelling. You just got back, and I–"

"Don't be stupid." She walks over to me and starts ushering me back to the door. "You should go. I'll be fine."

"Are you sure?"

"Yes, of course! Go! Have fun!"

She has me outside before I can protest.

"I'll see you later," she says with one of those rare genuine smiles. I hate that my instinct is to assume this happiness is fake, and it feels so wrong to walk out on her right when she's got home. But she's been in the hospital for so long now, she must have made progress. Right? If she were still a risk to herself, she wouldn't have been discharged. Right?

I've been excited for this date ever since Elliot asked me. If Mum is encouraging me to go, I can't miss my chance. "See you later, Mum."

When I finally reach Gusto, I'm sweating from running so fast. I take a moment to breathe and sort out my messy hair in the reflection of the window, regretting yet again that I didn't change out of my plain and baggy T-shirt. I already know that Elliot will look amazing. He'll have dressed smartly and combed his hair. When he sees me, he'll say I look fine but inside he'll be judging me. There'll be a click of confirmation in his head as he realises I can't possibly have nice clothes because I'm too poor to buy food. Even though I've got a nice shirt tucked away in my wardrobe at home. Even though I wanted to put in effort for him.

Or maybe I'm just overthinking.

I step inside, taking in the warmth and the smells and wondering if this is something Elliot is used to. I've never been here before. It's been years since I went out for a meal with Mum or Dad, and Carl wasn't really into restaurant dates.

A friendly looking man steps up to me before I can get very far.

"How can I help you?" he says, beaming.

"Er, Elliot Dove's table...please?"

"Right this way."

I'm led to the back corner of the room, and there he is. Elliot. Bright faced and smartly dressed and, despite how I must look to him, incredibly happy to see me.

"Hey," he says.

"Hey." I take my seat.

"Can I get you boys any drinks?" the waiter asks. He looks at the glass in front of Elliot–a clear reminder of how ridiculously late I am–and rephrases himself, looking at me, "Or just you, young man?"

"Just a water, please," I say.

He nods and speeds away, leaving me with my date. My cute-but-should-be-disappointed-in-me date.

"You look nice," Elliot says. A lie, but one I expected.

"You too. I love that shirt."

He blushes and looks around the room as if to check if we're being watched.

"Sorry again about being late," I say.

"It's fine! You needed to help your mum, I'm hardly gonna hold that against you." He'd said as much in his reply to the text I sent while running for the bus. "How is she, by the way?"

"She's good...at least, she seems good. It's always hard to tell, to be honest."

The waiter returns and puts my glass of water down in front of me. "I assume you need a little more time to choose your food?"

"Yes," Elliot says, "just a few minutes, please."

The waiter leaves again and I open the menu. It's leather bound, with a red ribbon hanging out of it–the fanciest menu I've ever seen. And holy shit, these prices! Some of the starters alone cost more than a tenner. I try to hide my shock from Elliot. If he weren't paying, I'd probably be dead from a heart attack.

"They do the *best* Bolognese," Elliot says.

"Will you judge me if I go for a pizza?"

Elliot chuckles. "No. The pizza's great as well."

"You must come here a lot."

"Just a few times. Family celebrations, that sort of thing."

"Are you close with your family?"

"Sort of."

Without having met them, I've already formed an image in my head of what Elliot's family must be like. A classic, happy family: a mum, a dad, Elliot and his brother. A life without worries. Without drama.

"How did they react when you told them you were...?" I let the question trail off, realising I don't actually know Elliot's sexuality. Whether he's gay or bi or pan or whatever else. "That you're into guys," I say instead.

Elliot fiddles with his menu, avoiding my eyes, and I realise what he's not saying.

"You're not out, are you?"

"Are you ready to order?" the waiter's voice explodes beside us without warning.

Elliot puts on a fake smile as he turns to him. "I'll have the Bolognese, please."

The waiter looks to me, committing the order to memory instead of writing it down.

"The Americana pizza, please."

"Will that be all?"

I nod.

"Yes, thank you," Elliot says. God, this boy is so polite. I wonder if he talks to his parents the same way.

The waiter bounces away and I can feel a blanket of tension settle over me and Elliot.

"No," Elliot says when I face him again. His cheeks are redder than I've ever seen them, and he looks weighed down by shame. "I'm not out. Except to a couple of friends. Sorry, I probably should have said."

"Don't be stupid. Coming out is tough and it's personal–it's none of my business how or when or if you do it."

He perks up a little at that.

"It's shit that we have to do it anyway. You don't see straight people tearing themselves up over how to tell people what gender they're into."

The redness fades as his smile returns. "Exactly," he says. "It's hard enough figuring out *what* I am, to be honest. There're so many labels, and I'm not always sure which feelings are real, and which just come from what I think I'm meant to feel."

"Been there."

I watch as he looks around the room again, checking to see if anyone's listening. There aren't many others in here, just a middle-aged couple, a family with two kids and a grandma, and a group of friends or work-colleagues.

They're all engaged in their own conversations, creating a low hum beneath the gentle, acoustic background music.

"When did you know?" he asks. "And how?"

It's not something I've been asked much before. My coming out story's not exactly one for the movies. Most aren't. The last time I recounted it was to Aym, the night she told me she's trans.

"I guess I knew when I was ten? At least, that's when I started figuring out the label. Before then, I'd always just been a bit different: friends with more girls than boys, not into playing with boys' toys. Not that that always means a kid is gay, but it definitely gets people thinking.

"When other kids talked about their crushes, I thought it was really weird. I didn't get it because I'd never been into any girls that way. And then in year six I really fancied this kid called Ben. I didn't tell anyone, because none of the other boys ever talked about liking boys, but I ended up finding out what the word 'gay' meant and realised that's what I was."

"Did you tell your parents?"

"Not straight away. Other stuff kind of got in the way." Like Dad leaving and Mum's suicide attempt. "But years later, yes. And to be fair to them, they took it well. I mean, I could tell Dad wasn't the happiest about it, but he'd left and his opinion didn't matter that much to me. Still doesn't. Mum was fine with it though. She told me it didn't change a thing about me and that all she wanted was for me to be happy."

Elliot smiles. "That's great. I'm not sure my mum would be the same. She's a bit more...traditional." He takes a drink.

"Whatever happens happens. At the end of the day, you can't change who you are. Your parents will just have to accept that. And if they can't deal with that, then fuck them."

Elliot snorts a laugh, almost choking on his drink, and spilling some down his shirt. A patch turns dark blue as it soaks in. "Shit," he whispers under his breath, grabbing his napkin and trying to wipe away the stain.

"Here," I pass him mine and fail to suppress a laugh. "Don't be hilarious while people are drinking: noted."

He keeps wiping, but it barely makes a difference.

"Shame we're in such a public place or you could take it off."

"Bet you'd love that," he retorts. There's a beat before his eyes dart up to mine and his face returns to its classic shade of red, like he just realised what he said and is shocked by his own attempt at flirting. This really is new for him.

"I won't pretend I wouldn't." I raise an eyebrow and sip my water, enjoying the awkward way Elliot doesn't know where to look. When I realise he might never work out what to say, I decide to change the topic. "So, remind me what subjects you did in school?"

"Holy shit," I say after my first bite of pizza. "Okay, I understand why you love this place so much. And why it's so expensive."

Elliot's face lights up like I'm complimenting him directly. "I'm glad you like it."

There's a spot of sauce just under his lip and, stupid as it sounds, I want nothing more than to reach out and wipe it away for him. To run my hand across his smooth face. But I don't. Instead, he catches it with his tongue.

"Do you think you'll go into music for a career?" he asks. "Ever since you played in the park that day, I've been imagining you up on stage performing for thousands of fans."

Now it's me who's blushing. "I don't know. It's a nice idea, but it's not exactly a stable plan, is it? Not that I know what 'stable plan' I'd go for. And anyway, I'm not a songwriter."

"Have you ever tried?"

"What?"

"Writing a song?"

"No."

"Then how do you know?"

I shrug. He may have half a point. Or less. Definitely not more. I've never really had enough belief in my own abilities to try writing a song. I play covers on my own in my house. That's all. Except for the busking.

"What about you?" I ask. "What do you want to do?"

He shrugs too. "My parents want me to go to uni, just like my brother, but I'm not so sure. I have no idea what I want to do, to be honest. My future's a blank slate." His eyes flash away at the last sentence, as though there's something behind those words that he doesn't want me to know. Or that he won't admit.

It's a look that intrigues me. It confirms what I think every time I look into his eyes–there's so much more depth in there than he lets on. There's a lot to Elliot that I don't know, a lot to learn and talk about, all of which I never really got with Carl. He was nice in the beginning, sure, but thinking back it all feels very superficial. Dates with Carl were more physical than romantic. We'd talk for a bit and then his lips would be on mine. It wasn't long after we first got together that we ended up having sex, and part of me (quite a large part, actually) wishes I'd waited longer. I wasn't ready. I'm not sure he was either. But we both thought it was the right thing to do.

It was after sex I told him I loved him. A spur of the moment stream of words that I didn't really understand. If there's one thing I regret about my time with Carl, it's that moment. The words were empty, but they kept me tied to him through every argument. It's not a mistake I'll ever make again.

But Elliot isn't like Carl. He's not someone who's just going to kiss me the first chance he gets–if he was, he'd already have done that. No, there's more to him. So much more.

TWENTY-FIVE

Elliot

It's raining when we leave the restaurant. Just a light drizzle, but enough for us to look at each other with horror.

"No chance you've got an umbrella?" Seb asks.

"Nope. And not a coat either."

"I should've checked the weather."

"I did. It didn't say rain." I sigh. "Guess we're running for the bus."

Seb turns to me with a grin that brings back those good old butterflies. "Is that a challenge?"

"It can be..."

"Hmm. Interesting." He looks out at the street, where the orange streetlamps form hazy rings in the drizzle, silent for a moment beneath the Italian-flag-canopy. And then he runs.

"Hey!" I shout, setting off after him. "Wait!"

"That's not how races work!" he shouts back, weaving expertly between the confused looking people on the pavement.

"Sorry," I mutter as I pass them, not that they'll believe the apology when I'm smiling this hard.

The drizzle is cold against my skin, and I can feel it soaking my hair–a recipe for a frizzy mess, but at least it's stopping me from sweating. I'm not too far behind Seb now. If I can just speed up a little more...

He turns a corner I don't expect, throwing me off course and making me stumble as I try to veer down the cobbled street he's racing along. The cobbles are slippery underfoot and I can't speed up anymore, but it looks like Seb can't either. He comes to a stop halfway down the road and leans back against the wall of a closed-down shop.

"This isn't the right way," I say, slowing to a stop beside him.

"I know," he says. "But I figured if you're not out then you'd probably want somewhere out of everyone's view to kiss me."

The world stops turning.

"If that's okay with you," he adds.

"I..." My heart, already racing from the exercise, goes into overdrive. I look around. He's right–this street is as private as things get in the town centre. It's just a bunch of closed shops. There's not even a streetlight to give us away. "Yes. Yes, that's okay."

"Are you sure?"

I nod. I can barely breathe, and my body is covered in goosebumps, and the drizzle has soaked my hair so much that there's water running down my face, but I want this. I *really* want this.

Seb steps forward, away from the wall, places one hand in the small of my back and the other gently on the back of my head. I don't know what I'm supposed to do, where I'm supposed to put my hands, whether I'm supposed to close my eyes. And then he brings his lips down to mine. And mine up to his.

And suddenly I don't need a Glimpse to see the future. Because how could I ever let go of this? This boy? This feeling? I could stay here all night with him pressed against me, our lips and tongues moving together. The taste. The thrill. The passion. All of it is perfect.

But it can't last forever. Seb moves back slowly, separating our mouths but keeping his hands on me.

"You're good at that," he says.

"I am?"

He nods. "Was that your first time?"

"Yeah."

"Impressive."

And then he moves in for another, which I welcome wholeheartedly. This time, I wrap my arms around him and pull him tighter against me, letting him know how much I love this feeling.

But again, it has to end.

"Yep," Seb says, letting go of me but grinning with joy, "very impressive."

We stay still for a moment, gazing into each other's eyes while the drizzle slowly soaks us. I don't want to go home. I want to stay with him as long as I can. Talking and laughing and kissing and kissing and kissing.

"We should probably head for the bus," Seb says, his words somehow making the drizzle feel colder.

"We probably should."

We head right to the back of the bus and sit beside each other, Seb's leg pressed against mine, sending shivers across my whole body. I hate that I do it, but I keep looking around to check if anyone's watching us. But our legs are out of everyone's eyeline. This moment is for us. A secret closeness that the world doesn't know about.

"Hey," Seb says. He places a hand on my knee and I flinch, my eyes darting to the other passengers and even out the window at the people passing by on foot. "No one's looking. Don't worry."

I wonder if Seb was like this when he first realised he was gay. When he dated Carl, did he spend every moment checking to see if he was about to be hate-crimed? He's not as anxious as I am, so it must get easier with time. But does it ever go away completely? It's not like other people's homophobia disappears just because you're comfortable in yourself.

"Sorry," I say.

He smiles. "Don't be." He gently rubs my leg, then removes his hand.

The bus starts moving, taking us up the main road out of town. The drizzle cascades down the windows and the more it collects, the blurrier the view becomes. Pedestrians and streetlights become formless blobs. I look instead to Seb, smiling up at his pale, chiselled face. And I stay like that, right until we reach his stop.

"I'll see you soon," he says as he rises from his seat. "Right?"

"Definitely." The word is laced with double meaning because I know the date of my Glimpse is less than two weeks away.

I watch him leave the bus and wave to him through the window as it sets off again.

And then, the exact moment Seb goes out of sight, I pull out my phone and call Callum. It barely rings before he answers.

"Tell me everything!" he says. I can hear his eager smile, and I know full well Nikita is listening too.

"It was amazing. He was amazing."

I hear Nikita cheering in the background.

"And? What did you talk about? How did it end? Is there going to be a second date?"

I glance around the bus again. Most of the passengers have left now–there's only an old woman and a teenager left, both of them too busy scowling at each other for either to be concerned with me.

"We talked about all sorts, we got the bus home together, and I'm pretty sure there'll be a second date. But...one second." The bus comes to a stop and I hurry off, thanking the driver before stepping back into the cold drizzle.

"You're killing us here, El," Callum says.

"Okay, okay, just had to get off the bus. Anyway, the headline–and you're going to want to sit down for this–is: WE KISSED!"

"NO WAY!"

"Yes way!"

I laugh at Nikita's background squealing.

"What kind of kiss?" Callum asks. "A proper kiss? A peck on the lips? Tongue? What was it?"

"Definitely proper. Yes, there was tongue. A lot of tongue, actually."

"Holy shit, El. I mean, I shouldn't be surprised–you two are having sex in what? Two weeks? But damn. This is big. Congrats, man."

"Thanks." I turn the corner onto my street. "Listen, I'm almost home now so I'd better go, but I'll talk to you tomorrow. Okay?"

"Sure. See you!"

"Bye."

I pocket my phone as I walk down the driveway, bouncing as I go. I'm alive with energy. Electricity sparks out of my skin with every drop of rain that hits me. I turn my key in the door and heave it open. Nothing can bring me down right now. Nothing.

"Hey bro, heard you've finally got yourself a girlfriend!"

It's Simon. All tall and well-built and wearing the cheesiest smirk in the world, stood just a few steps into the house. Like he's been waiting for me. I didn't even know he was coming home.

My face is on fire. "How did you-?"

"Mum and Dad told me," he says.

I take a moment to remind myself the lie I told my parents. What name did I use for the imaginary girl? Sophie? No, Sarah.

"She's not my girlfriend," I say. "We just...went on a date."

"And? How was it?"

I hesitate.

"Oh, leave him alone," Mum's voice calls from the living room. I hear her shuffle around, then she pokes her head out from the door behind Simon. "He doesn't have to tell you anything if he doesn't want to." She smiles at me, but her playful tone makes me think she's only saying it to coax more out of me.

"Exactly," I say.

Mum's face falters. Yep, she was definitely expecting me to tell her everything.

"I'm tired," I say, taking off my shoes. "I'll see you in the morning."

With that, I dump my shoes on the shoe rack, barge past my brother, and head upstairs. The joy I felt while I was with Seb falls out of me with every step. For the short time I was with him, and especially when we kissed, I felt free.

Truly free. But here? In this house? With me lying to my family? This is the opposite of freedom.

I spend an hour just lying in bed, facing the ceiling in the dark. Moonlight shines through the edge of my curtains so the ceiling has a soft silver glow to it. It's late enough that I should probably try to sleep, but I can't. In the moonlit haze, I can see my parents' disappointed expressions as I tell them I'm dating a boy. I can see Simon's shock. I picture them all exchanging glances and silent words of judgement. It's a vision I never want to come true. I don't want to be the topic of conversation at every family gathering. I don't want to solidify my role as the disappointing son–the one who never matches his brother's glory.

I know how I feel. And I know I'm destined to get even closer to Seb. I know the exact moment, the precise date and time, when that will happen. But I don't know if I'll ever be out to the world. I don't know if I'll ever tell my family the truth. They're not the only ones I'm lying to, either. Seb just gave me an incredible evening, but I was hiding the truth about us from him the whole time. I know I should tell him about my Glimpse, but what would that do to him? What would he think of me?

There's a buzz from my phone and the screen lights up, overwhelming the moonlight. I roll over, look at the screen, and for a moment my worries wash away.

Had a great time today, reads the text from Seb.

I pause, breathe, and try to think of a response that won't be too subdued or too excited. **Same. Definitely need to meet up again soon!**

Absolutely. My turn to pick the date?

Sure!

Typing...

Do I tell him how I'm feeling?

Typing...

Do I tell him how I lied to my family?

Typing...

Do I tell him that I'm scared I'll never fully leave the closet?

Typing...

Do I tell him about the Glimpse?

Sleep well x

A kiss. He wrote a kiss. A singular kiss. Two crossed lines that carry a whole bucket load of baggage.

You too, I type, and then to finish it off, **x**

Suddenly it's not my worries that are keeping me awake, but the memory of our kiss in the rain.

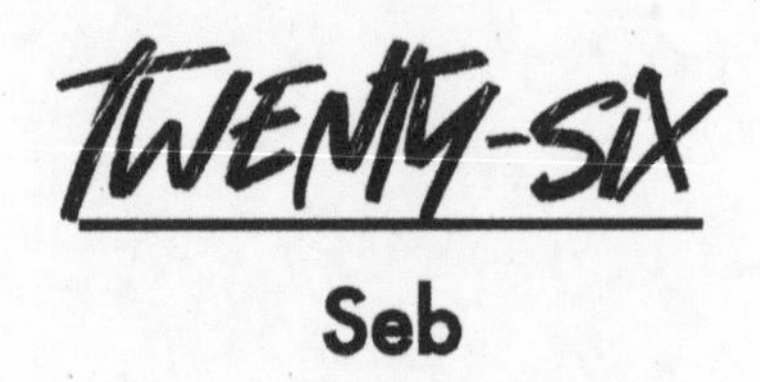

TWENTY-SIX

Seb

Aym has never looked as wild as this. In fact, I'm a little worried she might kill me.

"WHY DIDN'T YOU TELL ME AS SOON AS IT HAPPENED?!" her voice echoes around us, bouncing off the crags and into the village below, the mix of anger and excitement attacking every surface.

"I wanted to tell you in person," I say between laughs. "Now if you sit down for one second, I might tell you the details."

Aym got back from her retreat the morning after my date with Elliot, but she's been busy with her family for a couple of days, so I've been holding in the big news.

She sighs, rolls her eyes, then plants herself down beside me in our usual spot, legs dangling off the crag.

"Okay," she says. "Spill."

I launch into the story of mine and Elliot's date. Aym tries to maintain her fake-angry face, but it doesn't last long. Especially not when I mention the kiss.

"I know it's crazy to say after just one date," I say, "but I *really* like him. He's so different to Carl in all the right ways. He listens. And, God, he's a good kisser."

There's no hiding Aym's smile. "He sounds great. And you deserve someone great, especially after everything that's happened recently."

And there it is–that dark cloud that's always present, but sometimes forces its way into the limelight. Mum's depression. Her attempt to end it. All the stuff with Dan. While I didn't tell Aym about Elliot until now, I kept her updated about everything else.

Well...I left out some details. Like the brick through the window.

And the watch.

And the guitar.

"Yeah." I clear my throat to get rid of the sudden lump. "Anyway, second date is today."

"Today?!"

"This afternoon."

"What's the plan?"

"We're going on a walk."

It sounds dull, I know, but it was my turn to choose the date and pretty much everything I could think of would require money that I don't have. Elliot would have offered to pay, I'm sure, but I don't want to use him like that. He didn't even bat an eye when he paid for the meal the other day. I won't lie, it made me a little uneasy to see how casual he was when the bill came. He just handed over the money like it was nothing. Like he had no idea what I'd do to have even a sliver of that much spare cash.

So, the only thing I could think to suggest for our second date was a walk. I was worried he'd say it was a stupid idea, but instead he said "Sounds lovely," and that was that.

"Whereabouts?" asks Aym.

"I figured I'd take him to the woods by the golf course."

Aym raises an eyebrow, and I realise immediately what she's thinking. When they were kids, she and Carl used to run around the golf course and cause chaos, pissing off all the golf club members. It got to a point where the police were called to tell them off–trust the rich, snobby club members to treat a pair of kids like criminals–and they were basically banned from going there ever again. So, instead, they started playing in the woods that surrounded the course.

I know the story well, because Carl told me it when he took me to the woods one of the first times we were alone together. He led me in, along the dirt tracks, between the twisting trunks of old trees, to a clearing where he leaned me back against a tree and kissed me for the first time.

"I'm not trying to pretend he's Carl," I say before Aym has the chance. "It's just a nice place."

"Sure," she says without a hint of belief.

I shove her playfully. "I'm really not. Like I said, he's nothing like Carl."

Aym sighs and tosses her braids over a shoulder.

"So, anyway, how was the retreat?"

A grin spreads across her face. "It was incredible. The people were *painfully* arty–you'd have hated it."

She launches into her story, telling me all about the workshops she took part in and how beautiful her surroundings were. I listen, but a thought persists in the back of my mind–maybe Aym is right about my date. Maybe reliving my time with Carl isn't the best idea.

"You, er, know we're not going on a full-on hike, right?"

Elliot is stood at the end of my street, dressed as if he's about to head up a mountain. Fleece jacket, walking boots, backpack, and all.

"Always best to be prepared," he says.

"You sound like a Scout."

He goes quiet.

"Oh my God, you were a Scout, weren't you?"

He scratches his head. "For a few years, yeah."

"That's so cute, do you still have the uniform? With that little necktie thing?"

"It's called a necker, and the thing you put the ends through is a woggle."

I raise an eyebrow.

"Okay, yes I still have the uniform."

"You are definitely wearing that for me some time!"

He's blushing, but he's smiling too, and I can't help the urge to kiss him. I glance around to make sure no-one's looking, then rest a palm on his cheek and bring his face up to mine. It's quick but it sends electricity through me all the same. When I pull away, he's no longer blushing, and he looks at me the same way he did when I played guitar in the park. His wide, hazel eyes radiating warmth.

"Let's go," I say, heading off down the pavement with him beside me.

I'd love to hold his hand, but there's no way we won't see other people out here and I'd hate to make him uncomfortable. We're very close, though, and my arm occasionally brushes against his by accident. He doesn't react.

"So, what's in the bag?"

"Some snacks and a blanket. Thought we might want a mini picnic while we're in the woods."

And there's that confusing mix of guilt and shame again. A picnic is a lovely idea, but I didn't suggest it because I can't afford snacks to bring. Mum got her new benefits cheque yesterday, but that's only going to afford us what we desperately need. No snacks. No picnic food.

"Cool," I say, because what else am I supposed to tell him? A boy who has always had everything handed to him isn't going to understand why I find bag full of snacks so insulting.

We turn a corner to see the golf course. It's a vast, unnaturally green set of flat land and gentle slopes, so picturesque it looks edited, like a photo with a filter over it. The woods surround it on almost all sides, and a large dirt track goes down from the road where Elliot and I are to a big, country house where the club members go to do whatever rich people do. Probably laugh about poor people.

"My grandad was a member here," Elliot says.

Of course, he was.

"He had his seventieth birthday in the clubhouse. It was super boring."

I can't help but wonder if Elliot's grandad was one of the people annoyed by Aym and Carl. Could he even have been the one who called the police on them? I push the thought away. I know Elliot wouldn't do that, and that's all that should matter.

There are people scattered around the golf course, most of them barely more than a speck from this distance. I'm sure they'd all have words to say if they saw me sauntering down the track to the clubhouse, but I turn off with Elliot before we get too close, up a smaller path into the forest.

Pine trees surround us, their rough barks stretching up into the sky. At our feet are scattered pinecones, lying atop fallen needles and twigs. Sunlight decorates the ground, dappled bright spots breaking through the needled branches above. The sound of the road we left behind is dull and distant, and the occasional calls of the golfers are quieter than the birdsong.

"I think I came here once," Elliot says. "On a walk with Mum, Dad, and Simon. Long time ago."

I don't tell him I used to come here with Carl.

The trees are quite sparsely grown, so it's easy to see through the gaps and it's clear there's no one around to see us. I glance at Elliot and brush a hand against his. His fingers loosen, allowing me to slip mine between his. I watch the corners of his mouth curve up as he grips my hand properly.

"So, your brother's back from uni?" I ask, recalling a text he sent yesterday about how annoying Simon was being.

I feel him tense. "Yeah."

I lead him onwards along the path that's barely visible beneath the needles. "Must be weird after he's been away for so long."

"A bit. I mean, he always comes back during the holidays so it's not like I haven't seen him for years, but I get used to him not being around."

"It's nice to see him though, right?"

Elliot shrugs. "I don't know. My parents talk about him enough when he's not here, so when he actually is I basically turn invisible."

I've always been kind of jealous of people with siblings. If I'd had someone else close to my age around all the time when I was younger, it would have made all the shit with Mum and Dad a lot easier to deal with. Especially an older sibling. The weight would have been taken off my shoulders.

I once asked Mum if I'd ever have a brother or sister. I can't have been very old–maybe around seven–but I remember Dad overhearing and answering before Mum had a chance.

"We've tried," he said. "It's not going to happen."

Mum looked as if she might cry when he said that, so much so that I was afraid to ever ask again.

Elliot and I reach a small clearing with a solitary tree stump in the middle. The ground isn't quite as needly here and there are a few patches of undisturbed grass.

"Shall we stop here?" Elliot asks.

I nod, and he swings his bag of his back and pulls out a large, patchwork blanket which he lays gently on the ground.

"My grandma made this," he says, taking a seat. "We used to take it on our family camping trips."

"Scouting runs in the family, then?" I ask with a teasing grin.

"Shut up."

I sit down next to him, close enough that our shoulders are touching, and watch as he pulls crisps, biscuits, and bottles of coke out of his bag.

"I've never been camping," I say. "You'll have to take me some time."

"Er...yeah, maybe I will." His eyes shift awkwardly, as if I said something really weird. He hands me a bottle. "Coke?"

"Sure..." I take it from him, confused by his sudden change in tone.

There's a loud buzz from Elliot's phone and he pulls it out of his pocket. "Sorry," he says, glancing at the screen. His eyes widen. "Woah. Have you seen this?"

He turns his phone around to show me a news article:

BREAKING: PRIME MINISTER MARIA MCBRIDE URGES PEOPLE NOT TO PANIC AFTER STRING OF SUICIDES IN LONDON.

"What the fuck?" I say.

"There were rumours this morning, so I turned on my notifications for the news. A bunch of people jumped off major buildings in London as part of a protest."

"A protest?!"

"Because of the whole 'Last Day' thing. People are saying they don't want GlimpseTech to decide when they're going to die, so they're taking it into their own hands."

I feel sick. Something about that reasoning just doesn't sit right with me at all. When there are people out there like my mum, who attempt suicide because of genuine mental illness, how can people be so stupid as to throw their lives away just to make some bullshit philosophical statement.

It's not the first time something like this has happened because of GlimpseTech. Everyone knows the stories about the people who tried to prove Glimpses could be changed by killing themselves before their Glimpses came true, only for them to survive and end up severely injured instead.

But this is next level. Now people are actually dying.

"I'm sick of hearing about the Last Day," I say. "It's just another one of those stupid phrases we wouldn't have if GlimpseTech didn't exist."

Elliot looks at his phone screen again, concerned. "Does it not scare you a little, though? Like...what if people are right? What if the Last Day is real? What if we've only got these next few weeks left and then that's it? End of the world."

It's a thought that's crossed my mind a few times, I can't pretend it hasn't. No one can. The fact that no one has ever seen past July twenty-eighth in their Glimpses is weird and worrying. But the idea of it being the day the world ends is just one out of a hundred different theories, and none of them have any sort of proof behind them. So why believe the scariest?

"Sometimes," I say. "But then I think–isn't that the exact problem with being so obsessed with Glimpses? If we all live our lives based on what we think is going to happen in the future, we're not really living, are we?"

Elliot puts his phone away, but he doesn't look convinced. In fact, he looks less certain than ever.

"Don't you think it's better to live in the moment?" I ask, placing a hand on top of Elliot's. "Just say 'fuck you' to the future and be here with me."

His eyes meet mine, pupils widening, and I cup the back of his head. I'm close enough to feel his breath falter, and I see the exact flash in his eyes when he decides to let himself go.

He leans forward and kisses me, lips just as soft and gentle as they were the other day. I fall back against the blanket, letting Elliot take control. He swings a leg over so he's on top of me, kissing me, and running his hands gradually down my side. He's exploring my body, well, my upper body at least, while keeping his hands over my shirt and above my waist. I want him to go further. I want his hands to slip beneath the fabric. I want him to pull my clothes from me and see *everything*.

I slip a hand to the hem of his shirt, my fingers brushing against a sliver of exposed skin, but I feel Elliot flinch and move my hand away. It's not time for that yet. And that's his choice to make. Elliot is not Carl. That's never been clearer to me than in this moment, when his lips fall away and he rolls to my side and we look at each other, arms wrapped around each other, hearts beating in time. Just looking.

And even though I made that point about how I don't want to waste my life thinking about the future, I find myself believing I could happily spend eternity adrift in Elliot's eyes.

TWENTY-SEVEN

Elliot

You'd think we were hosting the Queen–the way Mum's been setting the table every day since Simon got home. This evening, she's got out the posh tablecloth with the fancy patterned edges and put Grandma's handmade placemats at every seat (even the two extra ones where no one ever sits). To top it off, she's set out the cutlery with the smallest on the outside and largest on the inside because, apparently, we're having multiple courses tonight.

"Mum," I say, taking my seat next to Simon and nodding at the extra placemats, "who else is coming?"

She's about to answer when the doorbell rings.

"That'll be them," Dad says, springing from his seat.

"Who?" Simon and I say simultaneously.

We don't get an answer, but when we hear two ridiculously posh voices, we don't need one.

"Oh, how delightful to see you," a deep voice with outstanding annunciation says.

It's followed by a higher, equally eloquent voice saying, "It has been far too long, hasn't it, dear?"

Simon gives me an 'oh, for God's sake' glance that reminds me we're not all that different. His face says exactly what I'm feeling. Uncle Andrew and Grandma Edith are here, which means it's time for an evening of endless judgement. Simon is going to receive a million questions about uni, and I'm going to be compared to him at every opportunity.

"Evening, boys," Andrew says as he walks in. He looks similar to Dad–same short ginger hair, same long nose, same chiselled jaw that Simon inherited but I didn't–but somehow dialled up. He's larger in both height and width, and always looks just slightly more put together than Dad. His hair is more recently cut. His clothes are more recently bought. I guess that's what happens when you own a global business.

"Evening, Uncle," Simon says. We always address him as Uncle, never by his name. I hate how happy it makes him look.

Grandma walks in after him. You wouldn't think by looking that she's well into her eighties. She stands almost as tall as Andrew, her white hair in short, carefully crafted curls, and wears a blue dress that probably cost more than Seb's mum receives in a year. There's that chime of privilege again. It makes me want to scream.

"Well, don't you look handsome?" she says, approaching Simon with open arms.

He forces himself out of his seat to hug her and she plants a kiss on each of his cheeks. I almost want to wipe my own cheeks in response.

"And Elliot..." She looks me up and down. "I do wish you'd cut your hair more often."

This is going to be a fun night.

About an hour later, we're waiting for Mum to bring out the dessert. Andrew and Grandma are listening intently as Simon talks about his internship with GlimpseTech–something I've heard plenty about this week already. I take the opportunity to get out my phone under the table and text Seb.

How about an escape room tomorrow? I text. And then, after a second's thought, **My treat.**

"So, what exactly is it you do for them?" Grandma asks Simon. "Do you guide people through their Glimpses? I remember this lovely young man who did mine–"

"No, I work on the GlimpseNet. They've just started letting me verify Glimpses. Basically, I go through the posts people have made, then watch their Glimpse to see if they're telling the truth, and then it gets verified and the post goes public."

Andrew scoffs. "Quite why anyone would want the details of their Glimpse publicly available, I don't know."

"There are lots of reasons. People see themselves dating someone they've never met, so they make a post to try and find them, or their Glimpse isn't very interesting from their perspective but it reveals something about someone else so they post it to let people know, and sometimes you get the really exciting ones–like the crimes."

I've never done an escape room before, Seb replies. **I don't really get it...like...do you just get locked in a room and have to get out? Is that fun?**

"Ah yes," says Andrew, "I've heard about this. The police can access all the Glimpses before they're even verified, can't they?"

"Yeah. If a person makes a post about a serious crime, that gets flagged with the police straight away before anyone verifies it. They can even use it as a warrant to arrest someone, without having seen the video of the Glimpse."

You have to solve puzzles and stuff. I did one for my birthday a few years back.

"Almost makes you want to make a post to get someone arrested," Grandma says with a chuckle. "I wouldn't mind posting about these silly protestors I keep seeing on the news."

Andrew laughs too, in the deep and phlegm-filled way that makes me want to stop eating. "I may have to join you on that, Mother."

"Well, arrests can be made," Simon continues, "but if a verification proves the claim false, then the person's free to go. Those ones jump right to the top of our priority list. I actually had to work on one yesterday–and it turned out the Glimpse was real."

"What was the crime?" Grandma asks a little too excitedly.

I tune them out, having heard the story from Simon yesterday. It's not even interesting. Just petty theft. I'm sure he'll add extra flare to impress Grandma and Andrew.

Sure, let's do it, Seb replies. **It'll be fun to be locked in a tight space with you.**

A laugh falls out of me, stopping everyone else's conversation. I look up from my phone to find all eyes on me. Even Mum, who just came in with dessert.

"It is rude to be on your phone during a meal, Elliot," Grandma says with a face of disdain I'm more than used to.

"Oh, leave him alone, Mother," Dad says, swirling his glass of wine. "He's probably talking to his girlfriend."

The attention on me intensifies a thousand times over. My heart races and I feel my cheeks cycle through ever darker shades of red.

"His girlfriend?" Grandma says. "Oh, how wonderful. Do tell us all about her, Elliot."

"I was wondering when you'd find one," Andrew says. "I worried you were a little *funny*, if you know what I mean."

There's a silence in the air as Andrew's words hang there, and I'm reminded of the moment, years ago, when he made a joke about how he wouldn't want any of us to 'come out.' Is that what he means by 'funny?' The silence does nothing to make me think otherwise.

My mouth is dry, but I manage to form words.

"I don't have a girlfriend, I'm just dating...someone."

The silence continues, but my family's eyes stay on me.

"I'm not hungry anymore."

I leap from my seat and head upstairs without another word. Everyone watches me leave, but I ignore them. I have to, because if I keep talking to them, I don't know what I might say.

Have I already said too much?

Does their silence mean they all suspect I'm *'funny?'*

How long can I keep pretending to be straight?

I lie on my bed and bury my face in a pillow. I'm still holding my phone, and I feel a buzz. A message from Seb. My overthinking stops as I read the only thing guaranteed to make me forget about the nightmare downstairs.

The door clicks closed behind me and Seb, plunging us into darkness for a second before the lights flicker on and bright red digital numbers start counting down from sixty on a screen above us. Gentle, twinkly music plays, and I take in the small room. The walls are made to look like rough stone, though one has a cabinet full of gemstones and glass bottles of colourful liquid. Occult symbols are carved on the other walls and a wooden desk adorned with sheets of parchment sits in the centre.

"What now?" Seb asks.

"We start looking around for clues or puzzles or keys or whatever."

Seb nods, but he looks baffled. It's kind of charming; usually, I'm the confused one. He gave the same fake nod to the woman who gave us an introductory talk. To be fair, her over-enthusiasm made it hard to take her seriously. According to her, this room is the cursed and abandoned workshop of a long-dead wizard, and now that we're locked in, our task is to find a way out.

I smirk at Seb and start exploring the room, heading straight to the desk. I scan over the sheets of parchment. Most of them have ink drawings of mystical creatures or plants, but the one that catches my eye the most is a sheet of writing, not that I can read it–instead of letters, there are runes.

"I reckon we need to translate this," I say, holding up the sheet. "It's just a bunch of runes."

"Like these?"

I turn to see Seb pointing at some runes carved into the door we came in through, which I completely missed.

"Exactly like those," I say, walking over to stand beside him.

A smile of pride flicks across his face and I feel my heart swell.

The runic writing on the back of the door matches that on the paper perfectly–except no, it doesn't.

"There's a word missing," I say, showing Seb the parchment and pointing at one of the runic words which is on the sheet but completely absent from the door.

"Oh yeah."

"So maybe we need to find that word somewhere? I don't know...let's look around."

Seb doesn't need to be told twice, he starts scouring every surface for clues, suddenly far more into this than he was before. It's cute, watching him getting hooked into the puzzle. So cute I can barely concentrate on searching myself.

"Over here!" Seb calls while studying the gemstones on the shelves.

I join him and follow his pointing finger to see that each gem or bottle of liquid is labelled with a rune. What's more, there's an empty shelf at the bottom, with five subtle circles carved into the wood.

"Maybe we're supposed to move something onto these circles," I say.

"Hmm."

I look back at the parchment, studying each runic word, particularly the one that's absent from the door carvings. A word made of five runes.

"Five..." I mutter.

"What?"

"There are five runes in this word," I say, pointing, "and five circles on that shelf...so..."

I hand Seb the parchment and start grabbing the items from the shelf labelled with the runes from the five-letter word. I place them on the circles, in the same order as in the word, and the moment I place the final bottle of glittering purple liquid on its circle, there's a loud click. The shelf-unit swings gently backwards, revealing a whole other room hidden behind it.

"Holy shit," Seb says.

The grin on his face is comically wide and I match it.

Two minutes left on the clock, and I'm stressed out of my mind.

"What do I do now?" Seb asks as he tries to manoeuvre the locked box through the maze in the wall.

"I don't know!" I scan my eyes over the page in the spell-book I'm holding for the hundredth time. "We're missing some of the directions!"

The clock keeps ticking down.

We must have missed something. Maybe there was a lock we missed somewhere. Maybe we didn't look through the cauldrons properly. Maybe there was a clue on one of the books in the second room. Or maybe the answer was in the first room all along.

"Can you not feel the right route?" I ask.

"I'm trying!" Seb has his hands in two of the holes on the otherwise blank wall, he's only halfway through the maze–the only hole big enough for the box to fit through is a metre to his left.

"Let me see if I can find something."

I head back into the third room, the one with all the cauldrons–too many to look through now. We're nearly on the final minute.

What haven't we tried? What might we have missed?

I sigh, ready to give up, but then I notice the painting on the wall. A painting of a wizard, stood in front of a blank wall. Well, blank except for the arm-sized holes. I get a rush of adrenaline, pull the frame from the wall, and get the painting out. It's the wall Seb currently has his hands jammed in. And on the back of the painting? A perfect diagram of the maze.

I dash back to Seb and thrust the image in his face.

"Holy shit," he says for what must be the tenth time today. He immediately focuses, moving the box as best he can through the maze, now with a map to guide him.

Forty-five seconds left.

"Quick!" I shout.

"Just one more corner..."

Forty seconds. Thirty-nine. Thirty-eight.

Seb reaches the largest hole in the wall and pulls out the box. I grab the key from my pocket and turn it quickly in the lock.

Twenty-six. Twenty-five.

The box opens and Seb pulls out a small scroll. He unravels it, revealing Latin words: a magic spell. And there's a drawing of a wand.

"We need the wand," Seb says, and I know that if anyone saw the look in our eyes right now, they'd think we were attempting to stave the apocalypse. I'd laugh if we didn't have so little time left.

"It's in the second room."

Without question, both of us start running.

Fourteen. Thirteen. Twelve.

We pass the cauldrons.

Eleven. Ten. Nine. Eight.

We're in the second room, with its rows and rows of books and the set of wizard's robes on the floor, atop which sits the wand.

Seven. Six.

Seb grabs the wand and we continue back through the secret door into the first room.

Five.

"Together?" he says with such sincerity. I make a mental note to tease him about how much he enjoyed this later.

Four.

He holds out the wand, pointing it at the door we first entered through.

Three.

I wrap my hand around his fist, so that we're both holding the wand.

Two.

In unison, we chant the spell on the scroll.

One.

"PATEFACIO SURSUM!"

The lights go out. The timer disappears. For a moment there is complete silence, save for our breathless gasps.

And then triumphant music flares up and the door opens.

"Well," the woman who first showed us into the room says. "You cut that a bit fine."

Seb giggles with childish glee. As we walk out, our hands stay together around the wand. And even though we're in full view of the woman, I don't actually care. In this moment, I feel free.

"For the record," the woman says, as she hands us signs that read, 'I BROKE OUT,' "you didn't need to go back to the first room. The spell would have worked wherever you were."

I feel myself turn red, imagining how unnecessarily intense we must have looked on the cameras.

"Yeah," Seb says, "but that wouldn't have been as fun."

He nudges me with his shoulder, still giggling, and we stand against the blank wall, holding up our signs as the woman readies a camera.

"There're some costumes there if you fancy putting them on," she adds, nodding to a box on the floor.

I'm about to protest, but the look on Seb's face tells me there's no way I'm getting away from this. He practically dives into the box and within seconds he's pulled out wizard robes and hats and is thrusting them towards me.

"I hate you," I whisper as he dons his robes.

"Aw. I hate you too."

We pose in costume, holding our signs while also holding the wand aloft, my hand around Seb's. And the picture is taken.

I stare at the photo in bed hours later. It's the perfect image: a moment of true happiness captured forever. No matter what happens at home–where Mum,

Dad, and Simon are being extra quiet around me since dinner with Grandma and Andrew–I'll always have this. A reminder of how happy it's possible for me to be.

You look so cute in that costume, Seb texts along with a winking emoji.

Not as cute as you.

Lies.

I bite my lip, a breathy laugh escaping me.

Guess it's your turn to pick the next date, I message.

Hmm. I wish we could do something longer.

What do you mean?

Like, longer than meeting up for a couple of hours.

Like a trip somewhere?

Exactly.

My heart starts beating faster. I know exactly where this is going. I've been keeping track of the days, and the events of my Glimpse are closer than ever. In four days' time, I'll be crossing a boundary I never thought I would with a boy. With Seb.

Only problem is everything's super expensive, Seb texts, **and I don't want you to keep paying for everything.**

My fingers hover over the keyboard. The Glimpse is absolute, so it truly doesn't matter what I type, and yet I'm scared to make the suggestion. It feels wrong to take matters into my own hands, like I'd be manipulating Seb through knowledge he has no access to.

Maybe we should just go on a walk or something, Seb says.

Or... My fingers are steered by destiny. Either that or I've wound myself up into such an anxious mess that I don't know what else to do but this. **We could go camping.**

TWENTY-EIGHT

Seb

"You're sure you'll be okay?" I ask Mum again.

"I'll be fine," she says. Her face is brighter than it's been in a long time. She's even washed and combed her hair. "It's one night. And you can't waste your life looking after me all the time."

I glance at the broken window, still boarded up since we can't afford to repair it. She's right, but after everything that's happened, I don't know if I can trust her.

"And he sounds nice, this boy," Mum says. "Even if you won't tell me his name."

I told her about Elliot when I got home from the escape room a few days ago. Every day since she left hospital, she's seemed a little better, but that also means she's noticing things that would normally pass her by. Like the fact I'm always texting someone with a huge smile on my face. Or how happy I am after getting home from a date.

It was only a matter of time before she worked out what's been happening.

"Who's the boy?" she asked me when I got back from escaping the wizard's workshop. She'd raised an eyebrow, but was also smiling, as if the happiness Elliot gives me is infectious.

It's been years since I came out to my mum, so I knew I wasn't about to get a talking to, and she seemed so excited it was impossible not to tell her. I kept Elliot's name out of it, not wanting to out him. There's no way Mum would ever end up spreading the news of Elliot's sexuality around, but it didn't seem right to take the power of coming out from his hands. It's his choice to make.

Instead, I gushed about all the things I like about him. His hair, his face, his eyes, the way he gets embarrassed so easily, how clever he is, the way he solved the puzzles in the escape room like I never could.

Mum took it all in, giggling with joy. Encouraging me all the way. And when I mentioned the idea of the camping trip to her, she didn't hesitate before saying I should go.

"What time are you heading out?" she asks now.

"Half an hour."

She's wrapped up in a dressing gown, sat on the sofa as the TV plays terrible daytime TV. It might be a sorry sight to some, but I know this is the best she's been in a long time. Her hair is clean, her eyes are without bags, and she's even eating a proper meal that she cooked herself.

"I'll be fine," she says again, knowing exactly what I'm about to ask.

I sigh, releasing the tension in my body.

Despite what she first thought, Aym has done a complete one-eighty when it comes to Elliot being a Carl replacement. I think it was the escape room story that changed her mind. We both know Carl would have thought the whole experience was boring rubbish. Elliot, on the other hand, has never been cuter than when he's in full puzzle-nerd mode. The way that boy worries about his exam results makes absolutely no sense to me.

Enjoy getting laid tonight ;), Aym texts.

I roll my eyes. **We don't know that's going to happen.**

Oh, please, as if you two will be able to keep your hands off each other all cuddled up in a tent.

I'd be lying if I said I haven't thought that's where things might go tonight. The condoms I just packed prove as much. But I don't know if Elliot will want to, and there's no way in hell I'd ever pressure him into it. Plus, I'd hate for his first time to be shit.

We'll see, I guess.

I put my phone back in my pocket and shove the last few things I need in my bag. The plan is to catch a bus with Elliot to take us further out into the countryside. Some guy out there who's friends with his dad used to let him and his family camp on some land he owns, and it seems he's willing to let Elliot go there with his friends too. That's the excuse Elliot's using–camping with Callum. No need to tell his parents I exist yet.

I check on Mum one last time before heading out. She's still on the sofa, happily watching TV. She gives me a cheery "Goodbye!" as I leave. No matter how happy she seems, I can't avoid the nervous sickness that washes over me as soon as I close the door.

But I can't keep focusing on that. And the moment I see Elliot, it gets easier to forget.

"Hey," he says, taking the seat beside me on the bus.

"Hey."

He's dressed a lot like he was when we went walking in the woods. All outdoorsy, ready for a full-on expedition, with the biggest rucksack I've ever seen and a tent-bag at his feet. I edge closer to him, leaning against his soft fleece jacket, and let my mind wonder what he looks like under all the layers.

This family friend of Elliot's must be rich as fuck. His house alone is impressive, but I can barely see it because we're so far out in the land he owns. The guy even has a little pine forest and a pond.

"How does your dad know the owner?" I ask.

Elliot is emptying the tent components onto the grass. We're in a field that's cordoned off from the ones around it. It's for the best, since there are sheep in the one to our right and the one to our left is just bare soil. This field gets rented out as a campsite during summer, but we're early to it since there's still a week before schools fully break up.

"He was friends with my uncle when they were kids," Elliot says. "I think he was best man at his wedding."

Elliot told me about his snobby uncle; it doesn't surprise me that he's best friends with a rich landowner. I wonder how he'd react if he knew his nephew was dating someone who sometimes doesn't have enough money to eat. Hopefully Elliot's dad isn't as stuck-up as his uncle.

"Right..." Elliot puts his hands on his hips and looks down at the poles, pegs, and sheet of orange plastic. Then he looks at me. "I'll be honest, I've never been good at pitching tents."

"I thought you were a scout!"

"I was." He starts kicking the ground lightly. "I just wasn't a very good one."

I walk up to him and muss his hair, ending with my hand on the back of his head. "Guess we'll have to figure it out together then." I pull him towards me and kiss him, feeling him melt at my touch.

When I let go, his hazel eyes catch the sun just right, transforming from what can sometimes be mistaken for brown into a mix of colours. Greens, golds, even a flash of blue. It's like the Earth itself is rotating in his eyes.

"You take half the poles, I'll take the others," he says, snapping me out of my trance.

I stand to attention and salute. "Sir, yes, sir."

He shoves me playfully in my side. "That isn't a scout thing, idiot."

"Not into roleplay. Noted."

Elliot grabs a bunch of poles and throws them towards me with a grin. "Shut up and get to work."

We lie side by side on a picnic blanket while the sun sets, tent far behind us. At our feet is the bank down to the pond, which looks almost cartoon-like as it reflects the pink evening glow. I slip an arm under Elliot's neck, resting my hand on his shoulder and hugging him to my side.

There's been no sight or sound from the landowner. Elliot said it was always the same when he camped here with family; the owner likes to let people enjoy themselves without being disturbed. All that surrounds us now is the darkening field and the distant sounds of farm animals. It's just me and Elliot. Completely alone.

"Are you happy?" I ask. "With me? With...whatever it is we're doing?"

Elliot adjusts himself, moving so that he's on his side. I do the same to face him.

"Of course, I am," he says. "Are you?"

"Very."

A breeze rushes through the pine trees in the distance.

"Why do you ask?" says Elliot.

I take a moment, not entirely sure myself. "I know it's the first time you've done anything like this. And I know I'm not the type of person you'd usually hang out with. I just want to make sure you're comfortable."

He smiles and reaches out a hand, tracing his fingers along my jaw. "I've never been more comfortable with anyone in my life."

I run my hand over his, keeping it against my face, gently stroking the smooth skin.

"I love this," Elliot says. "I love spending time with you. I love..." He pauses, and I feel my heart skip as my mind imagines the end of the sentence. "All of it. I love everything about what we're doing."

Was I really expecting him to say he loves me? After only speaking to me for a few weeks? Before we're even officially a couple? I guess that says a lot about me.

He kisses me, which stuns me for a moment before I let myself drink in his warmth. I don't know if I'll ever not be surprised when it's him who initiates a kiss.

We're still on the blanket an hour later, though now we're tangled far tighter together to keep warm in the night air. There's a full moon in the sky above us, and there's not a single cloud to obscure the stars. We're far from any town centre or main road, so there's no light pollution and I can see more stars than I ever have before.

"So that there is Ursa Major," Elliot says, pointing at the sky. "AKA the Great Bear."

"Where?"

"There." He traces the lines between the stars in the constellation. "You see those four bright spots in a kind of trapezium? And then a curved line coming off the top left star?"

I try my best to find what he's pointing at, but it's just a bunch of stars. I'm not seeing the shapes. Plus– "I'll be honest, I can't remember what a trapezium is."

Elliot breathes a laugh. "Okay, let's try again. You see the stars shaped like a saucepan?"

I look again, and there it is! Four bright spots forming the pan, and a trail of others forming the handle. "Oh shit. Yeah, I see the saucepan."

"That's it. That's the Great Bear."

I look back at Elliot with a raised eyebrow. "That's meant to be a bear?"

"Well, it's part of it. The rest is harder to see, to be honest. But the saucepan bit is called the Big Dipper or the Plough."

I turn to the sky again. "Definitely more of a saucepan."

"Agreed."

We stay like that a while longer, Elliot pointing out more constellations–he says he only knows a few, but a few is way more than I've ever known so I'm impressed anyway. Soon enough, the temperature drops, and it gets way colder.

"Reckon we should go in the tent?" I ask.

Elliot bites his lip and looks away. I'm not sure why. "Yeah. Probably for the best."

We roll up the blanket and take it back to the tent which, thank God, is still standing strong even though we put the poles in the wrong places an embarrassing number of times. It's Elliot's family tent, so it's big enough that four people could fit with space between them all. I don't think Elliot plans for there to be any space between us, though. While he did bring two sleeping bags, he only brought one mat.

We enter the tent, bumping against each other in the dark. It's pitch-black inside, so Elliot gets out his phone and uses the torch to find the battery-powered lamp he brought. The lamp fills the tent with dim, yellow light, and I notice Elliot is trembling slightly.

"You okay?" I ask, touching his shoulder.

"Hmm? Oh. Yeah. Just a bit cold is all."

He sets the lamp down in a corner.

I look at the sleeping bags on the floor-mat, and then to Elliot, and then back again.

"Shall we, er, lie down?" he asks. His voice is trembling too.

"Sure."

We cuddle together on the floor, just like we did on the blanket outside, but Elliot keeps shaking and I don't know if it's nerves or fear or both.

"Hey," I say, stroking his back to try and calm him down, "we don't have to do anything you don't want to, okay?"

"I..." His eyes keep shifting away from mine, as if he's worried they might betray a secret. "I want to... I want to do everything with you, Seb."

"You're sure?"

He nods, and his trembles lessen slightly. "I'm sure. I'm just...I'm nervous."

I kiss him gently and run my fingers along his cheek. "That's completely normal."

His eyes stare deep into mine, pupils wide, drawing me in. I kiss him again, more passionately this time, slipping my tongue between his lips. He kisses me back, and the tighter he holds on to me the less he shakes.

His hands move along my back, reaching the bottom of my shirt, hesitating at the hem. I pull back and look at him, seeing the excitement in his face which is matched by mine. And then I reach for the zip of his fleece.

We go slowly, kissing and caressing each other for a while before our shirts come completely off. We roll over each other, moved by desire, always together. And soon I'm on top of him, looking down at him in all his beauty, before returning to a kiss, and moving my hands towards his pants.

"Is this okay?" I ask.

"Yes," he whispers back.

And then there's no fabric between us at all and our hands are exploring everywhere they can.

It's perfect. And beautiful. And more than I could ever have hoped for.

TWENTY-NINE

Elliot

This is it. The Glimpse. It's no longer a vision of my future. It's the here and now. And from this moment on, nothing will ever be predictable. From here on out, it's just me and Seb, forging our own path, never knowing where we'll end up.

And it scares me.

But right now, in this moment, that fear is nothing compared to the joy that floods me. The euphoria. The complete and utter bliss.

Seb reaches for a condom, and soon we know each other more intimately than anyone.

And I never want to leave.

I never want to let him go.

I don't know what time it is when we wake up, but I don't care. Seb is still beside me, his skin soft and warm against mine beneath the unzipped sleeping bag. His eyes are closed and his breathing steady, occasionally rattling in his throat in a cute half-snore. I run my fingers through his hair, brushing the dark strands away from his forehead.

At that, his eyes flutter open.

"Morning," I say. "Or afternoon. I don't actually know."

Seb laughs before letting out a huge yawn and stretching himself awake. "How are you feeling?"

My smile is too big to hide. "Amazing."

"Me too."

He puts a hand to the back of my head and pulls me in for a kiss. His mouth tastes exactly how you'd expect in the morning, and I doubt mine is much better, but I don't care. He could have taken a shower in a sewer, and I'd still want to kiss him.

"We should check the time," he says when we finally stop.

"Do we have to? Can't we just stay here forever?"

"You're the one who sorted this whole trip with the guy that owns the place. You tell me."

He's right, and the agreement was just for one night. One night and then gone by the afternoon.

I sigh and reach for my phone.

"It's just gone two," I say.

"Two?!"

"I know. Quite the lie-in."

"Guess we should start packing up."

"I guess so."

We look at each other, and our eyes say the exact same thing. In an instant, our lips are locked together again.

Taking the tent down is somehow even harder than putting it up. It takes nearly half an hour just to figure out how to fold it correctly so it'll fit in the bag.

"Got it?" Seb asks, sat on top of the tent bag while I zip it up.

"Yep. Done."

"Thank fuck for that." He gets up and lifts the bag. "Shall we go?"

I nod and we set off back towards the road where, at some point, a bus will turn up. As we walk, a question weighs on my mind. One I don't really know how to ask because I've never had to before.

I guess it's obvious I'm stumbling over a question in my head, because when we reach the bus stop, Seb nudges me and says, "What's up?"

"Nothing."

He raises an eyebrow.

"Okay, something."

"Go on..."

I take a breath. "I guess...well, you know I've never *been* with anyone before, right?"

"Yeah."

"So, I don't really know what the rules are."

"Rules?"

"I mean...we've been going on dates, and now we've..."

"Had sex?"

I hate that I blush. "Yeah. So, what are we now? Are we just 'dating'? Or are we–"

"Boyfriends."

He says it so fast I feel like I've been hit by the bus that hasn't even arrived yet.

"If you want to be," he adds, scratching the back of his head and looking away from me, betraying nerves I so rarely see in him.

As if I'd ever say no.

I reply with a kiss, wrapping my arms around him, and even though I hear the bus pulling up behind us, I find for the first time ever that I don't care what people think. But maybe that's just because I know my parents aren't on that bus.

Boyfriends.

The word feels weird as I toss it around my brain. Foreign. Not a word I ever thought I'd use about a couple I'm in. Boyfriend, sure. I've always imagined I'd be someone's boyfriend someday. But for me to have one? For me to call someone else my *boy*friend? A part of me worries it'll never feel normal. Even if it's weird, though, it does feel right. It's what I want. Me and Seb. Together. For as long as we possibly can be.

My parents aren't back from work when I get in, and thankfully neither is Simon. He's spending the day at GlimpseTech and won't be finished for another hour. I wonder how many people are getting Glimpses today. They say the numbers are growing every day, what with the Last Day coming up. No matter how ridiculous people's Last Day conspiracy theories get, most seem to think we won't ever be able to Glimpse beyond that date. So, the closer we get to it, the more people grab their last chance at seeing their future.

I flick on the news when I get in the living room. As it's been for the last week, it's a bunch of dull stories interspersed with regular discussions about GlimpseTech and the Last Day. It's all protests here and suicides there, interviews with conspiracy theorists on one channel and interviews with scientists on the other.

I try to focus on the scientists.

"There is no evidence at all," one particularly passionate man on a discussion panel says, "nor has there ever been, that the Glimpses will lead to an apocalyptic event." He readjusts his thick-framed glasses beneath bushy grey eyebrows as he turns from the audience to the panel leader. "If I could cast everyone's minds back to the first particle collision experiments at the Large Hadron Collider, you may recall there were conspiracy nuts claiming the experiments would create a black hole that would swallow the Earth. And did that happen? No, it did not. In fact, if it weren't for research like that in particle physics, we would never have made the discoveries necessary for Glimpses to exist.

"The claims made about GlimpseTech come from people who have no scientific knowledge. They merely want to cause panic. And where has that led us? People have killed themselves, for God's sake. Even the prime minister has finally admitted that GlimpseTech means no harm and isn't hiding anything!"

There's a gentle applause from the audience.

"If I may counter," a red-haired woman sat beside him says, "it is a well-known and well-publicised fact that people have killed themselves, or at least attempted to, as a direct result of the Glimpses. You can't talk about the recent deaths without mentioning those too."

Applause again, but this time far louder.

The leader of the panel, an East Asian woman with dark hair tied up in a ponytail, raises her hands to quieten the crowd. I've seen her present the news many times before.

"I believe we have some questions from the audience," she says with a clear and authoritative voice.

She points at someone and the camera flips to show an audience member–young and wearing dungarees–being handed a microphone.

"My question is for Doctor Smith," she says. "What do you say to the claims that GlimpseTech is keeping us from having second Glimpses because they're hiding information about what happens after the Last Day?"

The camera returns to the thick-browed man just in time to see him sigh.

"GlimpseTech has always prevented people from having second Glimpses," he says, "but this is done to keep people safe. It is quite simple; early trials of the Glimpses proved that having more than one Glimpse can put a person at high risk of brain damage. GlimpseTech have never hidden that fact."

He's not wrong. I remember reading it in the small print when signing up to my own Glimpse. Something to do with 'temporal displacement of consciousness.'

A lot of the other questions get answered with similar ease. Doctor Smith has the facts which have never been hidden on his side. But he can't answer everything–mainly the one question providing the reason for this panel: why has no one ever Glimpsed beyond the Last Day?

No one knows. And it's that uncertainty which stops me completely ruling out the whole 'end of the world' theory. I'm not saying I believe it, but the thought is always there at the back of my mind. Now that my Glimpse has come true, I know with absolute certainty that Glimpses are legitimate. But that means there must be something stopping people seeing beyond the Last Day. The world might end in just thirteen days' time.

The shorter that time gets, the less abstract the idea becomes, and I guess that's why the protests keep getting bigger and why people keep taking stronger actions. It's fear. Fear that I don't want to feel but which is only growing.

Thanks to Seb, I'm happier than I've ever been. Thirteen days is nowhere near the lifetime I'm starting to imagine spending with him and there's no second Glimpse to give me hope.

Seb

Someone's been in the house. Someone other than Mum. If I couldn't tell by the smell of smoke, or the way the furniture's been moved, I'd know from Mum's face. The guilt. And it's obvious who it must have been.

"Dan's been here, hasn't he?"

Mum shrinks into herself, the shame making her almost invisible on the sofa. I've never felt less like her son. Right now, like too many times before, I'm the parent.

"Hasn't he?"

It's subtle, but she nods, and even though I knew I was right, I'm still crushed by her confirmation. It's like every bit of progress we've made has been stripped away, leaving me the same scared little boy staring at broken glass that I was almost three weeks ago. Little boy, teenager, and adult man all at the same time.

I dump my bag on the floor and try to get my breathing under control. I could scream or cry right now and I don't want to do either.

"Where is he?" I ask.

She says nothing. She doesn't even look at me.

"I want to know his address."

Still nothing.

"Mum! Tell me!" I step towards her with my fists clenched, rage rising inside me, fit to explode outwards and destroy everything in my path.

And Mum looks scared.

Terrified.

Because of me.

I'd never hurt her. Never, never, never. But how must I look right now? To make a woman scared of her own son? I step back, unclench my fists, and a lump rises in my throat.

"Mum," I say, voice softer. "Please." I kneel beside her chair, meeting her downward pointing gaze. "Tell me where he lives."

"Number seven, George Street," she whispers.

I should apologise. I should take a breath, sit down, and talk to her. Really talk.

But I don't.

Instead, I get back on my feet, head through the front door, and leave.

Number seven, George Street, the home of the man who's been terrorizing my family, doesn't match the man at all. It's large and detached, with a front and back garden, and an expensive looking car in the drive. It's secluded too, set far enough away from the other houses on the street and so surrounded by hedges that a person could get away with almost anything and not be seen. I feel sick thinking about where all the money he must have comes from, and that a man rich enough to afford this was happy to take my guitar from me.

As I walk towards the door, I see the cracks in the fancy-seeming surface of Dan's home. The garden is overgrown, the car is unwashed, and the windows of the house are dirty too. The smell of smoke hits me on the doorstep, a smell that sends me right back to the last time I saw Dan. In my head, I see him taking the money. I see his grubby hands on my guitar. Anger and fear mix in my chest, combining into determination.

I take a breath, clench my fist, and knock loudly on the door.

I hear Dan before I see him–his heavy footsteps approach from inside the house, and he hesitates at the door, probably looking through the peephole. It swings open, and he flashes a sickening smile.

"Didn't think I'd be seeing you again," he says. He's wearing a grease-stained vest, dark chest hair poking out of the top.

"You were meant to leave my mum alone." It's a struggle to avoid stuttering, and I have to keep my fists clenched to keep myself steady.

Dan snorts. "Yeah, I got that text from her saying she was done. Pathetic, really."

The lump in my throat returns; hatred, rage, and terror are fighting their way out of me, struggling for control.

"You got your money," I say. "She doesn't owe you anything."

He shrugs, smug faced.

"Please..." I'm losing control, the words aren't clear anymore. "Please just leave her alone. She's not well, she's..."

"Crazy."

Click. A switch is flipped.

Without hesitating, I drive my fist into his face, knocking him sideways. Pain shoots up my arm, but I don't care. Only one thought fills my mind right now. One desire. I want Dan to suffer.

He spits at the ground, leaving a red stain, and looks back at me. A trail of blood falls from his nose, running over his lips and dripping slowly off his chin to gather in his chest hair. His eyes are wilder than I've ever seen them. I go for another punch, so quickly Dan doesn't have time to react, but pain shoots up my arm when I make contact and I hesitate, which is my biggest mistake.

His hands are on me in an instant.

A fist collides with the side of my head.

A knee to my stomach.

I'm on the ground and the pain keeps coming.

Punches. Kicks. I can't tell the difference anymore.

My face is wet, but I don't know if it's blood or tears. Probably both.

No one comes running. No one tries to save me. I look up at Dan and see his yellow grin.

"You can beg all you want," he says. Blood is still dripping from his face but he does nothing about it. "Jane works for me. I own her, and I'm not letting her go." When he looks down at me, he has the eyes of a rabid dog. He spits blood to the ground beside me and marches into his house, slamming the door and leaving me gripping my side, tears streaming silently down my face.

Every step is agony. I barely get to the end of Dan's driveway before I collapse against a tree, clutching my ribs. There's no way I can get home without help. I know I should probably call an ambulance–hell, even the police–but I know where that would lead. They'd ask why I was at Dan's house, they'd find out about Mum, and then they'd take her away from me. My family would be destroyed forever.

There are only two people in the world I trust enough to call, and right now there's one face I want to see more than any other.

THIRTY-ONE

Elliot

My heart breaks into a thousand pieces when I see Seb. He's sat at the base of a tree in the setting sun, right beside someone's driveway, face bruised and gripping his stomach tightly.

"Oh my God." I kneel and make a move to hug him but stop when he flinches. "What happened?"

He was vague on the phone, telling me he needed my help and where he was. I could tell he was in pain from his voice, quiet and weak, but he wouldn't explain anything over the call.

He shakes his head now and says, "Help me up," reaching out a hand to me. I do as he asks, taking his hand and draping it over my shoulder as I help pull him up. There are whimpers from him, but he's keeping them quiet, suppressing them.

"You need an ambulance," I say.

"No!" He looks terrified, and I don't understand why. He can barely stand. "I'll explain what happened, but please don't call an ambulance."

"But you're hurt."

"*Please.*" His eyes are red and tear-filled, sadder than I've ever seen them, darting back and forth as he searches for something in my eyes.

"Okay," I give in. "Just tell me what happened."

And so, he does. Every last detail.

"This isn't my house," Seb says when I lead him through the front gate of a small terraced house a few streets away from his own.

"I know," I say.

I knock on the door and pray that the people inside won't mind us showing up unannounced.

"Elliot," Seb says, "who lives here?"

The door opens, revealing an overly-smiley, pale, bald man. Though the smile disappears as soon as he sees Seb.

"Who..."

"Sorry," I say. "We haven't properly met, but I'm Elliot. I'm friends with Nikita."

There's a pause as he studies Seb and me, completely baffled, but then, "Elliot? Oh, as in Callum's friend!" His voice is gentle, with a slight eastern European accent. I've heard it before in the background of calls.

"Yes," I say, "exactly, and this is Seb, I'm sorry to barge in on you like this, but as you can see, Seb is hurt and I know you used to be a doctor, so I was wondering if –"

"Elliot?" A new voice arrives. It's Nikita, running up behind her dad. "What are you doing here?" She notices Seb and her mouth drops open.

Her dad looks from her, to me, to Seb, and then finally says, "You'd better come in."

Seb glares at me as we enter, but I don't say anything. He's in pain but won't go to the hospital. This is the next best thing as far as I'm concerned.

We're led to the brightly decorated living room. It's exactly what I've always imagined Nikita's home would look like. Photos of her family adorn the vibrant walls: Nikita and her sister, who are a few years apart but look almost identical, and their parents. While her dad is Russian, Nikita's mum is Indian. I remember Callum telling me how Nikita's name comes from both her parents' cultures even though the origins are completely different. Back then, I thought she was just some girl he'd get over in a matter of days. I never expected to be bringing my own boyfriend into her house.

Seb and I sit on the sofa while Nikita's dad goes to fetch some supplies.

"So..." Nikita says, taking a seat across the room from Seb and me. Her eyebrows are raised in expectation. I can only imagine how she must be feeling right now. I'm not sure we've ever even had a conversation without Callum in the room, but I will admit I've felt closer to her recently. She even knows about my Glimpse, which I still haven't told Seb. I suddenly feel a lot more self-conscious.

"He got in a fight," I say.

Seb shoots daggers at me, but he doesn't need to worry. I won't betray him.

"With some guy from another school," I add.

I feel Seb relax beside me, a silent 'thank you' sent through the air as he exhales.

"Oh God," Nikita says. "Do you know his name?"

Seb shakes his head. It's a weak cover-up story, but it'll have to do.

Nikita's dad returns with a bundle of plasters, bandages, pain killers, and antiseptics.

"Let's take a look at you," he says with the gentle smile that only a doctor can conjure up. "And you can explain what exactly happened."

Seb uses the kid-from-another-school story, which I'm realising now we really should have planned out before we got here, but I guess I didn't give Seb much warning. Even if Nikita's dad doesn't believe Seb's story, he at least pretends to, only asking questions about the pain as he checks him over. Part of me is worried that as soon as we leave here, he'll be on the phone to the police. But I still don't think that would be the worst thing, no matter what Seb claims.

The sun has fully set by the time Nikita's dad has finished examining Seb, and the conclusion is no major harm has been done (thank God). It's mainly just bruising. Seb is guaranteed to wake up with a black eye tomorrow, but that seems to be the worst of it.

"Do you want me to call anyone for you?" Nikita's dad asks as he wraps up his supplies.

"No," Seb says.

"I'll get him home," I add.

"Thanks for everything," Seb says.

"You're welcome. It's been a while since I've whipped out my doctor skills."

Seb gives the weakest laugh I've ever heard. But a laugh is better than nothing.

"I'll see them out, Dad," Nikita says.

The moment her dad has left the room, Nikita glares at me and Seb.

"Are you both alright?" she asks. "And I mean *seriously*."

"We're fine," I answer.

Her eyes are thin, scrutinising my expression. I've never seen her like this, caring so deeply about how I feel. It's nice, in a way. I've often thought she only talks to me because of Callum, but after how she's responded to my whole relationship with Seb, and this evening, she doesn't feel like my best friend's girlfriend. She just feels like a friend.

"If you need anything else," she says, "just ask, okay?"

"Thanks, Nikita."

She nods and turns to Seb. "It was nice to meet you, Seb, though maybe not the best circumstances."

Seb chuckles, but winces in pain at the same time. "Yeah," he says. "Nice to meet you, too."

"And you're sure you're okay?"

Seb nods.

"I hope we get a chance to properly hang out soon. A double date maybe?"

"That'd be nice," Seb says. I know he means it, but there's not much joy in his voice.

Walking Seb home with his hand in mine is like hauling the weight of a hundred men. I can't even begin to imagine how he must feel. It's as if his emotions have gained physical mass. They're pulling him down, and he needs me to keep him afloat.

"I'm sorry for dragging you into this," he says as we turn onto his street.

"Don't be. I'm glad you called instead of trying to get home yourself."

"I shouldn't have gone to Dan's house."

I stay silent. He's right, but I understand why he went, and I'm not about to tell him otherwise.

We reach his house and I hear a loud sniff from him. He's fighting back tears.

"Hey," I say, putting a hand on each of his shoulders and moving him so we're face to face, sides to the door. "It's okay to be upset. This is shit. All of it. You're allowed to *feel*."

He nods, then leans forward and cries into my chest. I hug him, being careful not to press on any of his bruises, and let him fall apart. I'll be here to put him back together again.

"I was so mean to her," he mutters through sobs.

"Who?"

"My mum. You should have seen her face; she was scared of me. I don't know if I can face her."

I step back and run a thumb across his face, wiping away the tears.

"I'm going to stay with you, okay?" I say. "All night, if you want."

More tears come, but he nods and unlocks the door.

The house is quiet, and all the lights are off, but as we pass Seb's Mum's bedroom, we hear her slow, steady breathing.

"She must be asleep," I whisper.

The breathing falters, and we hear her tired voice call, "Seb?"

I look to Seb, seeing the fear in his eyes thanks to the dim glow from the window on the landing. I nod at him, and he pushes his mum's door open slightly.

"Hey, Mum," he says, poking his head through the doorway.

"You're okay." It's not a question, and I can hear her relief.

"I'm okay. And..." His voice shakes slightly. "And I'm sorry. For earlier. I just–"

"It's fine."

"But–"

"You had every right to be angry. It's okay."

He looks to me, fear replaced with surprise. I smile at him.

"I love you, Seb," his mum says. "Go to bed now, won't you?"

He pauses for a moment, but when he says, "I love you too, Mum," there's relief in his voice.

He closes the door with a quiet click and turns away.

Seb leads me to his room. It feels like a moment that should be exciting–my first time entering my boyfriend's bedroom–but after everything that's happened in the last few hours, excitement is nowhere to be found. It's hard to believe that just this afternoon we were waking up together in a tent after the most amazing night of my life.

The room is small and simple, but it feels comfortable. There's a single bed and a wardrobe and not much space for anything else. The walls are decorated with creased posters for bands I've never heard of, and in the corner, beside the door, is Seb's old, damaged guitar, leaning against the wall.

Without speaking, Seb lies down on top of the bed covers, fully clothed. He faces the wall that the bed is pushed against. I join him, lying behind him on my side and draping an arm across him. His hand grips mine, pressing it to his chest where I can feel his gentle heartbeat.

"Thank you," he whispers. "For everything."

"It's the least I could do."

Dim, artificial, orange light creeps in through the gap in Seb's curtains, casting a single line down the wall we're facing. I follow it with my eyes, from the top of the wall to the point where it jumps onto the back of Seb's head. It's like a slice across his skull. A bright wound.

Seb cries quietly as he lies against me. I tighten my grip on his hand. I want him to know I'm here, and that I always will be. As I ease my head into the nook of his shoulder, I block the line of light, letting it score its way across me instead.

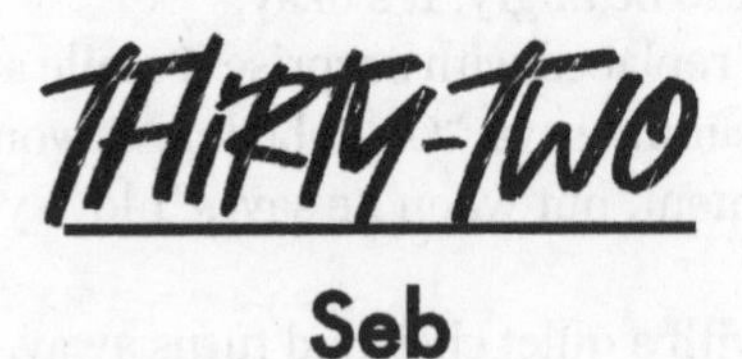

Seb

I know something's wrong the moment I wake up. I can feel it in the air. Beneath Elliot's quiet snores there's a silence that feels too strong. Like something's missing. A silence I've felt twice before.

I scramble out of bed. Elliot mutters something as I accidentally wake him up, but I ignore him.

I need to check on Mum.

A feeling of dread consumes me when I reach her door. I need my instincts to be wrong. I need her to be okay.

I open the door.

And she's not okay.

She's limp.

And silent.

Not breathing.

My vision is blurry.

And I'm falling.

Falling.

Down.

"Mum?" There's a voice in the distance. "Mum? Wake up!" It sounds familiar. But it's not mine. It can't be. Because I'm not speaking. Not doing anything. I'm just standing here, staring at the body.

And the pills.

"Seb?" And there's another voice. "Oh my God." And he's at my side. Elliot's at my side.

No. Not my side.

Some other boy's side.

Some dark-haired, skinny boy who's screaming at my mum.

Not me.

It can't be me.

Even if my throat hurts as if I've been screaming.

Elliot is talking to someone else now. I think he's on the phone. He sounds panicked.

Not like me.

And not like this boy who's still screaming over my mum.

There's a siren. And blue lights.

More voices. So many more voices.

Why are so many people putting their hands on Mum?

Where are they taking her?

People keep saying sorry. Over and over again. Like they've done something wrong. Like they've upset me somehow. But I don't even know them.

More phone calls. Elliot and these hi-vis wearing strangers. Adding even more voices to the mix. I think one of them sounds like Dad, but that doesn't make sense.

It feels like every time I blink there's something new to see. And it's all blurry because for some reason there's water in my eyes.

I'm tired, but I think it's the middle of the day because it's really bright.

Now it's dark. Or at least darker. And there's something soft underneath me. And someone has their arms around me.

"Hey," Elliot says. "Are you awake?"

"I..." I gather my thoughts. Even though they hurt. "I think so."

"Here." He passes me a glass of water.

I sit up and look around. We're in the living room, sitting on the sofa. We're as far away from her room as we can be in this house.

"What time is it?" I ask.

"Twenty-past seven in the evening. You've been asleep for a couple of hours."

He has bags under his eyes and his hair is flatter than I've ever seen it.

"She's dead, isn't she?" I ask.

I already know the answer, but my memories of what I think has been the rest of this day are all over the place.

Elliot just nods, like he's scared saying it out loud will hurt me. Too late for that. I can see the body in my head. Mum's body. Lifeless. Cold. I can feel the soreness in my throat from the screaming, my head is pounding, and I don't need a mirror to know how red my eyes must be.

There's a sound from the kitchen and I sit bolt upright, thinking for just a fraction of a second that it's all been a dream, that Mum is alive and well and just making a cup of tea.

"It's your dad," Elliot says, destroying the fantasy.

"My dad?"

I remember now. In the midst of the agony and tears, the paramedics got in contact with my dad to let him know what had happened.

"He got here while you were asleep," Elliot adds.

Dad must have heard us talking, because he pokes his head into the room and gives me a sad smile. I'm sure he means well, but it makes me feel sick. Seeing him here, in a house he hasn't entered in years, standing where Mum should be standing. Would be standing if I hadn't been so cruel to her.

A lump rises in my throat and tears fill my eyes again.

"Seb," Dad says, "I–"

"I don't think he wants to speak to you," Elliot interrupts. "Not yet."

I squeeze Elliot's arm to say thanks, throat too full of sobs for me to speak, and Dad goes back to the kitchen.

"It's my fault," I say in barely a whisper.

"What?" Elliot shuffles around on the sofa so we're properly facing each other. "No, Seb. It's not your fault. Don't ever think that."

"But it is."

He shakes his head.

"I shouted at her. I made her feel guilty. I made her think I hated her."

"She didn't think that."

"How would you know?"

Elliot's eyes shift away from mine and he sighs. "Because of what she said last night." He reaches into his pocket and pulls out a folded piece of paper. "And because of this."

THIRTY-THREE

Elliot

I ran into Seb's mum's bedroom as soon as I heard him screaming this morning. His agonised calls for her to wake up will be burned into my brain forever. It was obvious what had happened. Pill bottles littered the floor, she wasn't moving, and when I checked her pulse, I felt nothing. And there was Seb, crying, wailing, torn apart in a way I've never seen anyone like before.

I called for an ambulance, explaining what had happened, and while I scanned the room for any details they might need, I saw the note. A sheet of paper on the bedside table, covered completely in writing which began with two simple words: *Dear Seb*.

I didn't plan on reading the whole thing. It was addressed to Seb–the final ever words from his mother. It was his to read. His to absorb. His to treasure or despise. But I couldn't give it to him while he was in the state he was in most of the day. Maybe I would have if he'd responded to me, but every word anyone said to him seemed to fly past without notice.

And then the police came, and though the cause of death was obvious, they asked to see the note. So, I handed it over. They read it with blank faces. Detached. Unfeeling. I guess that's the state you have to put yourself in when dealing with things like this. Otherwise, the pain would be too much. In a way, I think that's what Seb was doing. In the moments where he was completely unresponsive, I don't think he was really there. He'd checked out. Left his body. I don't blame him.

The police stayed after the paramedics had taken the body away. They wanted to explain what happens next to Seb and, since Seb wasn't all there, me. I listened for Seb's benefit, but even I was struggling to stay present. All the pain around me was having an effect. I wanted to go home and cry while hugging my own mum, but I also wanted to stay with Seb.

Eventually, Seb drifted off to sleep and his dad arrived. The police left, and for a moment, I considered leaving too. But I looked down at Seb, asleep on the sofa. I saw the redness around his eyes, and the still-wet spots of tears on his cheeks. I could feel the suffering radiating off him.

So, I stayed. And that's when I read the letter.

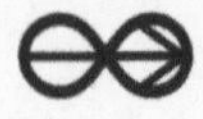

"What is that?" Seb says now, staring at the folded paper in my hand.

"It's from your mum." I hold it out to him. "It's addressed to you."

He doesn't take it from me straight away. Instead, he stares at it as if it's about to explode.

"You don't have to read it yet if you don't want to," I say.

"No." He reaches out a hesitant hand and takes it. "No, I want to." He unfolds it and his eyes move over the first few words, but tears start falling almost immediately and he stops to take long, deep breaths.

I give him a weak smile and run a hand along his arm. "Maybe it would be better to wait," I say, not just because I don't think he's in the best state right now, but also because I'm scared. Scared of how he'll react. The things in that letter...while they might convince him none of this was his fault, they'll hurt him a thousand times over as well.

He shakes his head. "I need to, but I don't know if I can."

"That's okay."

"Can you read it to me?"

"I..."

His red eyes stare right into mine and the pain in his next word breaks my heart. "Please?"

I take a breath. "Okay."

Dear Seb,

I know you're going to blame yourself for this, but I want you to know that it isn't your fault. I meant what I said when you came home tonight. I love you. I always have and I always will. You're my son. My only son. And you've done more for me than anyone else in the world. You've done things no son should have to do for their mother and there's no way I'll ever be able to make up for that.

I've been sad for a very long time now, and there's no one to blame for that but myself. My happiest memories, in fact my only happy memories, have all been thanks to you.

The truth is, I've known what's going to happen to me for a while. I never told you what I saw when I had my Glimpse. While your father's showed him in a new, happy, better life, mine showed me nothing. Complete darkness. I knew straight away what it meant, even before the doctor explained it to me. It meant I'd be dead before the date the Glimpse had shown me. Tomorrow's date.

I've tried to take my life before, as you know, but you saved me. You kept me going when I didn't think I could go on. And after the most recent time, when I realised just how close we were to the date of my Glimpse, I decided to do my best to stick around until the very end. So that's what I've done. I've stayed around for as long as I can. But now my time is up. I can't be alive tomorrow. I've known that for years.

Words can't express how sorry I am to leave you, Seb. You're the only thing that's kept me going all these years, and it breaks my heart to leave you. But I just can't do this anymore.

You are going to grow into the most incredible man the world has ever seen. You're going to be happy. You're going to fall in love with the man of your dreams, and he is going to feel so lucky to have you. You're going to grow old better than I did, and you're going to achieve your dreams. I don't need a Glimpse to know all that for certain.

Goodbye Seb.

All my love,

Mum

My voice cracks on the final words and though I want to stay strong for Seb, the tears start falling thick and fast. But it's nothing compared to Seb. He crumples into me, heaving sobs and heart-breaking cries filling the air around him. Around us.

I hold him close and let him lose himself completely. I let him give way to the grief. And I lose myself too. There are moments when I think I hear Seb's dad come back into the room, but if he says anything it goes unnoticed. The world around us has turned to dust. It's just me and Seb, adrift on this sofa. And I'm clutching him tighter than ever, to stop him from turning to dust too.

By the time I check my phone hours later, I have a bunch of missed calls. Mum, Dad, Simon, Callum, Nikita. And then about five more from Mum. And another coming through now.

I accept the call and don't get a chance to speak before her voice starts blasting through.

"WHERE THE HELL HAVE YOU BEEN?"

"I told you, I–"

"Don't give me any of this crap about being at Callum's house, Elliot. I know that's a lie! I've been worried sick. We nearly phoned the police! Where the hell are you?"

Seb stares out into space, not reacting at all to my mum's words which I'm sure he can hear even though she's not on loudspeaker.

"I'm with a friend, Mum." Now is not the time to come out to her. There's been enough emotional exhaustion already. "I'll be home soon, I promise."

"You'll come home right now! Send me the address, I'll pick you up."

"I can get home by myself."

"The address. Now."

"No."

"Elliot, don't you dare speak to me like th–"

I hang up. I was already bound to be yelled at when I got home, but now I've basically given Mum permission to execute me.

"You should go home," Seb mutters.

I cuddle up to him on the sofa again. "I don't want to leave you."

He shrugs. "I'll be okay. It's not like anything's gonna change." He looks over at the coffee table, where his mum's letter is half folded.

There's a creaking of floorboards above us. Seb's dad is up there. I wonder how he's feeling about all this. Is he in his ex-wife's bedroom? Is he mourning as strongly as Seb? He walked out on them all those years ago, but he must have loved them once, right? He must still be taking this hard.

"She didn't have to leave," Seb says.

"Hmm?"

"Mum. She didn't have to leave me. If she'd never had that stupid Glimpse..."

I press my forehead to the back of Seb's head. I don't know what to say.

"If she hadn't had that Glimpse, she'd still be here."

"I know. But she wasn't well, Seb. The Glimpse isn't the only reason this happened."

"She could have stayed around longer." He spits the words. "The only reason she's dead is because she knew the date of her Glimpse."

There's a shift in the air as anger pokes through Seb's sadness.

"Dad left because of his Glimpse and now Mum's left because of hers."

"Not all Glimpses are bad."

He glares at me. "Yeah? Well, they've fucking ruined my life, haven't they?"

He hasn't shouted at me like this since I caught him shoplifting. I forgot how much it hurts. "I'm just saying they're not all bad."

Seb scoffs. "How would you know?"

"They brought us together."

Silence.

Seb's eyes widen. I can see the thoughts cycling through his head. All the questions bubbling to the surface.

I immediately regret what I said. I don't even know why I said it. It's not going to make him feel better or do anything to help. Even though it's true.

"What do you mean?" he asks. His face is sapped of colour.

"Nothing." I turn away and stand up. "You were right, I should go."

He stands too and forces his way in front of me, not letting me look away.

"Elliot," he says, not a hint of uncertainty in his voice. "Explain to me now what the hell you mean."

This is it. This is why moving past my Glimpse was so terrifying. The unknown. There's no way of telling how he'll react to what I'm about to tell him. It's hard to believe it could be anything good.

It's time to tell Seb the truth.

"After prom, I felt awful," I say. "I'd started to question my sexuality, and that scared me. So, to clear things up, I had a Glimpse."

He's already piecing things together. I can hear the mechanics of his brain. At this point, it's not hard to figure out.

"And in that Glimpse," I continue, "I saw you. And me. Together. In the tent."

Seb steps back and his face changes. The anger he feels towards the Glimpses takes over, and I know it's now directed at me. He looks at me like I'm a stranger.

"That's why you started speaking to me," he says. It's not a question. "That's why you asked me out. All of this...you and me...you just used me because of your Glimpse."

"No, Seb, it's not like that, I swear. I–"

"It is like that, though. It's exactly like that. The whole time we were going on dates, you knew exactly what was going to happen. And you didn't tell me."

"I thought about it, but..." I trail off. Because I can't explain it. Because nothing I say is going to fix this betrayal. The way he's looking at me right now... I brought that on myself.

"Get out."

"Seb, wait, pl–"

"Get out of my house."

"If I could just–"

"GET OUT!"

He shoves me, but it feels like a blade to the heart.

"I NEVER WANT TO SEE YOU AGAIN!"

I can hear Seb's dad heading down the stairs, alerted by the noise, but I don't see him before I get to the front door.

I stumble outside and steal one last look at Seb before he slams the door in my face.

MEANWHILE

Agent Sigma

It all feels far more real as I help carry the bombs off the truck. My arms ache from the strain as I haul a crate towards the building. A woman with dark hair cut into a bob is holding the other side. Agent Kappa, I think she's called. It may be July, but the night air is chilly, and my muscles feel like they're about to seize up. We cross the threshold into the warehouse and set down the crate beside the others. Kappa heads out, but I pause for a moment, staring at the wooden boxes.

I've always known the grand plan involves violence. I've always known it'll lead to deaths, and I've been justifying them as a necessary sacrifice. But those deaths have been an abstract idea until now. Soon enough, these bombs in front of me will be moved and set in place. Ready for the moment where they'll end God knows how many lives. If I'm a part of that, am I really that different from the person who murdered my family?

"Sigma?" comes a voice from behind me. I turn to see The Instructor in the doorway, long coat waving in the cool breeze. "Come."

I follow as he walks towards the truck. He pauses, watching the other agents lifting the crates. I notice a crooked smile spread across his face.

"You had something to show me, correct?"

"Yes," I say, pulling the burner phone from my pocket, opening the photos. I pass it over to him and he flicks through the images, smile unmoving. The pictures show the central Glimpse machine in the lower levels of the Millfield GlimpseTech building. It looks like any other, but we both know it's so much more.

"And the Glimpse schedule?" he asks.

"A large number have been booked for the last day, just as you suspected." I pull my coat tighter around myself. Usually, I can't avoid looking at least a little smug when I tell The Instructor of my findings, but right now my mind is still on the deaths we will cause.

"Perfect," he says. "That's when we'll make our attack. The system will be at its most volatile and the increased number of protestors will provide better cover." He looks right at me with those captivating eyes. "Thank you again for finding us a way in."

It didn't take long for me to find the alternative entrance to the GlimpseTech building. It's a back door, hidden away from the view of pedestrians, used for maintenance staff and deliveries. We could have found it without someone on the inside, of course, but not the code to unlock it. I should feel pride at The Instructor's praise, but I don't.

"And what about the...what did you call them? The blinder-guns?"

The Instructor chuckles, amused by the name he gave the devices. "I'll show you." He heads along the wall to another entrance. As I follow, Agent Kappa glares daggers at me, no doubt annoyed she now has to move the crates without me. Or perhaps she's jealous of how close I appear to be with The Instructor. He has placed a lot of trust in me recently; I wonder how he'd feel if he knew the doubt currently swirling in my mind.

The meeting room is empty, save for the mismatched furniture. All the agents are busy unloading bombs or out on their assigned missions. The Instructor takes his usual seat, opening his laptop while I sit on one of the tattered sofas.

"It's taking longer than I'd hoped," he says, "but they should be ready for the Last Day." He turns the screen around to show me the blueprint of a blinder-gun. The components are labelled, but there are far too many for me to make sense of it. Outwardly, it'll look like any other gun, but it isn't a weapon. It's a tool, specifically designed to disrupt and destroy the Glimpse technology. The bombs will take down the building, but it's the blinder-guns that will do the real damage.

An email notification flashes up on the laptop screen, accompanied by a ping that echoes round the room. The Instructor spins the laptop back round to face him, but not before I've had a chance to read the subject heading: **Maria McBride Encrypted Files.**

He stares at the screen, reading the email, then looks at me. His face is neutral, so I have no idea how he feels about me having seen something I probably shouldn't. Usually, I'd move on, saying nothing and assuming if I've not been told something then it isn't worth knowing. But the bombs have ignited a spark of concern in my mind. I'm no longer certain that what we're doing here is right. I have to ask–

"What was that about?" I'm surprised by how confident I sound.

At first, The Instructor doesn't react, but then his crooked smile returns. "I was going to tell you all soon anyway," he says. "But some very interesting information about Maria McBride has come to light. Information that we will be leaking on the Last Day, right as the attack gets underway."

My eyes narrow. I remember the first time I set foot in this warehouse, The Instructor said he had agents in parliament itself, investigating the prime minister. I hadn't given it much thought at the time, but it's odd that an operation so focused on taking down GlimpseTech would bother with investigations into Maria McBride.

"What information?" I'm getting into dangerous territory, asking so many questions, but I can't help myself.

The Instructor's smile widens and he adjusts his glasses. I'd have thought he'd be annoyed by my impertinence, but he seems to enjoy it. "Maria claimed throughout her campaign that, once elected, she would launch an investigation into GlimpseTech, garnering her the support of every sceptic and protestor." He makes a few clicks on the laptop. "Meanwhile, she rode the high of her assured victory, thanks to the many GlimpseNet posts uploaded months before the election. It was clearly a strategy on her part, but according to some delightfully revealing emails, it would appear her scheming has been more elaborate than any of us could have imagined."

He rotates the laptop screen to face me once again, revealing an email between Maria and none other than the CEO of GlimpseTech himself, Gabriel Thompson. He stands up and passes the laptop to me. I'm surprised he's so willing to let me see what's on the screen, but I take it from him and start scrolling through an email chain that seems never ending.

"GlimpseTech's reputation has been souring for years," The Instructor says, casting a shadow over me from his high position, "just as long as Maria has been gunning for an election win. So, they teamed up."

I shake my head in disbelief while the incriminating emails shine into my eyes, almost blinding me.

"Maria offered Gabriel a promise," he continues, "she'd tell the public she'd investigate his company, only to reveal GlimpseTech's innocence, fixing their reputation once and for all." He moves forward and slams the laptop shut, still leaning over me but physically far closer to me than he's ever been before. Behind his glasses, his eyes are wide with excitement. "In exchange, Gabriel would orchestrate a series of fake posts on GlimpseNet, declaring Maria's win at the polls."

I can feel his breath on me in rapid, short bursts, fuelled by the adrenalin of dropping such a bombshell. It courses through me too, though not in the form of excitement. No, all this does is make me angry. I knew GlimpseTech were evil, but this is far worse than I suspected. The whole country has been tricked by their scheming. It's a disgusting abuse of power and it can't continue.

"But what if people didn't vote for her?" I ask through gritted teeth.

He steps back, taking the laptop with him. "They assumed people would vote for her simply because they wouldn't expect any other result. Or they'd stay home, knowing their vote wouldn't count. And it worked."

Well, it almost worked. Sure, Maria won the election, but the public's reaction to her declaration of GlimpseTech's innocence was laughable. Not only that, but the protests have continued to grow in size. And here I am, almost doubting my part in our goal to put a stop to all this corruption. I can't doubt myself anymore. GlimpseTech's empire is at a tipping point, and I will enjoy my part in bringing it down. No matter the cost.

There's a clatter from outside and my eyes, along with The Instructor's, snap in its direction. We rush out to find Agent Kappa frozen in front of a shattered crate, shining silver edges of the bombs just visible beneath fragments of wood. The other agents watch from the truck, all a good distance away from her as though worried they're in danger of the bombs going off.

Kappa looks at The Instructor, hands shaking slightly with shock or perhaps fear for how he might react.

"Is this your doing?" he says, nodding at the shattered crate. His voice is calm, but there's a sharp edge to it that isn't usually there.

She gives a timid nod.

"You stupid girl!" he shouts–something I've never heard him do before. He's usually so put together, but as he shouts it's like he's losing himself. "Do you have any idea what you could have done?"

"I'm sorry, sir," she says, voice shaking, eyes to the floor.

"Clean it up." He looks to the other agents, then back to her. "*Carefully.*" He turns around and walks back into the building, coat billowing behind him.

I move to assist Kappa. The bombs are safe to pick up, and I'm sure their design is complex enough that simply dropping them wouldn't be enough to set them off, but it was still a reckless error.

"This wouldn't have happened if you'd stayed to help me," she says, glaring at me with bitterness.

"I had important things to discuss with The Instructor."

"Yes, I noticed." Her words are petty, like those of a child. I don't know how she got into the inner circle with such immaturity.

Another agent –Epsilon– places a spare crate beside us and we start loading the bombs into it.

"Is it true what he said?" Kappa asks. She's no longer shaking. "The attack will be on the Last Day?" So, she was eavesdropping. Part of me wishes The Instructor had continued to shout at her.

"Yes."

"Isn't that a bit risky?" Her eyes meet mine. They're filled with doubt, much like I was feeling mere moments ago, before I learnt the full extent of GlimpseTech's power. "I mean, what if we strike too late?"

I roll my eyes. I may be one of the newer recruits, but even I know why we can trust The Instructor's plan with absolute certainty. It's the whole reason any of us follow him. The great secret he tells us when we join the inner circle.

Thanks to GlimpseNet, the public knows the latest time anyone has ever Glimpsed is seventeen minutes past three PM on the Last Day. That's the moment, so some theories go, that the world is bound to end. But the public are missing the whole story, because the true latest Glimpse has never been shared online. The true latest Glimpse belongs to The Instructor, which means he has the most foresight out of everyone on Earth.

Yes, his plan may involve violence, and yes it will take many innocent lives, but now I understand why. GlimpseTech is a plague that has infected the world and The Instructor is the only one bold enough to cleanse it.

I trust him with my life.

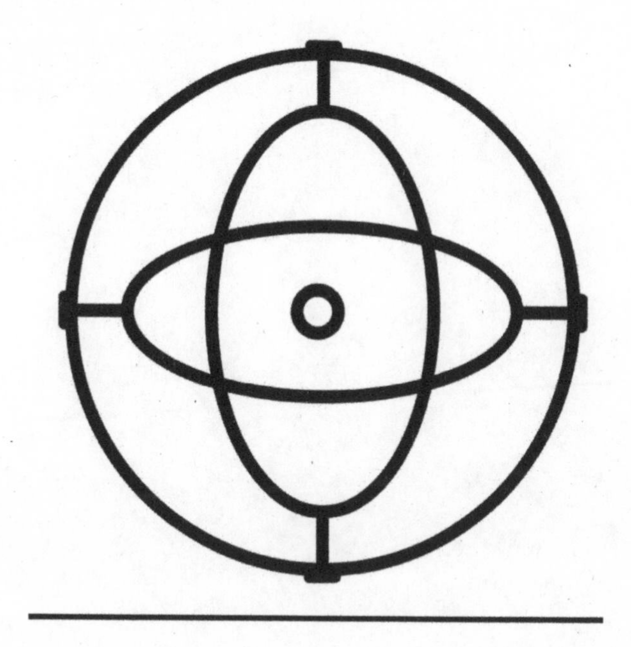

PART FOUR

GRIEVING

GlimpseNet Post #8531E6

Subject: Anonymous

Date Glimpsed: 16th July

Verification Status: Verified

I saw nothing. Just darkness. Silent, unmoving darkness. I know what it means, and I know there's no point in posting it on here. I just want to acknowledge it. To tell someone, even if that someone is a random person reading this on the internet. I haven't told my family yet. I don't know how to. I don't know if I ever will.

THIRTY-FOUR

Seb

The vodka doesn't taste as bad when I reach the end of the bottle. I like the way the glass shines in the sunlight. I stagger back, throwing the bottle, and laugh as shards of sunlight scatter through the air, some of them falling off the edge of the crags.

"Seb!" comes a voice from behind me.

I ignore it and lean back, closing my eyes and letting the sun beat down on my face.

"Seb!"

I start spinning, blindly twisting this way and that, making myself dizzy, feeling sick but still laughing. I'm getting closer to the edge.

But I just

don't

care.

"SEB!"

A pair of hands grab my shoulders and force me to the ground. I open my eyes and there's Aym, a blurry, spinning image of her staring down at me. She looks pissed off, which is even more funny.

"Sit up," she says, forcing me into an upright position and planting her ass on the ground in front of me.

"Oh, fuck off Aym, I'm having fun."

"You're drunk."

Another laugh. "And?"

She rolls her eyes and I copy her, which only makes her face sourer.

"I've been calling you for hours," she says.

"Cool."

"I was worried about you."

"Well, that's stupid."

"No, what's stupid is you out here drinking by yourself. You almost fell off the edge, for fuck's sake!"

I hold out my second bottle. "Fancy joining?"

She snatches it from me.

"Hey!"

"Where did you even get this from?"

"Stole it."

She shakes her head like a disappointed teacher. Or parent. Like a mother... Nope, not going down that road. I lie back on the ground a little too quickly, banging my head. The pain's not that bad, though. Probably thanks to the vodka.

"You can't keep doing this, Seb."

I've lost count of how many times I've gotten drunk over the last few days. I've lost count of the days too, to be honest. Days without Mum aren't ones I want to count.

I look at Aym and feel the frustration radiating from her, but instead of telling me how annoyed she is, she hugs me. The alcohol's been acting like a dimmer switch for my emotions, but at Aym's touch I feel the dial switch direction.

I'm sobbing into her shoulder, staining her denim jacket with tears. Aym doesn't say anything, just rests a hand gently on the back of my head and lets me cry harder than I ever have in front of her. Even harder than yesterday. And the day before. And the day before. I'm crying so hard I can't even keep my body still. I keep jerking forward, heaving as if I'm going to be sick, forcing Aym to move with me.

"I'm sorry," I say with a thick voice. "I'm so fucking sorry."

She strokes my hair the same way Mum did when I was a little kid. It just makes me cry more.

Aym passes me a mug of coffee and sits next to me on the sofa. I take a sip and it feels like it washes away the traces of vodka. I can think clearer. But that just means regret starts hitting me hard.

We're in Aym's living room, a cosy space with the softest sofas known to man. It's a lot tidier than my living room has ever been, but there are currently unfinished paintings leaning against one of the walls. They're in Aym's usual style: abstract, with raised areas that you want to run your fingers across.

I've always been good at keeping up with Aym's art–she's always posting updates to her Instagram–but I've never seen either of these paintings before.

"How long have you been working on those?" I ask.

"Started them on the retreat."

Long enough that she'll have posted about them, which means I just haven't noticed. Some friend I've been.

"They're great," I say.

"Thanks."

"What are they called?"

Aym always gives titles to her paintings, even if she hates them. She seems weirdly hesitant to answer when I ask, though.

She points at the one on the right: swirling strands of pastel pink, white, and blue. "That one is 'Unmasked.'" Then she points at the other: rough, ridged blackness, with a single bright spot in the very centre. "And that one's called 'Hope.'"

Her eyes dart away from mine when I look back at her, and I think I can guess why. 'Hope' is undoubtedly a painting about struggling, and after what happened to Mum, I can't help but think that's where Aym drew some inspiration. If only Mum's bright spot had kept her going.

I take another sip of coffee, if only to distract from my thoughts with its scalding heat.

"How's your dad?" Aym asks.

"Fine," I say, even though he probably isn't. The truth is, even though Dad's been living with me since Mum died, I've barely spoken to him. He offered to take me to his house to stay until we 'sort something out' but I told him no and have been mostly ignoring him since. "He wants me to help him plan the funeral."

"And are you going to?"

I shake my head. "I don't see what needs planning. It's not like I'm gonna make a speech or anything. I don't care what happens."

Aym doesn't respond. She drinks her coffee and we stare at the paintings.

"Seb?" Aym asks after the silence stretches just a little too long.

"Yeah?"

"Can I ask...what happened with Elliot?"

I knew this question would come up at some point. Since Mum's death, I haven't spoken Elliot's name once. I haven't seen him. I've certainly thought about him, but every time I do, I just feel angry. And sad. And confused. So, the last Aym heard we were very happily packing up a tent. If things had turned out differently, I'd probably have spent a whole night gushing about him to Aym. It's hard to imagine that now.

"I don't want to talk about it."

"Okay."

"We're over. That's all there is to it."

Aym nods.

There've been moments over the past few days where I've considered texting Elliot. Brief seconds of stupid thoughts, usually while drunk or after a heavy session of crying. Sometimes in those moments I remember how happy

I felt with him–an emotion that feels so distant now I can't quite fathom that it was barely a week ago. It's like a snapshot of a completely different life. A world without problems. A world where my mum was alive, and I had a boyfriend who I was starting to fall in–

No.

I wasn't falling in love. I was being lied to. Manipulated. Used. All thanks to the same technology that killed my mum.

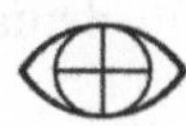

A couple of days ago I was walking through town, no destination in mind; I just needed to walk somewhere. I ended up heading down the street where GlimpseTech is. I didn't realise until I saw the glass shards pointing up at the sky. I would have realised I was getting near it sooner if I'd been listening, because there was a chanting hoard of protesters on the march.

Their chants and signs echoed what I'd been feeling about GlimpseTech. What I'm still feeling now and probably always will. That they should be closed down. That the Glimpses ruin lives. The protesters would eat up my story and use it as fuel for their fire. More ammunition to fire with on their picket signs. It could even become a discussion point on one of those debate shows on TV.

Despite all that, though, I had no desire to join them. Because here's the thing, if what people say about GlimpseTech causing the end of the world is true, then maybe I don't want GlimpseTech taken down. Maybe I want the Last Day to be exactly what it says on the tin. The Last Day anyone will ever live. Because I don't know how I'm supposed to keep going in a world that takes away everything I care about.

THIRTY-FIVE

Elliot

Mum's calling me from downstairs.

"Tea's ready," she says in the half-demanding, half-wary tone she's been taking with me for the last week.

When I first got back from Seb's that awful night, she launched straight into a screaming rage, telling me I should be ashamed of myself, that I'd made her, Dad, and Simon worried sick. But then I burst into tears. I thought I could hold it in at first, since I'd been crying the whole way home and thought I'd worn myself out. But no. The tears came in an uncontrollable stream. And Mum's screaming stopped as quickly as it had begun.

I haven't told her what happened, despite the number of times she's asked. In fact, I've barely spoken to her at all. Or anyone else, for that matter. I've mostly stayed in my room, keeping to myself, sometimes crying, sometimes just staring at the ceiling and feeling nothing at all, only going downstairs to eat and to prove to my family I'm still alive.

There's so much darkness swirling around me, keeping me away from everyone else. The relationship I had with Seb, which brought me more happiness than anything in my life, is over. But that's not the worst of it. What hurts the most is knowing what Seb is going through, and not being able to do anything about it. He's all alone without his mum, and all I did was make things worse.

Callum's tried calling a few times. I answered a couple of them, but I couldn't bring myself to tell him everything out loud. It hurt too much. So, I texted him instead, giving him as much detail as I could without it making me want to scream until my lungs collapse. He responded just how you'd expect: reams of sympathy, telling me he'll always be there for me.

But none of it helped.

I drag myself downstairs now, wading through the feelings that make it so hard to move these days. Mum, Dad, and Simon are all at the table, already digging into their food. They look up at me when they hear me come in, give their usual concerned smiles, then return to their food.

Mum's been extra generous with my serving today, as she has been for the whole week. It's like she's worried I'm starving myself, which I suppose isn't entirely untrue. While everyone's at work during the daytime, I tend to let myself go hungry.

I take my seat next to Simon, fully aware that everyone is still looking at me, even if they're doing it more discreetly. I start eating, which gets rid of some of the attention.

"This is lovely, Mum," Simon says.

"Thanks," she says. "Thought I'd try making something different. Do you like it, Elliot?"

I nod, which is as much of a contribution as I've given recently.

She turns back to Simon, "Do you know who I bumped into when I was picking up ingredients earlier?"

"Go on," Simon says.

"Tracy Benson! And Emily was with her. You remember Emily, don't you?"

"Of course, I remember Emily."

"You two used to be inseparable." Mum smiles in the way she always used to whenever Simon brought Alyssa over. "That little romance you had going on in high school was the cutest thing."

Simon rolls his eyes.

I remember Emily too. She was Simon's first girlfriend. He used to spend every minute with her until it ended after just a month. I feel a sharp pain in my chest at the thought that Simon doesn't even talk about that relationship anymore; is that what's going to happen with me and Seb? Am I going to roll my eyes at the sound of his name?

"She's doing well," Mum says. "In fact, she's engaged!"

"Jesus." Simon almost chokes on his food. "She's a bit young for that."

Mum shrugs. "Young love is a powerful thing."

It's only for a fraction of a second, but Mum glances at me when she says, "love." She's been doing things like that a lot this past week. Whenever there's a mention of girlfriends or love or whatever, she flashes her eyes at me. I know why. She thinks she knows the reason I'm so sad. She thinks it's because I broke up with my fake girlfriend. So close to the truth, yet so far.

Maybe that should change.

"Mum," I say, looking up from my food. "Dad, Simon..."

They all stare at me. Waiting.

I haven't planned how to do this. I don't know what I'm supposed to say. And I'm still scared of how they'll react. But I ruined everything good in my life last week because of a lie. Because I wasn't honest with someone I cared about. And if there's even the slightest bit of hope that I might salvage what I've lost, I think I have to start by telling this simple truth.

"I'm bisexual."

The silence seems to last forever. At first it feels like I'm being crushed beneath it, but the more I say, the lighter I start to feel.

"I don't have a girlfriend. I never did. That was a lie."

Their faces are hard to read. Blank. Taking it all in.

"I had a boyfriend...or at least a boy I was seeing...but that's over now."

Mum clears her throat. "Is that why you've been so...?"

"Sad? Yeah." I don't include all the other stuff. It's Seb's life. His trauma. My family don't need to know about that.

"I see."

Silence again.

"What..." Dad starts, "what do you mean? Bisexual?"

"It means he's into guys and girls, Dad," Simon says. He turns to me, and I'm surprised by how much he seems to care. "Right?"

"That's one definition. I think I prefer 'same and other genders,' but yeah."

"Isn't that more like pansexual?"

Again, I'm taken aback by Simon. Since when does he know this much about queer identities? I barely know all the definitions myself.

"I, er, maybe? I'm not sure..."

"Where has this all come from?" Dad says, eyebrows knitting together like this is a puzzle he's struggling to solve.

"He was obviously born like this," Simon says.

"Oh," Mum says, "I'm not sure that's how it works, darling. And are you sure you're not just gay, Elliot?"

"No, I'm–"

She doesn't give me a chance to finish. "You know I'd really like for you to be able to have children. I'm not sure this is the best way to–"

"Jesus Christ, Mum!" Simon cuts in. "You work in a school, and you spew this bullshit?"

"Don't you dare talk to your mother like that!" Dad says. "Besides, I think he's just confused, I didn't raise my boys to be–"

"SHUT UP!" I shout. The words tear through my throat, propelled by all the anger and pain I've felt since Seb told me to leave. "All of you, just shut up!"

Silence again, but now Mum and Dad look appalled.

"Look," I say, "whatever you think about all this, you can't change it."

No one responds, but I'm done. I'm not going to argue anymore. I've said my piece. I've exposed my biggest secret to them. They can judge me however they want, at least I don't have to hide anymore. I get up, leaving my half-eaten food where it is, and head to my room.

I can't make out what they're saying, but I can hear my family's muffled voices coming up through the floor beneath my bed. They go on for ages, sometimes getting loud with anger, and at one point I think I can hear Mum crying. I feel strangely calm. After everything that happened with Seb, an imperfect reaction to me coming out doesn't feel like that big of a problem. It's painful, sure, but it's hardly the most painful thing going on right now.

Eventually, everyone downstairs goes quiet, and I hear footsteps come up the stairs. There's a knock at my door.

"Come in," I call.

Simon pokes his head in. "Hey."

I sit up in bed as he walks in and closes the door behind him.

"How're you doing?" he asks.

I shrug. "I've not been thrown out, so I guess I'm fine."

Simon laughs quietly and sits down beside me on the bed. "They'll understand eventually."

"Maybe."

"Nah, they will. Especially Mum. She's already regretting what she said, trust me."

"At least I've guaranteed you your 'favourite child' title forever."

Even sat down, Simon's taller than me, and he's never felt more like a big brother than he does now, looking down at me with concern. He frowns and looks away in thought.

"I failed half of my exams this year," he says, and it's so matter of fact that it takes me a second to register.

"Wait...what?"

He smirks. "Yeah. Failed half my exams, and I broke up with Alyssa too. Well, she broke up with me."

I stare, open-mouthed.

"And to be honest, I've been debating whether I want to finish this degree. I mean, don't get me wrong I'm loving this GlimpseTech internship, and I know I could probably get a job in something similar with my degree, but I don't know if I'm even capable of passing final year."

I don't know what to say. Simon's had his sights set on university for as long as I can remember, and after his Glimpse showed him at Oxford...that was it. His destiny was confirmed. And now he's changed his mind? It doesn't make sense.

I shake my head. "Why are you telling me all this?"

"Because I'm not the golden child Mum and Dad think I am, and I hate that you think I'm the favourite."

"But–"

"And I'm not saying that me failing at uni is in any way the same as you coming out–I mean, your sexuality isn't something you can control or something to be ashamed of–but I'm not living up to Mum and Dad's expectations either, so don't go thinking they love you any less. They're our parents, they're not us. They don't get to decide how we live our lives."

Every feeling of jealousy I've ever had towards Simon suddenly seems pointless. For the first time since we were young kids, I find myself reaching out and hugging him.

"Now," he says when he lets me go. "Tell me about this boyfriend you had."

Seb

There's an uncomfortably clean feel to the funeral director's building. Clinical. It reminds me of a hospital, which seems odd since one is a place of healing and one is a place of death. Not that the hospital did much to heal Mum. If they had, she'd still be here.

I'm sitting with Dad, waiting to be called through for a talk about funeral arrangements. The chairs are lined with smooth, red vinyl. I feel like I'm slipping off it, ready to be devoured by the floor below. On the wall is a noticeboard, covered in various flyers. One reads **'Glimpsed your own death? Get ahead of the game and plan your own funeral today!'** I wonder how often people take up that suggestion.

"Mr Glass?" says a kind-faced, middle-aged woman from a door on the opposite wall.

Dad and I look up.

"Come on through."

We follow her into a room that's clearly been made to feel calm and comfortable, a way of distracting people from their grief. It's small, probably to give it a cosy vibe, with an old wooden desk with a computer, various pamphlets, and a box of tissues on it. The walls are covered in testimonies from people who've used this director before.

'Haysmith and Co made my father's passing as stress free as possible.'

'We'd known our son didn't have long left ever since his Glimpse. Haysmith and Co helped us prepare from very early on.'

I wonder if Mum ever considered getting in touch with this place after her own Glimpse. Did she accept the fact of her death immediately, or did she go through a period of denial? I guess finding out you're going to die doesn't exactly put you in the right headspace for organising your own funeral.

Dad and I sit across from the woman and she starts talking through the arrangements Dad has already sorted with her. I barely listen. It's just noise. I don't care what happens at the funeral; it's not like Mum will be able to see it. Funerals aren't for the dead, they're for the living, and I couldn't give a shit what words are said, what songs are played, or whether she's buried or cremated. It makes no difference.

The only reason I joined Dad today is that Aym convinced me I should. She thinks I'll regret it if I don't get involved. I disagree, but she made the point that my dad is probably hurting a lot too, and he'd probably feel better if I helped him however I can. Not that I think he deserves to feel better. Sure, he might be hurting, but he left us. I stayed with mum while he made a new life for himself. This is my pain to feel, not his. But if I said that to Aym, I'd sound cruel, wouldn't I? So here I am, helping by being present, but still not listening.

The funeral is in three days. And the Last Day is in four. It's strange to think about, I mean, if the world is going to end in four days, then most people seem pretty calm about it. Not that I've been paying much attention to the world around me recently. I guess it's only one small theory among many that the apocalypse is approaching, and you'd think there'd have been more signs by now if that were true. The so-called experts were saying there's nothing to worry about when I last checked. Still, the closer it gets, the more I find myself wondering what's going to happen.

I've even wondered who I'd spend my final moments with if it is the end. Aym, I guess. Dad has his other family, and Aym doesn't exactly get on with hers, so it seems right that we'd face the apocalypse together. And yet, I keep thinking about Elliot. If things last week had gone differently, if Mum hadn't died and I'd never found out why Elliot started talking to me in the first place, I imagine we'd have spent the Last Day with each other.

But last week didn't go differently. I can't just forget the way he used me because his Glimpse told him to. Even if, in the moments when I'm saddest, my mind keeps flashing back to the time I spent with Elliot. To that perfect night in the tent.

THIRTY-SEVEN

Elliot

Her name is printed in black and white. Jane Glass. Seb's Mum. And below it, the time, date, and place of her funeral. I've been checking the obituaries every day since last week, scanning through Dad's newspapers once he's gone to work.

It's in two days, the day before the Last Day, at Millfield Crematorium. I don't know if I should go. I never knew her, and Seb doesn't want to see me, but I can't bear to think of him facing the funeral alone. He'll have his dad and Aym, I suppose. Maybe that will be enough. If we were still together, I know I'd be there with him, holding his hand, absorbing his pain. Doing everything I could to make him feel better.

"I'm late!" Simon shouts as he bursts into the room, as though announcing it will make it any less true.

I look up from the newspaper, watching as Simon grabs his bag from the floor and hurriedly tucks in his shirt. He races past me but pauses at the door.

"You okay?" he asks.

I hold out the paper and despite the fact he's running late, Simon walks over and takes a look.

"Jane Glass... Seb's Mum?"

I nod. I told Simon everything–well, almost everything–when he was with me in my bedroom two nights ago. The only part I left out was Dan and what Jane did for him. It felt wrong to tell him such a private part of someone else's life.

"You gonna go?"

"I don't know. Do you think I should?"

"I think it's up to you. Whatever you choose, I'm sure Seb would understand." He checks his watch. "Sorry, but I really need to go."

"It's fine."

"Sorry." He darts out of the house, leaving it empty except for me. Which means I'm free to do the same walk as yesterday without anyone knowing.

I hadn't planned to end up here yesterday. I'd been walking to clear my head, just absent-mindedly strolling along random streets, when I found myself somewhere familiar. It was the trees that did it. The tall, sturdy oak tree which I last saw when helping a beaten Seb get back on his feet. The tree just outside Dan's house.

I couldn't help myself then. I had to walk over to it. I had to peer down the driveway at the huge house where Dan lives. The houses on George Street are so spread out that it's easy to find areas where no one can see you from their windows. I stood in the shade of the tree, just behind Dan's garden wall and watched. And waited.

And there he was. A grim, unwashed man who you'd never think could afford a house like this, opened the front door, got in his car on the driveway, and drove off. I made sure to crouch out of sight when his car passed, then got up and stared at the house once again, an idea starting to form.

So here I am again today, peeking over the garden wall at exactly the same time I did yesterday. And there Dan is, leaving his house and getting in the car at the same time. A pattern. Only a two-day pattern so far, but a pattern, nonetheless. And that might be the key to my idea.

This time, I don't stay hidden once he's driven away. Instead, I head down the driveway and take a look at the house, inspecting it from as many angles as I can. There are no cameras, thank God, and as far as I can see there's no burglar alarm. The windows are dirty, but when I get close enough, I can see inside.

Dan's living room is a mess. Random trash is scattered all over the floor, mingling with expensive items like a leather sofa and a huge TV. I dread to think how much damage Dan's caused to such a nice house. I wouldn't be surprised if rats are living under all the junk. One thing grabs my attention more than anything else, though. There, in the corner of the living room, right below another window, is Seb's guitar. It's hard to see clearly from where I am, but I recognise it instantly.

My mind is thrown back to the last time I heard that guitar, as Seb played it for the small crowd in the park. I can hear his raspy singing voice coat every inch of my brain, igniting every feeling I have towards him. Feelings that haven't gone away, and I can't imagine ever will.

I make my way around the house, to the window right above the guitar. It's as grimy as the rest, but as I grasp my hands against the sides, I find it moves ever so slightly. It isn't locked. My heart races, but I take a breath to calm down. If I'm not careful, I'll mess everything up.

I wiggle the edge of the window a little more, until it finally gives way and opens outwards. I can see the top of the guitar. If I wanted, I could just take it right now. But then what would happen? Dan would come home and find it gone. He'd report a theft or go after Seb. I can't risk that. Instead, I take the small window key that's sitting on the windowsill. It's still a risk, but it's a lot less noticeable than a missing guitar, and I need the window to stay unlocked tomorrow.

I pocket the key, close the window, and leave.

I get home before anyone else to make sure no one asks where I've been. Beneath all the sadness that's been consuming me, I'm angrier than ever before. Angry that I'm not with Seb. Angry at what happened to his mum. Angry he was beaten up by a man who got away with it. A man who has done so much harm in Seb's life. Where else can I direct my anger if not at him?

I remember the night Seb first told me about Dan. We ate pizza and watched TV, and when it ended, I asked Seb on a date. It's the night everything really began between us. Sure, we'd spoken before that, and I'd had my Glimpse, but that night was the moment a spark ignited. Despite how sad he was about his mum and the loss of his guitar, he felt enough of a connection to agree to a date with me.

Then Dan brought it all crumbling down, which is why I need to do something to get back at him. I'm going to get Seb's guitar back...and I'm going to get Dan sent to prison. Everything just needs to go according to plan, even if I don't have a Glimpse to guarantee it.

As the sun sets, a text comes through from Callum.

Results day afterparty, you in?

I almost laugh as I read it. Results day... I'd completely forgotten about it. After the whirlwind of the last few weeks, the whole idea of exams and grades completely slipped my mind. It's only now, thanks to this text, that I realise how bad the timing of results day is.

It's the same day as Seb's mum's funeral, I text back.

My phone immediately lights up with an incoming video call from Callum. It's far from the first time he's tried that in the last few days, but I guess I can't ignore him forever.

"I'm sorry, man," Callum says when his face fills the screen. "I had no idea."

"It's fine. Not your fault."

"Are you planning on going? To the funeral, I mean."

"Maybe. Probably. I don't know." I run a hand through my hair. "I'll be able to come get results in the morning though."

It feels wrong to say, as if I'm agreeing to two contradictory things. A day of celebration and a day of mourning. It feels so long ago that I did my exams, even though it's only been a few weeks. But that was before I ever spoke to Seb. Results day is a reminder of my life before him. A life where I didn't truly know myself.

"You sure?" Callum says. "You can just get them online if you're not feeling up to going into school."

"Yeah, I'll be fine."

Callum's got his concerned face on, wide eyes and scrunched up mouth. "Have you heard from Seb at all?"

Just the notion causes my breath to catch.

"No," I say. "And he's blocked me."

Callum sighs. "That sucks. But he's going through a lot right now, so maybe he'll come round when the worst is over."

"Maybe."

But Callum didn't see how angry Seb was when he told me to leave. He didn't see all the affection drain from Seb's face. There's every chance he'll never forgive me. Even if tomorrow goes right. Speaking of which–

"Hey, Callum, could you do me a favour?"

THIRTY-EIGHT

Seb

Aym lies beside me on top of the bedcovers. It's the second night in a row she's stayed over, and it's definitely helped. I still cried myself to sleep last night, but there were fewer tears than usual. She does what my dad can't. She makes me feel less alone.

"I miss him," I say, mind on Elliot, just as it is whenever I'm not thinking about Mum.

Aym rolls over, hands beneath her cheek, facing me. "Have you spoken to him, since everything?"

I shake my head.

"Have you forgiven him?"

A deep sigh escapes me. I've asked myself the same question so many times. "I don't know if I can."

I still don't know exactly what Aym thinks about Elliot's lie. When I told her, she did her usual thing of listening without judgement, letting me rant.

"It's just..." I continue, "I feel like everything bad in my life has been caused by the Glimpses, so the fact that I would never have even spoken to Elliot if it hadn't been for his Glimpse..." I trail off. My anger is hard to put into words, like I don't even know what I'm mad about.

"I get it, but I'm not sure if you can really blame the Glimpses."

The urge to argue rises in me. Like an instinct. But this is Aym, and she always talks sense. I'm willing to listen.

"Take your dad, right? If he's shitty enough to leave you and your mum because of a vision he saw, then he can't have been that great a guy to begin with."

Some people would call that an insensitive thing to say, especially in the current circumstances, but Aym makes it work. She has a point.

"And... your mum... she wasn't well, Seb. You know that. Her Glimpse didn't help, that's for sure, but it's more complicated than one vision sending her over the edge."

I know she's right. Whether I'm ready to accept that is another question.

"And Elliot..."

My heart races at the sound of his name.

"He wasn't even out before he met you, right?"

I nod.

"So, before he had his Glimpse, he might not have even thought about his sexuality, and then he saw himself being intimate with a boy. That's bound to mess with someone's head. He should've told you, sure, but at the end of the day I think it was just a stupid, stupid mistake."

"But–"

"I saw how happy he made you, Seb. I hadn't seen that in a long time."

I can't deny that. What she saw was what I felt. My moments with Elliot were the happiest I'd ever felt. They still hold that title, too, even if it hurts to think about them.

"And," Aym continues, "well...you know what my Glimpse did for me. They aren't all bad. I wouldn't be who I am today without them."

I sigh. "So, what do I do now?"

"You get through tonight. You get through tomorrow. You get through the funeral. And then, when you're ready, you decide what to do about Elliot."

"Okay."

She rubs my arm and smiles.

"What would I do without you?" I ask.

"You'd be a complete mess."

For the first time in days, I laugh.

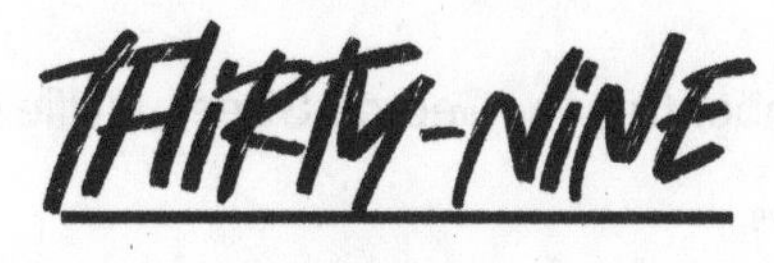

Elliot

I take a deep breath as I stand at Dan's garden wall. It's the last barrier before I do what I've planned. The last place I'm safe. I'm doing everything I can to stop my body shaking with nerves. In my hands, the GlimpseNet webpage lights up my phone screen. I'm logged into my account and my thumb is hovering over the 'post' button beneath my Glimpse entry. My fake Glimpse entry.

It's partially thanks to Simon that I'm here. I'd never have had this idea were it not for what he said at the family dinner last week: 'If a person makes a post about a serious crime, that gets flagged with the police straight away before anyone verifies it. They can even use it as a warrant to arrest someone, without having seen the video of the Glimpse.'

That's the key to my plan. I never made a post about my actual Glimpse, so the one entry to GlimpseNet that I'm entitled to is still available. My timing needs to be perfect, though. If I'm to post a fake Glimpse, it will be removed from the system as soon as someone attempts to verify it. The police will see the post immediately, but if I post it too early then they'll get here too quickly.

I reread my fake entry.

GlimpseNet Post #7128X0

Subject: Elliot Dove

Date Glimpsed: 26th July

Verification Status: Unverified

I saw myself at Number Seven, George Street, Millfield, being assaulted by the man who lives there.

I've debated adding more detail, but everything I add makes things more complicated. If I give Dan's name, that'll call into question how and why I know him. If I'm more specific about the assault, that'll determine what has to happen to me. This fake post is enough to get him arrested on suspicion, but I need there to be a reason to keep Dan in custody. And that can only mean one thing.

I'm going to need to be assaulted by Dan.

It's a huge risk–I'm well aware of that–and posting a fake Glimpse that leads to someone's arrest could get me in all kinds of trouble. But I have to do something. If Dan can't be arrested for ruining Seb's life, he deserves to be arrested for something else.

Dan's door opens at the same time it's done for the last two days. He locks the door, gets into his car, and drives away.

I pocket my phone, entry still not posted, and run to his house. I head round the back, to the window above the guitar. I left the key at home, figuring if anything goes wrong it's probably best not to be found with it on my person. Besides, I don't need it. I only took it to make sure the window would stay unlocked. Which it has, thank God.

While my heart races, I swing the window open with ease, and once again there's the top of the guitar within reaching distance. I take a deep breath, grasp the guitar's neck, and carefully lift it up and out of the window.

I take a moment to look at it: the way the sun bounces off the rosewood, the shining strings Seb played so beautifully. I hear the music in my head. It calls to me, begging to sweep me away. I could let it if it weren't for the fact I don't have much time.

I swing the guitar over my shoulder, press the window closed again, and run back around the house and up the drive. It won't be long before Dan gets back, and I need to make sure I intercept him before he goes inside, and I also need to get the guitar somewhere safe. In less than a minute, I'm turning onto another street, and then another, and another, until I finally see Callum waiting exactly where I asked him to.

"Hey," he says, smile disappearing as he takes in my breathless face.

"Hey." I pass him the guitar.

"This is what you want me to take home?" His eyebrows knit together in confusion. "Why?"

"Like I told you yesterday, it's complicated. I'll explain everything later, I just need you to keep it safe for me."

"But–"

"It's Seb's."

"Oh." He looks at the guitar again. "But why do you have it?"

I look back towards the house. I'm running out of time. "*Please*, Callum. Just trust me. Okay?"

He shakes his head, but says, "Okay."

"Thank you."

And just like that I'm running back to Dan's.

My thumb is hovering over the 'post' button again. I'm standing on Dan's doorstep, waiting, tapping my foot. He came home at around the same time yesterday and the day before, so if I'm right, then I only have a few minutes. Which means I need to nail the timing of this post. If I'm too early, the police will arrive before Dan does anything. If I'm too late, I'll have been beaten to a pulp.

The time ticks forward one minute. I hit 'post.'

And then I wait.

And wait.

And wait.

Until there's a crunching of pebbles beneath the tyres of a car.

Until the engine switches off and the door opens.

Until I'm facing the man who attacked my boyfr-

The man who attacked Seb.

"Can I help you?" he asks, combing a hand through his thin, greasy hair. Being this close to him after everything he's done is terrifying. It breaks my heart to think of Seb, scared and intimidated by Dan in his own home. He suffered all of that and I just made things worse.

I keep my fists clenched to avoid shaking and clear my throat. "I'm looking for Dan."

"Oh? And why would that be?"

This is the part I haven't planned. I don't know what to say. I don't know what to do. I just need to provoke him somehow.

He steps closer to me. I can already smell the alcohol.

"I know Jane Glass," I say.

He laughs. "Popular woman, isn't she? You a friend of her son? He came snooping around here and that didn't do him much good."

I grit my teeth, picturing Seb's bruises. "Jane's dead."

He doesn't reply. Just stares at me. I can't read him.

"She killed herself."

Still nothing.

"Because of you."

Now he reacts. In the most disgusting way possible. With a smile, which turns into another laugh. "There I was thinking she was just ignoring my calls."

In the distance, I can hear the faint sounds of police sirens. Are they because of my post? Has it worked?

"If you don't mind," Dan says, "I'd like to get in my house."

Are they getting closer? I can't tell.

Dan steps forward.

"You ruined her life," I say. It bursts out of me, driven by my hatred of him and everything he's done. "And her son's. You took advantage of her when she was at her lowest. She attempted suicide and you swept back in while she was recovering."

Dan shrugs, which makes me feel sick. How can someone care so little? "She was messed up in the head. It was only a matter of time before she offed herself."

My eyes start to tear up, but it's not just from sadness. It's rage and guilt and sorrow. Hatred and vengeance. The knowledge that if it weren't for this disgusting excuse for a human, Seb would still be happy. His mother would still be alive.

It's more than even that. I'm angry at myself for not doing more, for not treating Seb with love and kindness from day one, for not being more honest with him or myself. We could have had so much more time together. We could have had forever. The floodgates are open, and nothing's being kept buried anymore.

I spit right in Dan's face and shout, "Fuck you!"

And that does it. Within seconds, I'm on the floor, right ear ringing from the blow he serves. And now there's a kick to my stomach. And his knees are on top of me. And is that a siren or just the ringing? And there's a fist to my face. A siren. Must be. Another punch. Two. Three. There are voices shouting in the background. Dan is being pulled off me. Hands grab me from every angle, but they're gentle. Their voices ask if I'm okay.

I'm in pain all over. But I'm alive. It worked.
I'm okay.
I'm okay.

Seb

"You know," Aym says as she readjusts my tie, "I thought when I started presenting femme, I wouldn't have to deal with ties anymore."

I laugh. It's weak, but it's there. I doubt I'll manage many more laughs today.

"Thanks, Aym," I say, taking a look at myself in the mirror. My bruises aren't all gone, but the worst are hidden by the long sleeves of my blazer. Aym helped pick off the school badge from the pocket yesterday. Dad offered to buy me a new suit, but I refused. I'm already being forced to live with him, I don't want to accept anything else he offers.

Aym is wearing a simple black dress and her braids tied up in a bun. She rests her hands on my shoulders and smiles at me in the mirror.

"Ready?" she asks.

I don't answer, because of course I'm not. But I take her hand anyway.

We head downstairs, where Dad waits beside the open door. A hearse and a large black car are parked just outside. I can't look directly at the hearse. Not when the coffin is right there. Instead, I keep my head low and walk straight to the second car, getting into the backseat along with Aym before Dad joins us.

Aym keeps her arm wrapped around mine for the entire journey. I stare out the side window, ignoring the hearse in front of us and focusing on anything and everything else. It's a bright summer's day, with a gentle breeze moving through the trees and smiling people walking around in T-shirts and shorts. A cheerful world unaffected by Mum's death. Well, at least cheerful in parts.

A few minutes into the drive, I hear the chants everyone has become too familiar with recently. The happy pedestrians give way to protestors holding up placards and we slow to a stop, blocked by a picket line.

"For fuck's sake," Dad mutters.

Aym grips my arm tighter, and I glance at her to let her know I'm fine. As I said before, funerals aren't for the dead. They're for the living. A delay isn't going to ruin anything for Mum.

The driver says something under his breath, then turns sharply and takes us down an alternate route. It's a lot busier here, what with people heading toward the protest. I can't avoid the look on their faces when they notice the hearse in front of us. Their smiles falter and they glance through the window at me, offering some weird fake sympathy.

I lean back and close my eyes.

The crematorium is nothing special, just a plain-looking building set back from the main road, with swathes of green grass on either side. We have to wait for the previous funeral to finish before we can go in. People arrive in dribs and drabs–some of them I recognise, relatives I haven't seen in years, others I don't know. Dad told me who he knew would be coming, but I wasn't listening. As far as I'm concerned, if I don't know them, they can't have meant that much to Mum.

A large crowd files out of the building, wearing dark clothes and sombre expressions. A few are crying. It's a lot more people than are here for Mum. The officiant steps out and greets me and Dad with a handshake and an "I'm so sorry for your loss," then steps aside to let us in.

I've never set foot in a church, but I imagine this room is what one feels like: a little too big and filled with too much air. There are rows of chairs laid out, facing the front, where Mum's coffin stands on a raised platform. I already feel sick.

"There are too many chairs," I whisper to Aym, who is holding my hand as we walk down the aisle.

Music starts playing from a set of weak speakers at the front–it's a song Dad chose, which, according to him, Mum loved. I can't say I've ever heard it before.

Aym leads me to the front row, and we sit down. On every chair is a small booklet with a photo of Mum on the front. Black text above and below her reads, **In Memory of Jane Elizabeth Glass**. A lump rises in my throat.

"I can't do this," I whisper.

Aym puts her arm over my shoulder and pulls me gently against her. "You can."

It's too much. The music. The coffin. The booklet. Even the officiant's face as he arrives at the front of the room. I can't do it. I can't just sit here and listen to this stranger talk about my Mum as if he knew her. I can't sit here while everyone sheds tears for a woman they barely knew. I turn around, taking in just how many empty chairs there are. The people here for Mum fill less than a quarter of the available seats. And none of them *knew* her. Not really. None of them knew her like I did.

I feel like screaming at them. I want to tell them all to leave. I want to grieve in peace. To cry until I'm out of tears. To fall and fall and fall and never rise back up. Why are these people even here? Why did they–

My eyes stop at the door, where the final person is entering the room.

Elliot. Dressed in a suit, awkwardly fiddling with his hair, and about to take a seat when his eyes meet mine. Eyes filled with sympathy.

Then he smiles.

And everything feels just a little bit more okay.

FORTY-ONE

Elliot

His eyes leave mine and he turns to face the front again. I don't know how he feels, whether he's glad I'm here or if my presence has made everything worse. But I can't worry about what he thinks of me right now. This isn't the time. The music fades and the officiant clears his throat.

"To lose someone dear to us is one of life's greatest pains," he says. "It is an event that makes us all ask 'why?' Why them? Why now? And no matter how hard we may try, the truth is that there is no reason. No justification to ease the suffering of those left behind. So, what can we do when we lose someone?" He casts his eyes over us all. "We can remember them.

"When speaking with Jane's family, I learned all about the incredible woman she was, through the memories people have of her. Those of you that knew Jane in her younger years will remember her as a fun-loving girl who loved music and dancing. She was always happiest at a party with her friends, or a concert where she could lose herself in the music she adored."

On a screen behind the officiant, images start fading in and out. Photos of Seb's mum when she was younger, her hair wild as she danced with friends, pure joy spread across her face. It's hard to fuse the girl in these pictures with the woman who raised Seb. My heart aches at the thought that Seb never knew his mum during her happiest days. I stare at the back of his head, seeing Aym sat beside him. I can't even begin to imagine what he must be feeling.

"It was through this love of music," the officiant continues, "that Jane met Steve, and eventually brought her greatest love of all into the world: her son, Sebastian."

I watch as Seb's head lowers, and I know the faint cry I hear is his. Aym wraps her arms around him while the officiant continues to speak. I'm no longer listening. I hear the words, but they're not going in. My focus is entirely on Seb. On the pain that pours from him and washes across every person in the room.

I shouldn't be here. I'm intruding on something I'm not supposed to be part of. I never knew Jane, and yet here I am among people who did. People who are grieving. I take a breath, and rise from my seat, ready to leave.

The chair scrapes on the floor. It's not overly loud, but when only one person in the whole room is speaking, it's impossible not to hear it. People flinch, but most keep their focus on the officiant. Except for Seb.

He turns and stares at me, then looks to the door, then back at me. He shakes his head and mouths the word 'stay.'

So, I do.

FORTY-TWO

Seb

When the officiant's empty words have finished and my tears have dried up, Mum's coffin is removed through a curtain in the wall, and we all file out of the room. Dad and I stand at the exit and listen as each attendee gives us their condolences. Dad thanks them, but I don't give much more than a nod. Until the final person.

"Hey," I say when Elliot approaches.

"Hey."

Now that he's close, I notice bruises on his face. There aren't many, but they're fresher than mine.

Elliot looks to my dad and says, "I'm sorry for your loss."

"Thank you," Dad replies.

I reach out and take Elliot's hand, and he reacts as if he's had an electric shock, almost jumping out of his skin.

"Can we talk?" I say, nodding to a clear area away from the crowd. "Over there."

Elliot nods. I let go of his hand and walk away with him, glancing back at Aym to give her a tight smile that says, 'I'll be okay.'

Elliot and I stop at the edge of a path that leads into a set of gardens filled with bright flowers. For the first time in what feels like forever, we're alone together.

"Thank you," I say. "For coming. You didn't have to."

Elliot shrugs. "I wasn't sure if you'd want me here."

I run a hand down his arm. It feels both right and wrong at the same time. "I'm glad you came."

We stand in silence as a warm breeze passes over us, ruffling Elliot's hair. The quiet chatter from the group at the building is fading fast as more and more people leave. I'm sure I'll see some of them again in a few minutes at the wake, which I'm dreading. It's yet another of Dad's decisions for the funeral that I don't want. At least Aym will be there to distract me. For a moment, I think about asking Elliot to join us, but I'd rather be alone with him. To properly talk.

"What happened to your face?" I ask.

"Long story."

"Seb!" calls Dad. He and Aym are at the car, waiting for me.

"And it doesn't look like you've got much time," Elliot adds with a frown.

I want to stay here with him all day. I want to hear his voice and feel his warmth. I want him to hold me close and tell me everything will be okay.

"Before you go," Elliot says, "I need to say, I'm–"

"Are you free tonight?" I cut him off.

He looks taken aback. "Yes."

"Come to mine? We can talk there."

He nods and then hesitates, as though debating whether or not he should do what he's thinking. And then, as if nothing has changed between us, his arms fold around me. But it only lasts a moment.

When I pull away, there are tears in my eyes, and in Elliot's too.

"I'll see you tonight," I say, before returning to Dad and Aym.

The wake goes by in a blur. Only a tiny fraction of the already small congregation turned up. Mainly the ones I vaguely recognise, like distant relatives. It all goes far slower than I want it to, especially when no one has much to say, but eventually the house is empty except for me, Dad, and Aym. The sun is starting to set, and Aym and I are slumped into the sofa, half-watching the news. It's wall-to-wall coverage about the Last Day. They've even got a speech from the prime minister, with her telling everyone to stay calm and trust the experts: the world won't end tomorrow.

Dad's on the phone with Samantha. She didn't come to the funeral, but I know she wanted to. I heard her say so on a call with Dad a few days ago. But he shot her down. He didn't ask me about it, but I know he did it for me. He does care about me at least a little. More than a little, Aym would say. I might admit that one day.

"I'll be home soon enough," he says. "I promise. I just don't want to leave him on his own tonight, and I don't think he's ready to live with us."

I roll my eyes. The thought of living with Dad and Samantha makes me feel ill, especially since they'll be welcoming a baby in a few months. But there's not much else I can do. Not quite yet anyway.

"You can leave me on my own tonight!" I call loud enough for Dad to hear.

Dad's voice stops and he pokes his head into the living room.

"I'll be okay," I say. "I've got Aym with me."

"Are you sure? I can stay if that's–"

"Really, Dad. It's fine." I look over at the newly replaced window. "I'll be safe."

He hesitates, tossing the idea over in his head, but he knows full well I've basically looked after myself for the last few years anyway.

"Sam," he says down the phone, "I'll be there soon." He mouths his thanks to me while the call wraps up and he searches for his keys.

Once he's got his coat on, he pauses, looking at me. I know he wants to say something, but he can't find the words. Aym, ever the expert in reading the room, goes to the kitchen, leaving me alone with my dad.

He's silent for another moment, rubbing his hands awkwardly on the front of his coat, until eventually he says, "I love you, Seb. You know that, right?"

I don't know what to say.

"I know I've not been very good at it. But I do." His voice gets thicker and his eyes glisten. "And I'm going to be a better dad. For you." He glances at one of the funeral booklets on the coffee table. "For her."

For the first time in a very long time, I believe him. If I say too much, I'll start crying again, so I opt for, "Thanks, Dad," and give him a quick hug before he heads out. I sigh deeply as the front door closes. There are harder conversations to come tonight.

Aym walks back into the living room and studies my face. I can feel her working out exactly what I'm thinking. The ends of her mouth curve up in a smirk.

"You want me to go too, don't you?"

I scratch the back of my head. "Well..."

"Is Elliot coming over?"

My smile, which feels so wrong on a day like today, gives me away, and Aym looks like she might cheer with joy.

"You're sure you're ready?" she asks.

"I'm sure. I need to speak to him. Properly."

Aym nods. "If you need me, just text me. I'll be here as quickly as I can." She starts gathering her stuff together but pauses. "And even if you don't need me, you'd better tell me exactly what happens!"

I laugh. "Will do."

She gives me a final hug and leaves.

An hour passes before there's a knock at the door. An hour of arguing with myself in my head, debating what I want to happen. An hour of replaying the conversation I had with Aym two nights ago about whether the Glimpses are really to blame. An hour of trying to understand what I feel for Elliot, all while knowing there's only one word I could possibly use.

I open the door, and there he is. Freckled face. Hazel eyes. Ginger curls. He's changed out of his suit and is now in the same, button-up, short-sleeved, blue shirt he wore on our first date. And despite the tired, reddened eyes that I'm sure I'm displaying too, and the bruises, he looks just as beautiful as he did that night.

I'm about to speak, but then I notice what Elliot's holding. I can't quite believe it. It's impossible. But that dark rosewood... I'd recognise it anywhere. Elliot looks from me to the guitar and back, eyes somehow both hopeful and nervous.

"H..." My throat seizes up, like the words can't get out. "H... how... how did you...?"

The bruises. Of course.

"Dan..." I say. "You got it back from him? And he did that?" I point at Elliot's face.

"Yeah. But then he got arrested."

"What?"

He smiles. "Told you it was a long story."

He holds out the guitar with both hands, and even though it's right in front of my eyes, I can't believe it's here. The guitar I'd wanted for so long. The last gift I ever received from my mum. I thought I'd never see it again, but here it is along with this beautiful, amazing boy.

I hesitate but reach out and run a finger down one of the strings. I pluck it, and the D note rings out, bouncing off the walls around the doorway, coursing through me and igniting a flame deep inside my chest. I take the guitar in my hands and stumble backwards, a lump rising in my throat.

Elliot steps inside and closes the door behind him. And with that, the tears just pour. I can't stop them. The guitar draws everything out of me, every bit of pain for the loss of my mum, and every bit of joy the guitar was supposed to bring. Too many emotions demand to be felt at once. Elliot catches me as I fall to the ground, cushioning my fall and protecting the guitar. He sets it aside and hugs me close, letting me cry into his shoulder just like the night Mum died.

He whispers softly to me, telling me it'll be okay.

We stay like that a while longer, Elliot holding me together as I sob, until I'm able to stand up again. I wipe my eyes and lead Elliot to the living room, where we sit, side by side on the sofa.

"Okay," I say, voice still thick from all the crying. "So, what happened?"

He tells me what he did. Every detail. Watching Dan's house for multiple days. The fake GlimpseNet post. The unlocked window. The way he got Dan to attack him. It was a stupid, risky plan, and part of me wants to slap him for even considering it. But somehow, it worked.

"But...the police," I say, "surely they had questions about your GlimpseNet post? They'll know it's fake as soon as someone tries to verify it, right?"

Elliot nods. "They would, yeah. Except I told them the post was fake."

"Isn't that–"

"Illegal? Turns out the laws are a bit messy on the subject. GlimpseNet only came out in the last few years, right? Before that, people just had Glimpses and kept them to themselves. And since Glimpses can be verified, there aren't really any laws against posting fake ones. Plus, they saw Dan beat me up. That kind of took priority. A grown man assaulting a teenager is hard to justify."

I wish I could clean his bruises away with a wave of my hand. "So...you're okay?"

"I'm okay."

"And you knew all that beforehand, right? You knew you wouldn't get in trouble?"

He hesitates. "No. I didn't know."

"But you did it anyway?"

He nods.

My hands slide into his like they belong there. "For me?"

"Of course. And I'm sorry, Seb. I'm so sorry for everything. I should have been honest with you from the start. I was never doing anything just because of the Glimpse, I swear. Everything I felt for you was real. *Is* real. I never meant to hurt you and I wish I'd just–"

I can't help it. Despite everything that's happened, despite how stupid Elliot's been and how I'd never have let him take such a risk if I'd known about it... I lean forward and kiss him. And for a moment, for one perfect moment, I forget everything and everyone else. Elliot's here. With me. And now I can confess how I feel about him.

The words come easy because they're true.

"Elliot," I say, pulling back from the kiss and gazing into his eyes. "I love you."

FORTY-THREE

Elliot

You always hear in books and movies about how much weight those three words carry, but I don't think you really understand until you hear them spoken to you. As the last syllable leaves Seb's lips, I feel like I've been thrown right back into my Glimpse–that moment of true, unquestionable happiness. Bliss.

It's not just a declaration of love. It's forgiveness. It's an invitation back into Seb's life. It's something I'd hoped for with every fibre of my being but never quite believed would happen. And my response comes to my lips in seconds.

"I love you too."

He kisses me again, colliding with me and sending us both floating into space. We shine and spin around each other, locked in orbit, bound together as we hurtle past sprawling galaxies and vibrant nebulae. Meteors fly by, burning up into nothing as they're drawn towards planets, but we remain bright and strong, taking our place among the constellations, the ones I showed Seb that night beside the tent. We go beyond space and time, transcending past and future, locked in an instant that's also an eternity.

"Will you stay with me?" Seb whispers.

I place a hand on his cheek, running my fingers down his perfect jaw. "I will. For as long as you let me."

I feel his smile before I see it and kiss him once more.

Nearly an hour passes and we barely say a word to each other. I don't know much about love, but I think this is part of it. Feeling happy and content just being *with* the other person. No words necessary. Just closeness. I could lie here for hours just as I am now, on the sofa, arms around Seb, his head on my chest, his hands holding mine.

Eventually, Seb sits up and reaches for the guitar. He looks it over, running his hands across its smooth surface, his eyes wide with adoration. Then, he puts the strap over his shoulder, manoeuvres his fingers to form a chord, and strums the strings. The rich sound cascades over me, the same way it did the last time I heard him play.

The joy on his face as he strums makes my heart swell a thousand times over. I watch him forget all his worries as he moves into a song, the same song I first heard him play what feels like a lifetime ago. He relaxes into the rhythm instantly and closes his eyes as his head falls back. He keeps his voice quiet to start, humming instead of singing, but the further he gets into the song, the clearer his voice becomes. Soon enough, the raspy voice I fell in love with fills the room.

When he finishes, he lets the final chord ring out, making the hairs on the back of my neck stand on end. His eyes flicker open and meet mine.

"I've missed this," he says.

I watch him set down the guitar with the gentle hands I know so well. "So have I."

"I never asked," Seb says quietly, "after you left...the last time you were here...how did you explain it to your parents? I remember your Mum was so angry on the phone."

"Yeah, she was pretty mad. I didn't tell her everything, but...after a few days, I did end up coming out to her."

Seb's jaw drops. "Really?"

I nod. "Yeah. And my dad, and Simon. It's not a secret anymore."

"Oh my God, Elliot that's amazing!" He throws his arms around me, almost knocking me to the floor. "I'm so proud of you! How did it go?"

I shrug as he lets me go. "Could've gone better. Could've gone a lot worse. Simon was great about it though. You should've heard the things he said to my parents when they disapproved."

"That's good. Are your parents still not okay with it?"

"I think it'll take time. They're definitely improving. They're going to have to, anyway, now that you're..." I trail off, realising we haven't actually discussed what we are to each other now. I mean, I know what I assumed, but– "...my boyfriend again?"

I hesitate, scared of messing everything up again. "If that's...what you want?"

Seb laughs and shoves me playfully. "Of course it is, idiot."

I breathe a sigh of relief right as my heart grows a thousand times bigger. "Just wanted to be sure." I shove him back. "Anyway, they seemed fine with me when I got my exam results this morning."

"Oh, shit. That was today, wasn't it? Did you do okay?"

"Yeah. I did better than I expected."

It was a very weird morning, with almost everyone in my year walking into the school library to get their results, all excited or nervous, some cheering when they opened their envelope, some crying. And there I was, feeling indifferent about it all. With the funeral only a few hours away, I wasn't exactly feeling hyped about my GCSEs.

Callum understood, thank God, so he didn't try to enthuse me. But I didn't stop him celebrating his own results. He'd done just as well as his Glimpse had shown him, and if I showed any excitement, it was for him rather than me.

Still, my results were good. I didn't fail anything, and I did really well in maths and science. Mum called me as soon as I texted her and was practically singing with joy.

"Nice," Seb says. "Well done."

"Thanks."

"I guess mine have been emailed to me." He looks at his phone with a sour face.

"You don't have to check them now. Not today or even tomorrow. Not if you don't want to."

He sighs a laugh. "It's been an exhausting day already, I guess. And hey, the world might end tomorrow."

I shove him again. "No, it won't."

"You don't know that for sure."

I pause. "When did you get into Glimpse conspiracies?"

His eyes falter, flashing away from mine, and I regret my words instantly. "Sorry. Stupid thing to say. We shouldn't talk about Glimpses."

"No, it's fine." He looks back at me. "I talked to Aym about it, and... I don't think I can blame the Glimpses anymore. I mean, they brought us together, right? I love you, Elliot. I can't be mad at the thing that made us meet."

I run a finger across the back of his hand, tracing a circle.

"You know," he continues, "I heard one theory that tomorrow's a sort of reset day for the Glimpses–that people will be able to see further into the future if they get Glimpses from tomorrow."

"Yeah, I heard that too. I think it's more likely the Glimpses just won't work after tomorrow. Simon said loads of people have booked appointments for tomorrow because of that. A last chance sort of thing."

Seb nods and looks off into the distance, deep in thought. "A last chance..." he mutters.

"Yeah."

As if a bolt of electricity flows through him, his eyes dart to mine, fixing my gaze, and he says his next words with a certainty I never imagined I'd hear from him.

"I want to have a Glimpse. Tomorrow."

FORTY-FOUR

Seb

Elliot wasn't wrong about how many people have booked Glimpse appointments for today. When I tried the website last night, every appointment was already taken. I thought maybe someone would cancel and a new one would show up this morning, but as I scroll through the page on my phone, it's looking just as fully booked as it did last night.

"Morning," Elliot mumbles beside me, rubbing his eyes and rolling over. He's still fully clothed like me, but we're under the covers of my bed, barely fitting on the single mattress. "No luck?"

I shake my head. "Nothing."

"And you're still sure you want to do this?"

"Certain."

It was as much of a shock to me as it was to Elliot when I said I wanted a Glimpse. For as long as I can remember, I've said I'd never get one, always blaming them for my parents' breakup. But something about Elliot being here, the one good thing the Glimpses have brought me, made me change my mind.

There's every chance the Glimpse won't show me anything useful, most likely it'll show me some mundane moment from later today. But my life has been all over the place recently. An unpredictable mess. Now that Elliot's come back to me, I'm scared I'll lose him again. I'm scared another shitty thing will happen and I'll lose the best thing in my life. A Glimpse–even if it doesn't show me something beyond today–would give me something solid to hold on to. As bullshit as it sounds, I think seeing myself with Elliot in my Glimpse would be like a message from the universe, telling me we're meant to be.

"Well," Elliot says "I was gonna suggest this last night, but I could always ask Simon. He works at GlimpseTech. If there's a way for us to get you in without an appointment, he'll know."

"Oh my God, yes, that would be perfect."

Elliot grins and gets out his phone.

"Hey," he says when the dial tone ends, "Simon, I've got a favour to ask..."

Town has never been as busy as it is this afternoon. Nor as loud. We're still a five-minute walk from GlimpseTech and already the crowd is too big for us to get through. Simultaneous chants overlap each other, forming a blockade of confused and angry noise. Pickets and flags emblazoned with phrases and symbols are everywhere. All anti-GlimpseTech. It's strange; not too long ago, I felt a kinship with the protestors. I thought I agreed with everything they stood for. Now, I'm not so sure.

"It's like this all over," Elliot says, angling his phone towards me so I can see the news report: **Protests Rage On at Every GlimpseTech Building in the Country**.

"Couldn't have picked a better time," I mutter, staring at the solid wall of people in front of us.

"Hey." Elliot rubs my arm. "It'll be fine. Don't worry. We'll find a way through, come on." His hand slides into mine and he leads me to the left, around the crowd, searching for the slightest break.

It takes a while, and we have to take multiple different streets, but eventually we find enough gaps to get through. The broken-glass-like building comes into view. Bright shards glistening above the hoard of protesters.

"We need to get to the back," Elliot says.

A large, bald man aggressively shouting "down with GlimpseTech" nudges his way past me, forcing me to collide with Elliot.

"You okay?" Elliot asks, gripping both my arms.

"Yeah. Let's just get round."

As we move, I catch sight of the front door of the building, where armed police are standing guard to stop people getting too close. I go cold, worried that we'll find the same defences at the back. Elliot's brother said it would be fine, but what if they've added more security than he expected?

The crowd gets thinner and thinner the further round the building we get. I guess it makes sense for them to focus on the front, especially since the back door is plain, barely noticeable, and presumably locked. A severe-looking woman in a navy boiler suit walks up to the door, taps in a code, and enters the building.

"Now what?" I ask.

Elliot gets out his phone, taps on the screen, and puts it away. "Simon will be out in a second."

We approach the door. From this side of the building, the noise of the protesters is much more bearable. Still constant, but less deafening. I wonder, if things had gone differently, might I be among the crowd? Would I be waving a picket sign, red-faced with fury?

There's a click, and the door opens. For the first time, I'm faced with Elliot's brother in the flesh. He's dressed all in black and keeps checking over his shoulder to see if he's being watched. It's clear he and Elliot are related–they have the same fiery hair, same hazel eyes, even the same nose. But Simon's taller, his hair is straight, and his jaw is much more defined. I guess he's what you'd call classically handsome, but I wouldn't trade away Elliot's cute, freckled face for anything.

"You must be Seb," he says, nodding at me.

"And you must be Simon."

He holds out a hand for me to shake, and even from the side I can tell Elliot's rolling his eyes. I shake it anyway and step inside as he makes room for us. The door closes as soon as we're in and the natural light gives way to flickering neon tubes above our heads, lighting up the black and grey surfaces around us. It's like we're in a cave.

"It looked a lot different the last time I was here," Elliot says.

Simon laughs. "You'll have come through the main entrance, it's all fancy up there with the huge windows and white tiles. Down here's the bit the public never sees. This door's basically just for cleaners and maintenance workers. Anyway, we don't have long. Follow me."

He starts leading us down what looks like an endless corridor. It occasionally branches off to areas full of metal boxes or cannisters of God-knows-what. There are a couple of people in navy boiler suits–the same woman I saw earlier and a man. The man is tall, pale, and blond. He watches us pass, but tries to do it discreetly, attempting to pass it off as just a quick glance. But his eyes stay on us for a second too long.

"You're not risking your job for this, right, Simon?" I ask, ignoring the boiler-suited man.

"Nah. I mean, this isn't technically allowed, but one of the machine operators owes me a favour and we have a spare Glimpse room that's mostly used for tests. I heard it's some special version of the machine or something, I don't know. If we're quick, it should be fine. Everyone's way too busy upstairs to notice anyway."

The corridor ends with a big metal door that Simon heaves open. And there, in the centre of the circular room, is the Glimpse machine: a golden hemisphere, surrounded by a control panel with hundreds of buttons, switches, and levers. It looks like the console for the time machine in that goofy sci-fi show Aym watches. A young, blue-haired woman stands beside it, rolling her eyes at the sight of us.

"Finally," she says. "You're really pushing this favour, Simon."

"I know, I know," he says, walking over to her. "But you love me anyway." He nudges her and a slight smile flicks across her face.

I look at Elliot and raise my eyebrows. He does the same. Not just me detecting the flirting, then.

"Elliot, Seb," Simon says, "this is Julia."

She clears her throat.

"Sorry," Simon's cheeks redden, just like Elliot's always do, "this is Doctor Taylor. She'll be operating the Glimpse."

"Indeed, I will, but we don't have much time so let's get to it." She takes a seat at the edge of the control panel, then looks at me. "I take it you're Seb?"

I nod.

"Amazing. Well, Seb, bit of standard procedure for you: I am obligated to mention that you undertake this process at your own risk, and GlimpseTech takes no blame for anything you might see, or indeed not see, during your Glimpse."

"Understood."

"There are very rare instances where a person will see nothing at all during their Glimpse. Many people interpret this to mean they will be dead, but not enough tests have been carried out to prove this as true."

I bite my tongue to avoid saying anything and just nod. My mum was one of those 'many people.' A too-short life turned into a statistic for them to throw at everyone who comes here.

"Now, if you could just scan your thumbprint here." She flicks a switch, and a small panel lights up.

I place my thumb on the panel and a moment later my face flashes up on the screen, poking out of the control desk in front of Julia. She flicks another switch and a vial containing a swab rises up from a hole.

"Now I need to take a DNA sample." She grabs the swab. "Open wide."

I open my mouth and she rubs the swab across the inside of my cheeks. She then returns it to the vial, lowers it, and presses a button. The hemisphere whirrs to life. Everything's going a lot quicker than I anticipated.

It's not until Elliot grabs my hand that I realise I'm shaking.

Julia looks at me. "Ready?"

"I..." As soon as I go through with this, there's no turning back. Whatever I see will be set in stone. "Has anyone seen past today? The people who've had Glimpses today, I mean. Has anyone's taken them further into the future?"

Julia sighs. "I'm afraid I'm not at liberty to say."

Elliot and I tried looking it up this morning once people started having Glimpses, but the amount being posted made verifications extra slow. People were claiming all sorts on message boards. One guy claimed he saw Jesus floating down from the sky to take his loyal followers to heaven. The only official verified posts we could find were mundane snapshots of today.

Elliot squeezes my hand tighter. "You don't have to do this if you don't want to."

"No. I want to." I look at him, fixing my eyes to his. "I'm ready."

"Well then," Julia says, holding up a weird golden helmet. "Let's get going."

I take a seat in front of her and let her place the helmet on my head.

"The Glimpse will last forty-four seconds exactly," she says, "but you can end it early by removing the helmet."

"Okay."

"Ready?"

No. "Yes."

She flicks more switches, pushes buttons, pulls levers. Her chair moves around the desk so that she can press more things on the other side.

The hemisphere in the centre opens up, revealing a bright light and spinning rings. The helmet vibrates.

Julia wraps her hand around a lever. "Here we go."

She pulls it.

I'm scared. Terrified, in fact. Shaking with fear.

I'm still in the Glimpse room, but the helmet is in my hands and Julia is frantically flipping switches as the hemisphere slowly closes.

"Seb?" Elliot says.

He grabs my arm and I spin to face him. I'm on my feet. I must have jumped out of the chair, though I don't remember doing it. Elliot stares at me with wide eyes.

"What happened? That was way shorter than it was meant to be."

"Oh my God" I say. "It's now."

"What's now?"

I look down at the helmet in my hands and throw it to the floor, where it lands with an almighty clang.

"What the hell?" Julia shouts. She lunges towards me, but Simon stops her. "That's expensive equipment, you can't just throw it on the floor!"

I ignore her, somehow knowing it doesn't matter. None of it matters.

"Seb?" Elliot says again.

"We need to go," I say. "Now!"

But it's too late. With a crash, the door to the room swings open, revealing two people right behind it. A man and a woman. In navy boiler suits. Holding guns, raising them up, pointing them right at us. Ready to fire.

"NO!" I shout, pulling the helmet off.

I hold it between my hands, shaking. That can't be the future. It can't be. But Glimpses always come true.

I look up from the helmet to see Julia flicking switches like her life depends on it. The hemisphere is still whirring like crazy, but it's starting to close. Slowly.

"Seb?" Elliot says.

He grabs my arm and I spin to face him. I'm on my feet. I must have jumped out of the chair, though I don't remember doing it. Elliot stares at me with wide eyes.

"What happened?" he says. "That was way shorter than it was meant to be."

No.

No no no.

"Oh my God," I say, realisation setting in. "It's now."

"What's now?"

This can't be happening. It can't be. I've just signed away our lives. I look down at the helmet. This stupid, fucking helmet that's forced us all into this fate. I should have taken it off sooner. Before the guns. Before any of it.

I throw the helmet to the floor, willing it to shatter, part of me hoping destroying the machine will save us all. It rings out as it hits the ground, the sound mixing with the whirring from the hemisphere.

"What the hell?" Julia shouts. She lunges towards me, but Simon stops her. "That's expensive equipment, you can't just throw it on the floor!"

It's too late. The Glimpse is unfolding right in front of me. It only sent me mere seconds into the future. And now we're all going to die. And it's my fault. It's all my fault.

"Seb?" Elliot says.

And he looks at me with such worried eyes, my fear passing into him. He doesn't even know why. I need to save him. I can't lose him too.

"We need to go, now!" As soon as the words leave my mouth, I realise they're meaningless. I said them in the Glimpse. Which means –

The door swings open with a crash. And there they are. The boiler-suited man and woman, guns raised and ready to fire.

But I stopped the Glimpse before they pulled their triggers.

And they're hesitating at the sight of us.

Which means I have a chance.
A moment of uncertainty.
Undestined.

I throw my arms around Elliot and force him down to the floor.

MEANWHILE

Agent Sigma

This room is supposed to be empty, so the presence of these people makes me hesitate. The woman beside me does the same, waiting for my command before taking action. I may have been part of the inner circle for less time, but The Instructor gave me this role over anyone else. He knows how devoted I am to the cause, not to mention I now know this building like the back of my hand. It's thanks to me the others knew where to place the bombs. Without me, the entire plan would fail.

And yet I haven't accounted for this. No one has. Two teenage boys and a pair of staff members face us, as shocked to see us as we are to see them. It's no matter, though. Countless people will die today. It will be a huge loss for many, but it will serve the greater good. The Instructor's Glimpse takes place hours from now, so if we act quickly, the world will be saved. That much is guaranteed.

As the dark-haired boy tackles the redhead to the ground, I pull my trigger. Pellets fire from my gun and lodge perfectly in the Glimpse machine, some of them even making it into the almost-closed hemisphere. The woman follows suit, firing hers as well. And then the pellets begin their job, sending electrical impulses through the machine, perfectly crafted to disrupt and destroy the technology.

I can't pretend to know the ins-and-outs of how the Glimpse technology works, but I know the importance of this machine. All Glimpses, the world over, utilise this central machine. If it goes down, so do the rest. They hid it away in this unremarkable town, but we found it. *I* found it.

Sparks fly from the machine, and I watch gleefully as the two staff members and the boys stare in horror. The whirring speeds up, but it sounds far different to its usual tone. It wavers and changes in frequency. Lights flash across the control desk, and the wires that connect it to the hemisphere release unnatural cracking sounds, like lightning ripping through them.

"What have you done?" the female staff member asks.

"Saved the world," the woman beside me says.

I pull my phone from my pocket and send the signal that will activate the bombs. Pride swells in my chest. I turn to my companion.

"Go," I say. "You don't have long."

Her eyes widen, puzzled. "Aren't you coming?"

I turn back to the sparking machine and smile. I've played my part, but I have never planned on surviving this. "No."

The woman hesitates, but she doesn't question me again. After a moment's thought, she darts out of the door and runs down the corridor, heading for the only safe exit. The locks should have activated on the main entrance by now, trapping people inside and keeping others out.

It's necessary, I remind myself. All of it. Necessary.

The hemisphere explodes in a burst of light, sending chunks of metal across the room. I hear the screams of the others, and when the light dies down, they're cowering on the floor with their hands over their heads. The metal pieces have narrowly missed them.

A memory stirs. Seeing these people, cowering, terrified, reminds me of my parents. Their slaughtered bodies on the living room floor on that fateful day. I never heard their screams or saw their fear, but in my nightmares, it looks similar to this.

What will their families feel when they hear of their demise? How will the world react when the bodies pile high from what I've done here today? The world will not remember me fondly, even if my actions have saved it.

I stare at the two young boys. Not even adults yet. If they stay here, they'll never see the new world I've helped to create. They'll never get a chance to live their lives unbound by fate. What has this all been for if I deny them that?

The longer I look at the boys, the more time seems to stretch, like the sparks of the machine are cascading across the room in slow motion. In this moment, they cling tightly to each other. I can feel their love radiating from them. The same love that was torn away from my parents, The same love that will be lost by so many once the bombs go off.

I can't stop the detonation.

But I can spare these lives.

"Run," I say.

The boys look up, eyes filled with tears, and the older pair listen too.

"All of you, out the back! Run as fast as you can!"

They all stare, dumbfounded.

"Run! NOW!"

There's another explosion from the control desk, and all four of them jump to their feet.

They run.

I watch through the open door as they flee down the dark, endless corridor, until they're so far away that I can no longer see them.

"Keep running," I mutter, voice masked by the sparking of the console. "Don't stop." I pray that they keep moving even when they reach the exit. I pray that they make it out in time. Perhaps I should run too, but where would that leave me? A criminal in the new world, still without my family. No, this is better. I will die here in the rubble that I've helped bring down. I will pass on and see my parents again. The new world will go on without me.

There isn't long until the bombs go off, now.

Not long until the end.

Before the building falls.

Before–

PART FIVE

LIVING

GlimpseNet Closing Statement

It is with a heavy heart that we announce the closure of the GlimpseNet website as part of the wider closure of GlimpseTech as a whole. Our deepest condolences go out to all those affected by the attack on the Millfield GlimpseTech building, words cannot make up for the profound loss of life.

It is now understood that the reason no one could see beyond the so-called Last Day was, in fact, due to the destruction of the Glimpse technology. We regret that we didn't understand this until it was too late. We know that you will have many other questions, but we cannot answer all of them. For latest updates on investigations into the organisation who orchestrated the attack, we recommend following reliable news sources.

ONE MONTH LATER

Elliot

For the first time in a long time, the election coverage on TV makes sense. No one knows who's going to win. There's still a whole month before the election actually takes place, but after weeks of talking about what happened to GlimpseTech, it's the new dominant topic on the news. Well, that and the downfall of the prime minister, but that's exactly why we're having another election.

It all came out bit by bit in the days after the bombing. First was the shock that spread across the world, and the realisation of what the Last Day truly meant. I didn't really know how to feel at first. Seb and I were both in shock, I guess. As was Simon. And Julia.

I'll never forget how I felt as we ran out of the building that day. We were all driven by fear. I held Seb's hand the whole way, adrenaline distracting me from how out of breath I was. Once we were out the door, we kept running. The sounds of the protesters were still loud as ever, and I'm not sure I'll ever shake the guilt of the fact we didn't try to warn any of them. Seb tells me all the time that there was nothing we could do. We didn't know the extent of the attack. We had no idea about the bombs. But still, it hurts.

We ran along the streets, cutting corners, putting as much distance between us and the building as possible. And then we heard it. We felt the shockwave. The bombs went off, ripping the GlimpseTech building apart, killing everyone inside. Shards of glass went flying, injuring the protesters within range.

The four of us turned to face the explosion. We saw the smoke, and the fractured shards of glass within it, still glistening. I turned to Seb, and we wrapped our arms around each other and cried.

In the chaos that followed, it would have been easy to pretend we were never there. Easy in practice, at least. Not emotionally. But we didn't stay quiet. All four of us told the police what we knew. We described the man and the woman we saw, and exactly what they did. We also had to explain why we were there in the first place. Trespassing in a building that had become rubble was hardly something they were going to punish us for at that point, though.

We didn't hear from the police after that, but I saw on the news they caught the woman a couple of days later. It goes way beyond her though, not that the mastermind behind it all has been found. Others from the terrorist organisation have been caught and all of them tell the same story about some creep they call The Instructor. I read one article that said The Instructor claimed to have had the latest Glimpse, but people are saying that was probably a lie. God knows. Whatever he claimed, he got people to follow him, and now he's got gallons of blood on his hands.

I thought it would be done after that. Everyone did. But then came the anonymous leaks about Maria McBride and her shady deal with Gabriel Thompson. I guess it's a good thing no one will be able to pull something like that off again, not with the Glimpses gone for good.

"All this science jargon is too much for me," Mum says when the election coverage turns into a report on the post-Glimpse coma patients. There aren't many, but some of the people who were midway through their Glimpses at other facilities during the bombing have been unconscious ever since.

"Julia says the central machine was like an internet server," Simon says. "All the others around the world were connected to it. But instead of hosting the internet, it hosted human consciousness during temporal displacement."

I roll my eyes. As if that's less jargon than what's on the news.

He continues, "Once that central machine went down, so did all the rest. And some of those who were mid-Glimpse might have lost consciousness forever."

Yet more victims on the list. If we'd gone to a GlimpseTech building in another city, Seb could be in that comatose state right now. If we'd not been using the central machine at the Millfield site, we'd have all died in the explosion. I'm forever grateful we made it out unscathed.

Seb

"Dad," I call from the front door, "I'm heading out!"

"See you later!" he replies from the living room, where yet another broadcast about the election is playing on the TV.

"Be careful!" Samantha adds.

"Always am." I shut the door behind me and head down the road, past all the detached houses with their huge gardens, to the nearest bus stop.

It's a pain, living a whole hour away from Aym and Elliot, but it's not been as bad as I thought it would be. I was ready to absolutely hate Samantha when I moved in, but she's actually not that bad. I'll never consider her my new mum, but I don't think that's what she's trying to be. She even offered the biggest of the two spare rooms to me, even though it was meant for the baby. I thanked her, but turned it down, figuring if I'm only here for a couple of years, I can cope with a smaller bedroom. Even the smaller one is bigger than my room in Mum's house, anyway. And though I miss my old home, it's nice to not be in a house that has sadness painted on the walls.

There's a buzz from my phone.

Set off yet? reads a text from Elliot.

Just waiting for a bus.

See you soon x

I smirk. Elliot's taken to adding kisses to the ends of texts recently. I think he's trying out different 'couple things.' A couple of weeks ago he went down the whole 'no, you hang up' track while on a call to me before bed. I think it's a tad ridiculous, but it's cute all the same, and I'm hardly going to stop him figuring out his 'thing' in his first ever relationship.

A bus approaches and I hold out my hand to stop it. The driver greets me with a smile as I flash my bus pass. He's gotten used to seeing me these last few weeks. I've spent nearly every day heading over to Millfield to meet up with Elliot. Or Aym. Or both. Or, like today, Elliot, Aym, Callum, and Nikita.

I'd never have imagined such a group forming a year ago. Back then, Callum was some guy who occasionally spoke to Carl, Nikita was one of the popular girls who I was probably invisible to, and Elliot... well, he was a boy I recognised and nothing more. And yet, the first time we all met up felt perfectly natural.

It was a couple of weeks after the bombing, when things had settled down, Elliot and I finally felt like going outside to be around people other than each other again. Elliot said his friends would love to properly hang out with me, and suggested I bring Aym along too. We met in the park, far enough away from the remains of the GlimpseTech building so we didn't have to think about the last time we were in town. After a couple of awkward introductions, everyone pulled out bags of snacks and things felt instantly calmer.

We're meeting at the same park today, and it's a good day for it. The skies are clear, and the temperature is soaring. I sit beside an open window, letting the wind tousle my hair as it goes. The bus takes me down country roads and awkward bends, and even passes the place where Elliot and I camped for one night (my favourite part of every bus journey). We've been talking about doing that again soon. Not necessarily camping, but a holiday. Just the two of us, completely alone together for a few days. Even the thought has me biting away a smile.

Elliot

I arrive at the park early, but not as early as Aym. She's already waiting in the same spot we've hung out the last few times. A cool spray washes over my face as I pass the fountain and head up the slope to meet her.

"Hey," she says, smiling wide and practically glowing in her bright pink top.

"Hey. Seb should be here in a few minutes, says he's almost at the bus station."

"I know," she says, waving her phone at me.

Some people would probably feel jealous seeing how close Aym and Seb are–not that there's even the slightest chance of them getting together. I'm not sure even Callum and I are as close as them. But I've not felt jealous at all. In fact, it's been quite nice getting to know someone who knows Seb so well.

"How's the painting coming along?" I ask, planting myself down next to her.

She smiles. "Almost finished."

She holds out her phone to me, showing a photo of the painting. I've seen it a couple of times before, and each time it looks entirely new. She calls it 'Hope,' and apparently it started out as a canvas covered in black with a single bright spot in the centre. Now, though, the bright spots are everywhere. It's like a night sky, but the stars aren't just white; they're gold, silver, vibrant blue, and striking green. There are swirling galaxies of orange and purple. Infinite points of light in the darkness.

"It looks amazing," I say.

"Thanks."

"Hey!" calls a new voice.

I turn to see Callum and Nikita approaching, hands linked as usual. When they reach us, Callum throws down a rucksack overflowing with snacks.

"The party has arrived," he says.

Seb

My heart leaps when I see everyone in the usual spot. It's only been a couple of days since I last saw them, but if I could spend every day in their company, I would. Elliot jumps to his feet as soon as he spots me. He runs at me full speed, then collides with me and sends us both spinning in a hug. As we steady ourselves, I kiss him.

"Missed you," he says.

"Missed you, too."

We join the others. Callum's lying on the grass, sunglasses over closed eyes while he sunbathes. Nikita and Aym are chatting about their plans for next year. Turns out Nikita is going to be doing an art A Level at Nikita's college. Last week, Aym told her about the retreat she went on, and Nikita had her mouth open in awe the whole time.

Elliot passes me a can of coke.

"Cheers."

"How're your dad and Samantha?" he asks.

"Good! Really good, actually. They helped me decorate my room yesterday."

"Oh, nice. Fancy inviting me over to see it?"

"I don't know, I've got my other boyfriend visiting for a whole week."

Elliot shoves me playfully. "Shut up."

"Make me."

Callum clears his throat and sits up right before Elliot has a chance to kiss me. "You know," he says, "I'm starting to get how Elliot must have felt when me and Nikita were flirting around him all the time."

"Took you long enough," Elliot says, sniggering.

"Don't you two start competing!" Aym cuts in. "I'm not about to be a fifth wheel."

"Maybe you should invite Tim along next time," I say, grinning.

Aym blushes.

"What's this?" Nikita spins on Aym. "Tim? Who's Tim?"

Aym turns to Elliot. "Remind me to murder your boyfriend later."

Nikita starts tapping Aym's legs. "Who's Tim?"

She rolls her eyes. "Just some guy I met at the retreat."

I fake a cough. "Some guy who she's been messaging every day since the retreat."

"WHAT?" Nikita shouts. "Tell all, right now!"

"Seb," Aym says, trying to shoot me evils but unable to hide her grin, "I officially hate you."

I raise my can for a cheers. "I'd expect nothing less."

Elliot laughs and nuzzles his head onto my shoulder. We stay sat like that while Aym tells the group all about Tim, the cute, dungaree wearing, artist/poet/activist boy of her dreams. She told me all about him a couple of weeks ago, and I asked just as many questions as Nikita is asking now. Where's he from? What does he look like? Are you dating? When can we meet him?

I can't help but smirk at the 'I'm so done' look on Aym's face.

Elliot

When Nikita's finally exhausted all her questions, Aym suggests they go to the nearby ice cream van.

"It's hot as fuck out here," Aym says.

"Good plan. Boys, any of you want to join?"

Callum jumps up. "I will."

"Seb?" says Aym. "El?"

"I'm alright," Seb says.

"Same," I add.

The three of them head off, leaving me and Seb on the grass, the back of my head on his stomach, surrounded by bags of unfinished snacks. In the distance, I can hear the sound of someone busking. They're using a recorded track, rather than playing an instrument, and it sounds like they're in the spot at the top of the park, the same spot I took Seb to when he was busking.

"You should've brought your guitar," I say.

"Yeah, coz a bunch of teenagers in a park with a guitar doesn't say cringe at all."

I laugh. "Okay, fair point."

Seb runs a hand through my hair, and I roll my head to the side so the fountain is in full view. On its base, there are traces of the graffiti someone sprayed all those weeks ago on the last day of exams. It's been scrubbed enough that you wouldn't notice if you hadn't known it was there, but I can still picture the words 'END FATE, RESTORE FREE WILL.'

"Do you think things are better now?" I ask. "Without GlimpseTech?"

Seb

It's a big question, and it hits harder for me than I think it would most people. The Glimpses weren't just an unremarkable quirk of the world, they shaped my whole life. I don't blame the Glimpses for the end of my parents' marriage, or even for Mum's death anymore, but I can hardly say they didn't have an impact.

In the days after the bombing, when everyone realised the Glimpses were gone, I spent a lot of time wondering how my life might have been different if the same thing had happened before I was born. Would my parents have stayed together, despite being unhappy? Would Mum have stuck around a little longer? I guess I'll never know the answer.

"I don't know," I say to Elliot. "Maybe."

I sit up, forcing Elliot to do the same. We face each other, cross-legged on the grass, and I take his hands in mine.

"I think it forces people to live in the moment," I say. "And that seems better to me."

Elliot nods. "I sometimes wonder what it would be like if we knew for a fact that we'd be together forever."

I smile. "I've thought the same thing."

"Really?"

"Yeah." I run a finger along his arm. "But here's the thing; if we knew where we were heading, then in the end we wouldn't know if we stayed together because of love, or just because we were told that's what's supposed to happen."

"I suppose." He looks down as he speaks, and he sounds uncertain.

"Hey," I say, tapping the bottom of his chin so he looks up and faces me. "Maybe we will be together forever, and maybe we won't. I can't tell you if it's destined or written in the stars. But we're together right now. I love you, and you love me. Isn't that all that matters?"

He doesn't answer right away, but as his eyes stare into mine, I can see his worries disappear. His mouth curves into a grin. "When did you get so profound?"

I laugh. "Probably when I met you."

Elliot's hand moves to the back of my head, bringing me in for a kiss. Our lips connect, the distant music keeps playing, a breeze cooled by the fountain washes over us, and it feels like this moment could last forever.

ACKNOWLEDGMENTS

I began writing *Against The Stars* at the very end of 2020. It was a turbulent year for the whole world, with COVID and lockdowns, but for me it also brought a move to a new town and a career change. I was submitting a manuscript to agents for one book, and was 12,000 words into another when an idea formed. Two and a half years later, that idea is now a published novel, but it took a lot more than just me to make that happen.

First, I have to thank Everett O'Donoghue. If it hadn't been for your enthusiasm when I first suggested the concept of this book, or the constant demands for more chapters to read, or the brutally (and beautifully) honest feedback, it simply wouldn't exist. Oh, and it wouldn't have its title either!

This is my first published novel, but it isn't the first I've written, and there's only one person to have read both of my unpublished attempts. Thank you, Sol Cotton, for being that person. Your feedback helped me find what works and what doesn't, and hopefully that shows in *Against The* Stars and everything that follows.

Thank you to Zee Y and Morel O'Sullivan, whose support as best friends, flatmates, and fellow queer creatives has been invaluable. I would not be the person (or indeed the writer) I am without you both.

Thank you to A Peschanski, Jenna Rennalls, and Hannah Barnes, who all read this book before it found a publisher. It's a very scary thing to share an early draft with others, but I loved hearing your thoughts!

Thank you to all the wonderful people at Ruckus Retreat, but especially to Rowan Ellis and Krish Jeyakumar for creating such a diverse and welcoming creative environment. My confidence in my writing has come a long way thanks to the Ruckus workshops.

I've been a writer, or at least a storyteller, for as long as I can remember. Thank you to my family for always encouraging my creative outlets and for surrounding me with books from a young age. Mum, in the nicest way possible, I hope this book made you cry!

A book is nothing without the team who work on it behind the scenes, so thank you to Julia Wortman and Tim Frost for your invaluable comments and edits. Thanks also to Lewis Hughes and

Kylie Koews for your work on the marketing; and to Jeremy Gibson and Travis Burmeister for your contributions. Thank you, Samantha Lee, for the absolutely gorgeous cover art - I will never get over the experience of seeing Seb and Elliot visualised and I love that I can tell which is which even in silhouette form.

And, of course, a truly massive thank you to Joshua Perry, the Tiny Ghost Press founder and editorial director. I had started to lose hope of ever seeing *Against The Stars* in print after endless rejections, and I was delighted to find a home at Tiny Ghost Press. Thank you for everything you've done to get *Against The Stars* into the world. Your enthusiasm for this book, and for queer books in general, is so genuine and I couldn't dream of a better person to work with.

Finally, to you, the reader: thank you. I hope Seb and Elliot's story resonated with you in some way.

Lightning Source UK Ltd.
Milton Keynes UK
UKHW041106250123
415936UK00003B/10/J